SINISTER REFUGE

A BOYD AND ABBOUD MYSTERY

RICK E. GEORGE

This is a work of fiction. Any resemblance to any persons, living or dead, or to any business establishment, is entirely coincidental.

Sinister Refuge

COPYRIGHT © Rick E. George

No part of this book may be reproduced or transmitted in any form or by any means without written permission by the author.

Cover Art and Interior Design by Laura Boyle

Knapweed Press
P.O. Box 1882
White Salmon, WA 98672

First Edition 2021

Print ISBN: 978-1-7376782-1-2
Digital ISBN: 978-1-7376782-0-5

Library of Congress Control Number: 2021916509

Published in the United States of America

"No one leaves home unless home is the mouth of a shark."

—Warsan Shire

"Refugees are not terrorists. They are often the first victims of terrorism."

—António Manuel de Oliveira Guterres

CHAPTER ONE

Russell Boyd squeezed between two Seattle PD vehicles and stepped over the crime scene tape. Thirty yards in front of him, law enforcement officers stood guard around a circle of portable partitions outside the tinted windows of the Elliott Bay Hotel and Condominiums. A jagged hole gaped from a glass canopy above them. On a balcony nine stories up, a technician collected prints from the rail. Higher up, a cloud the shape of a running greyhound drifted in a deep blue sky radiating a warmth that didn't belong in November.

Gawkers hovered behind the right side of the tape, the Puget Sound blue and sparkling beyond them. To his left, past the partition, Seattle PD Detective Angela Sherman gave him a nod, and he veered toward her.

She had with her the potential witness she'd told him about, a Muslim woman who stared through the windows into the hotel's empty lobby. A turquoise hijab covered her head, and an eggplant-colored abaya hung to her black high-heeled shoes. Sherman hadn't known what language the woman spoke—probably Arabic, but Boyd knew it could have been Eritrean, Malay, Uzbek, or dozens of other tongues.

"Should've seen her ten minutes ago," said Sherman when he reached her. A seventeen-year veteran working the Vice and High-Risk Victims Unit, Sherman had short fingernails with white polish, and she kept her black hair in a bob.

She gestured toward the woman. "Kept saying *I know I know*, pacing back and forth, gasping, crying, like she was trying to find somebody to talk to. I don't know how I convinced her to wait. Gave her a hand gesture, and she must have understood."

"Agent Roshan is bringing an Arabic interpreter," said Boyd. "I'll try to talk to her, verify if that's her language."

He looked toward the woman. He hadn't spoken Arabic in three years. "Salam."

She turned from the window. Strands of toffee-colored hair and silver drop earrings peeked from her loosely wrapped hijab. Her eyes flitted to the scar near Boyd's right ear, a one-inch raspberry blot nobody could pretend not to notice. It made him look like a hitman in a two-bit Italian mobster movie. He wished he had the money to make it go away.

He clasped his hands. "Assalaamu Alaykum." *May peace be upon you.*

She replied with a burst of Arabic. Her tone was grim, her eyes glassy and red.

He held up a hand. "Aasef." *Sorry.* Hoping she'd understand he meant the interpreter would arrive soon, he pointed toward the street and waved a hand. "Motarjimi," he said. *Interpreter.*

Her eyes showed recognition. "Motarjimi?"

"Na'am." *Yes.*

What the hell was the word for *soon*? He'd known it in Iraq, but he couldn't remember it now. Funny—he'd forgotten so much, but what he wanted to forget, he couldn't.

She turned to the window again.

"She wants to tell us something," said Sherman. "What we know already is that the room is in the condominium part of the hotel and the owner of it is a forty-seven-year-old man named Phillip Buchanan, primary residence in Reno, Nevada. We've got people searching for him. We have no idea who the girl is. When she went off the balcony, on her own or with assistance, she didn't have on a lick of clothing. She left behind an abaya, a hijab, shorts and a tee-shirt, underwear. What she didn't leave was anything to identify her. No purse, no wallet."

"Any guesses about her age?"

"I'd say sixteen at most."

He reached into his windbreaker, took out an opened pack of Neccos. The flavor on top, clove, prompted a silent groan, but he popped the wafer in his mouth.

"She never had a chance to start her life," he said.

"My guess is she didn't have much of a life to begin with." She raised her head and gestured. "Here's your interpreter."

Boyd glanced toward the street. Agent Toni Roshan and a woman wearing a maroon hijab strode down the steep hill, then crossed toward them.

He spoke to the witness. "Fathleki. Motarjimi."

The woman turned from the window. "Motarjimi?"

"Na'am."

"Hot damn, Boyd," said Sherman. "You do fine in Arabic."

"Not really. Just enough to cause trouble."

Roshan and the interpreter ducked beneath the crime scene tape and hurried to them. In addition to the hijab, the interpreter wore black running shoes, navy blue slacks, and a blue blazer over a black turtleneck sweater. Boyd guessed she was almost his age, late twenties, perhaps, yet she seemed older. Her face was serene, as though she were coming to the hotel spa for a massage, not to the scene of a homicide.

Roshan stopped a few feet in front of them. Nearly six feet tall, she had a prominent nose and sandy blonde hair. Like Boyd, she wore a blue FBI windbreaker. After peering down the wall of windows at the partitions and the balcony above it, she nodded toward the Muslim woman. "This our potential witness?"

"Maybe," said Sherman. "She definitely wants to talk."

The interpreter turned her attention toward the woman. She placed a hand over her heart. "Na uzo billah," she murmured—an expression of sorrow or commiseration. The last time Boyd had heard those words, he'd …

No. He pushed the memory out of his head. It had no place here.

The two women exchanged words until Roshan put a hand on the interpreter's shoulder.

"Hold on a moment." She looked at Sherman. "What do we know so far?"

Sherman relayed the same information she'd given Boyd.

Roshan shook her head. "Jesus. Oh—by the way, this is Nawar Abboud. We pulled her from translating cellphone transcripts to bring her here."

"Pleased to meet you," said Abboud in a British accent, "though I wish the circumstances were different."

"As do I," said Boyd. Something about her—was it her voice or her demeanor?—struck him. He wondered what her story was, how she ended up in the U.S.

She spoke to the witness, eliciting a torrent of words and the dribbling of tears.

After a minute, Roshan interrupted. "Abboud, please bring us in on the conversation."

"Of course. We are only introducing ourselves. She is Syrian, as am I. May I present to you Mrs. Katya Al-Salek."

The interview resumed, along with pauses for Abboud to translate what the woman said. Mrs. Al-Salek had been reading in the lobby when a figure came crashing like a boulder through the glass canopy. She had no reason to think that the victim was the teenage girl she'd met on the ninth-floor hallway, but she felt certain that it was. She had rushed to the window and nearly fainted at the naked figure smashed onto the sidewalk.

Earlier, in the hallway where she met the girl, Mrs. Al-Salek sensed something was wrong. A twentyish woman accompanied the girl. The pair of them could have strolled the runway of a fashion show in Beirut or in Damascus before the war. The teen wore a lemon-yellow hijab and an azure abaya with rose-hued floral designs on the bodice. Her makeup was flawless, her lips pink like flamingos. The woman wore a dark blue hijab and a black abaya with a silver neckline, and she had also taken pains with her makeup.

One detail caught Mrs. Al-Salek's attention. The girl wore gold-hoop earrings filled with a white resin and black hand-painted Syrian eagles, stylized like the ones embossed on Syrian coins. This prompted Mrs. Al-Salek to stop them.

In the midst of translating these last details, Abboud's voice broke—a small rip in the air of serenity she'd been exuding.

"I am sorry," she said. "It is close to my heart. Mrs. Al-Salek asked them if they were Syrian. The woman said nothing. The girl stared at her feet and said, '*Za'atari*.'"

"What's that mean?" asked Sherman.

"It is where I lived before I came here. It is a place for refugees."

So, thought Boyd—Nawar was a refugee. He would have never guessed that.

Abboud turned back to Mrs. Al-Salek, whose eyes narrowed as she recounted the next part.

"She says the woman pulled the girl away, but the girl looked back. She thinks the girl was terrified. The encounter felt bad."

Mrs. Al-Salek clasped her hands together and pressed them to her chin. She spoke quietly, and Abboud nodded.

"Mrs. Al-Salek says she was not at Za'atari, but she was in Beirut. She knows what can happen to refugee girls."

. . .

Boyd took out his phone to check the time. He'd been sitting on his ass for twenty minutes in the Elliott Bay Hotel and Condominiums lobby. Assigned to accompany Abboud while she obtained a written report from Mrs. Al-Salek, he couldn't participate because he didn't know the language, and he couldn't get a cup of coffee because he'd have to leave the lobby to do it.

Meanwhile, Roshan and Sherman were on the ninth floor where the real action was taking place. He imagined a crowd of law enforcement types and technicians examining the clothing left behind by the girl, collecting hairs and fluids, discussing hypotheses. Maybe some techie had rushed into the condo with hallway surveillance footage he'd copied from the hotel CCTV, and his more seasoned colleagues had dashed out of the building, on the chase for someone connected to the tragedy.

"We are finished." Abboud picked up the notepad onto which Mrs. Al-Salek had been writing in Arabic.

"You've got her contact information?" he asked.

"Yes."

"Would you please translate the statement for me?"

Abboud read it in her British accent.

"It sounds quite thorough. Good job. She can go."

Abboud exchanged words with their witness, who left the lobby, pausing to show a policeman at the door her identification, a requirement now for everyone entering or leaving the building.

He stood up from his chair and typed a text to Roshan. Maybe she'd have him come up to the condo. More likely, she'd ask him to accompany Abboud back to the office or to wait in the lobby.

A rope separated the lobby from guests checking into the hotel or with other business at the front desk. Except for a pair of cops stationed to ensure civilians didn't breach the barrier, Boyd and Abboud were alone. While he typed, she walked to the window and peered toward the partitions twenty feet to the left beyond the lobby.

"What will happen to her?" she asked.

"You mean the girl?" he said.

"Yes. What will they do with her body if no one can identify her?"

"When they're finished with her here, they'll bring her to a hospital where they'll perform a forensic autopsy."

Abboud nodded. "As I thought. Then I must see her

before they take her away."

The demand surprised him. What did she have in mind? Why would she need to see a dead body? "You can't. Even I can't. The techs have her now."

"Perhaps I have seen her at the mosque."

"I doubt she's been to the mosque. If what happened to her is what we think happened, the ones who controlled her wouldn't have let her go anywhere, let alone a mosque."

Abboud took a step, hesitated, then marched toward the entry. Did she think she could just storm ahead and bull her way right past the barriers? Boyd sprang forward, but he couldn't intercept her before she ducked under the rope.

"Wait," he called.

She allowed him to catch up with her. "I need to see her. There are reasons of faith."

"No offense, but faith matters to us, too. And right now the religion is forensic science. You go charging past those partitions, they're going to excommunicate us when we get back to the office."

"I thought I was finished with this."

"You are. You did a fine job. You put the woman at ease … well, as much as you could, given the circumstances."

"I do not mean that." She hurried out the door and whirled toward him when he caught up just outside the entry. "The war has followed me. In Za'atari I watched these girls disappear. Their families married them off much sooner than they would have before the war. Thirteen, fourteen years old."

"Then how'd she get here?"

"I do not know, but as for her location now, I believe she jumped."

"Because?"

"What does your forensic faith tell you?"

"It tells me …" He thought for a moment. "I want to stop the people who did this. That means keeping my job. You go charging past those barriers, this could end up being our last day working for the Bureau."

"In our nation she would be buried within a day. Her body would be washed and an imam would say some prayers. Can we not arrange for such prayers at least?"

"I'll talk to Detective Sherman. She'll figure something out."

"I hope you will understand. She needs a prayer before they take her away."

She darted a few steps forward. Boyd kept pace. "Stop it, Abboud."

Twenty yards from the partition, he grabbed her arm. She glared at him. Her eyes were moist.

"Can you say the prayer from here?" he asked.

"The prayer needs to be in the presence of the body."

He let out a long breath. Here he was, back in the States, repeating the same kind of scene he'd experienced in Iraq. What he did next would matter to Abboud the same way it did years ago to the Iraqis. There was something about her, some scar he couldn't see, that made her this way.

"I'll try," he said. "But if it doesn't work, you have to promise me that you won't go past the partitions anyway. You could be arrested if you did that. Doesn't matter that you work for us. Maybe they wouldn't ultimately charge you with a crime, but they might lock you in the back of a squad car until they're done here. So what's your answer?"

She pressed her lips together, considering. "Thank you for trying," she said. "I will not go inside unless you receive permission."

"I didn't say I'd ask for permission." He let go of her

arm, and they walked to the policeman on their side of the partitions.

"Good morning, patrolman," he said, projecting confidence that he didn't feel. "I have with me Nawar Abboud. She's a specialist in Muslim culture. She's going to step inside for a moment to say a traditional prayer. This is what we do when the victim is Muslim. Do you understand?"

The patrolman, who appeared to be on the younger side of twenty-five, hesitated. "That's not—"

"Do you really want to interrupt Detective Sherman? I can call her right now."

God, he hoped not. Sherman would never approve.

"No," said the cop. "You can go."

"Thank you," said Abboud.

They entered the sanctum via a gap between overlapping partitions. A woman in a Tyvek suit looked up from the body and glowered.

"Pardon us," he said. "My colleague is a specialist in Muslim culture. There's a prayer she needs to say, and then we'll get out of your way."

The victim lay face down, legs bent halfway to her chest, arms outstretched above her head. Dark hair, lush and silky, flowed across a shoulder and onto the sidewalk. Were it not for the pool of blood around her head, she might have been sleeping.

Abboud knelt to her knees. She recited the words of a prayer he had heard far too many times. He remembered part of the translation, and so now, half a world away and yet far too close, he whispered the English.

Oh, Allah, forgive her, wash her with water and snow and hail. Cleanse her as white cloth is cleansed of stains.

CHAPTER TWO

The Hawk savored what he knew would be his last look out the glass wall of his twelfth-floor business. A quarter-mile offshore, a white triple-decked Washington State ferry skimmed the cerulean blue Elliott Bay on its jaunt to Bainbridge Island. A green-hulled ship stacked bejesus high with containers waited to disgorge its cargo.

If he didn't abandon this waterfront penthouse pronto, his new view would be from inside an eight-by-eight-foot concrete cell. But there were problems with the evacuation plan. For starters, he had a fucking idiot john whining in a chair a few feet away, a john whose attentions to the new girl Amal had inspired her to pancake herself off a ninth-floor balcony. This john—Roger was his name—didn't even know she'd taken the fast elevator down. While The Hawk's surveillance video captured Roger in the kitchen digging into the refrigerator, the bedroom camera showed Amal dashing to the sliding glass door of the balcony. She opened it and disappeared.

Seven thousand bucks—that's how much he'd invested in Amal.

By the time The Hawk and his executive assistant Jack reached the condo, Roger had figured it out. He had his pants on, his white dress shirt half-buttoned, shoes and socks still on the floor. He was in a sweat, didn't bother asking how the hell The Hawk already knew what had happened. Blubbering about how his life and his marriage and his career were finished, the chump could hardly move.

Now, here in The Hawk's office, the little whiner had transformed into a demanding shit. "You need to get me the fuck out of here," said the john, as though The Hawk were one of his employees.

The Hawk worked for no one. He walked back to his desk and settled into his chair. He crossed his arms, leaned on his elbows, and gave this sniveling john his best mafia don stare.

"Jack is reporting that there are cops at every entrance. They're looking for a middle-aged man with a fleshy nose, a bit of a paunch, blonde hair with a bald patch at the top, last seen wearing black slacks and a white dress shirt. Does that sound like anyone you know?"

"Holy shit! How do they know?"

"Hallway surveillance video. It's only a matter of time until they figure out there's a connection between this penthouse and that condominium unit. You aren't the only one that needs to get the hell out of here. I told you I'm making arrangements."

"I want my money back, too."

"I don't have to give you shit. You got what you wanted."

"I didn't ask for a girl who'd jump off a balcony."

The Hawk made a show of rubbing his chin. "Do you

know how doctors get rid of hemorrhoidal tissue, Roger? Don't be a pain in the ass." He held an open hand across the desk. "Hand me your phone."

"Fuck you."

The Hawk retrieved a Glock from its holster beneath his sports jacket, and he pointed it at the john's chest.

Roger's eyes went wide. "Okay." He reached into the pocket of his slacks and set a phone on the desk. The Hawk picked it up and rose from his chair.

"Stay put, Roger. I'll be back."

. . .

The Hawk put the pistol back in its holster and walked down a hallway. He had long accepted the advice that in case of fire, every home should have an evacuation plan. Although this afternoon's incident had burned his ass, he wouldn't be going up in smoke, and neither would his business.

He reached the lounge. On a white sofa, each holding a full daypack on her lap, sat his most important employees.

Dima wore a carnation hijab with white polka dots, but Jannah, Amelia, and Razaan were bare-headed. All four were about to have an unexpected vacation. He'd check them into a low-budget SeaTac hotel where they'd be ignored, but he couldn't tell them that, even if he wanted to. He didn't speak their language and they didn't speak his, except for vocabulary related to the trade.

Standing between them and the door, Shayma lowered her head and stared at her feet.

He glared at her. "You said Amal was ready."

Shayma did not look up. "She did everything we told her to. She made him feel at ease. She was lively."

"You tell her to jump?"

Shayma shook her head.

The Hawk picked up the nearest thing at hand—a coffee table book featuring photos of yachts—and he hurled it at Shayma. She ducked, and the book smashed against a painting, knocking it to the floor.

The girls' eyes widened.

"That's right! We're not planning a fucking party." It didn't matter that they couldn't understand the words. He'd made sure they understood the gist.

Shayma stayed in a crouch.

"Stand up!"

Shayma complied.

"Tell the girls we're going to move to a bigger and better place. But first we'll be staying in a motel. Tell them it's a vacation. I'm not going to have them entertaining men in a fucking dive."

Shayma smiled. "This is why I stay with you. You care about the girls."

It would be beneath both him and Shayma to let loose the ironic laugh that rose in his chest. Shayma knew what would happen if she tried to leave. Everyone did.

"Yes, I care about them," he said. "Tell them it won't be long. I've been looking for a new place. We're expanding. Now's as good a time as any to let them know you'll be bringing back some new sisters. As for Amal—tell them she had a terrible accident and now she's dead. Emphasize that if she hadn't disappointed us, she'd still be alive. We want to protect them. We want them to have good lives."

Shayma hit some sort of internal switch, and a smile lit up her face as she relayed The Hawk's words in Arabic. The Hawk glanced at his phone—no message yet from Jack.

If they didn't get out of there ASAP, it wouldn't matter what The Hawk planned.

CHAPTER THREE

As Boyd and Abboud made their way back to the Elliott Bay lobby, he received a text from Roshan.

Report to the Mt. Baker Conference Room ASAP. Bring Abboud.

He sighed. "We're supposed to report to Roshan. I think she knows."

"Knows what? That I said a prayer?"

"That you and I interrupted the examination of the body."

"I am not worried. Someone had to do it."

He sighed. "There's a word for that. Audacity."

"I prefer *necessity.*"

"Brazen."

"Intrepid."

"Cheek."

"Grit."

He couldn't hold back a smile. Who *was* this woman? "Where did you learn that kind of vocabulary?"

"Where did you?"

"Come on. Let's go face the music."

Roshan nodded when Boyd and Abboud entered the conference room, then returned her attention to a pair of laptop computers situated at the head of the table. Special Agent in Charge Fisk, who supervised the Seattle bureau, was also in the room, along with Detective Sherman and a half-dozen others Boyd didn't recognize.

Abboud nudged his arm. "You may stop digging your grave now," she whispered.

"Back it up," Roshan said to a tall man with tightly curled hair. "Go to the interaction in the hallway with Mrs. Al-Salek before she enters the condo. Boyd, tell me what you notice."

He moved closer, as did Abboud.

The interaction lasted less than a minute. Mrs. Al-Salek gestured toward the girl's earrings, visible because she wore the hijab loosely. The downward angle of the camera made it difficult to discern body language, but the girl had a slight smile that seemed stitched in place. When the chaperone grasped her arm and pulled her away, the girl turned her head back toward Mrs. Al-Salek, and this time the smile was gone.

"What do you make of that?" said Roshan.

"The girl looks less than enthusiastic," said Boyd.

Roshan nodded. "Jump to the single man entering the condo."

A man in dark slacks and a white shirt walked into the camera's field of vision. He knocked on the door and walked in when it opened. Three minutes later, the chaperone exited via the same door.

"Twelfth floor now," said Roshan. "Show us what you put together."

They turned their attention to the second laptop. The same chaperone exited an elevator and walked toward the CCTV camera. She passed by a seating area of light-colored furniture before entering a different unit.

"Now show the men," said Roshan.

On the first computer, thirty-seven minutes after the chaperone departed, two men walked into view, one stocky and the other lanky, both wearing ballcaps that hid their faces. Almost immediately afterward, they left with the man who'd been in the room. This time, the man wore a ballcap like the two who'd retrieved him. He carried his shoes. They reappeared on the second computer, exiting an elevator and entering the penthouse.

"Are they still there?" asked Boyd.

"We don't know," said Roshan. "Eight minutes after this scene, the CCTV went dead."

"I've got two plainclothesmen up there right now watching the place," said Sherman. So far no one has entered or left. A SWAT team has assembled in the conference room next to us. They're got the manager of this place with them. They're studying floorplans and developing their strategy. I expect they'll be ready pretty damn quick."

"Sherman has another team reviewing surveillance video from the past week," said Roshan.

Sherman nodded. "I counted as many as seventeen men admitted into the penthouse in a single twenty-four-hour period. Also, several young women, might even be teens, leave at various times from the penthouse, reappear on the ninth-floor camera, enter the same condo with the same woman acting as a kind of chaperone, apparently. Then a dude shows up and the chaperone skedaddles. It looks like we've got activity in the penthouse as well as this ninth-floor condominium."

Roshan gestured toward Abboud. "That's why we need you here. We don't know whether any or all of these other girls are Syrian or Arab, but a lot of times that's how these trafficking operations work, specializing in a certain nationality. We want you ready to go, right after the SWAT team secures the penthouse. The girls are likely going to be hysterical. It's not exactly translating documents, Abboud. You up for this?"

"I would rather deal with the traffickers," said Abboud, "but I will settle for speaking with the girls."

Both Sherman and Roshan glanced at Boyd, a question in their eyes. He shrugged his shoulders. *Hey, I just met her,* he wanted to say.

Fisk broke the pause. He was a broad-shouldered man, fiftyish, with thinning hair and what Boyd had long ago concluded was a permanent scowl. "I understand you have reason to feel that way," he said to Abboud. "Especially if these other girls are also Syrian." He nodded toward Sherman and Roshan. "Continue."

Sherman introduced the other individuals in the room. Four worked for the Seattle PD Vice and High-Risk Victims Unit. Two were Washington Anti-Trafficking Network counselors.

"Surveillance video also shows three different men coming and going from both the penthouse and the condo," said Sherman. "They're either running the show or serving as muscle. By the way, surprise, surprise: none of them is Phillip Buchanan, the supposed owner of the condo. Mr. Buchanan died of heart failure twenty years ago at the ripe age of six. Whoever these men are, we'll separate them into different rooms, advise them of their rights, ask them what the hell's going on. See if they hang themselves. My people will do the questioning. Agent Fisk, would you like to join Agents Roshan and Boyd to observe?"

Fisk picked up a baggie that contained a single earring with the eagle that Mrs. Al-Salek described. "If these girls *are* Syrian, I want to know how the hell they got here. I don't see how an official refugee ends up in a high-priced brothel. A legal refugee would be connected to a support group, and we'd be keeping track of her. We can't have people from that region slipping into the country and we don't know about it. It's bad enough to have a girl trafficked like that. But she didn't blow herself up in the lobby. That's the potential we're talking about here."

"I'll interpret that as a *yes,*" said Sherman.

. . .

Fifteen minutes later, after taking the elevator to the eleventh floor and the stairs to the twelfth floor, Boyd and Abboud, along with Sherman and the others in their group, stopped and waited. Shortly afterward, an eight-person SWAT team emerged from an elevator on the other end of a short corridor to their right.

The SWAT team turned a corner in front of the stairwell and went down a hallway before gathering on both sides of the penthouse door. Their leader pounded the door with an open palm. "Police! Open the door."

Ten seconds passed. Boyd's body tensed. His mind blinked back in time to a concrete hovel on a packed dirt street early in his first stint in Iraq. It had been 3 a.m. local time. His squad was looking for bombs, not girls. Nobody inside opened the door. Only two of the residents walked out alive.

It was the first time he'd ever killed a man. He got used to it. He didn't like the part of himself that got used to it.

The SWAT leader nodded at a beefy-sized cop, who swung a battering ram hard, busting open the door. A half dozen officers burst into the penthouse.

"Front room clear!"

"Clear!"

"Clear!"

"Clear!"

Nobody was home.

CHAPTER FOUR

Three days later on the other side of the world, Lely Khayat sat on a mat in a trailer so small she could walk from one end to the other in nine and a half steps, but it was her home now, one among thousands crammed into the Jordanian desert below the remains of Syria. She wore her best abaya, the black one with turquoise patterns along the shoulders and around the cuffs. Although it was only mid-morning, stale heat extracted sweat from her body.

The terms *refugee* and *orphan* still did not take residence in her mind. Those words applied to other girls, and yet each day she woke on a little pad in this trailer with someone else's family. It was unreal, like a mirage, like this entire city, Za'atari Refugee Camp, an ellipse of tents and trailers encircled by walls and concertina wire. But those two words brought them a visitor on this morning.

First to the Grand Qadia and second to Lely, Mama Amena handed out tea in Styrofoam cups—nobody brought real cups out of the wreck that had once been Syria, only clothing, pictures, jewelry, old coins, maybe a silver bowl, although Lely had never seen a silver bowl. It was an object named in novels. She herself had no small valuables, not unless she counted the two bangles on her right wrist, one a cobalt blue and the other red like her favorite kind of gumdrop, and for those trinkets she couldn't obtain two Jordanian dinars even if she wanted to sell them.

Her real mother gave them to her. Before the thing that happened.

So, yes, Mama Amena was a queen for taking Lely into her care, but Lely quite honestly would have deeply preferred to have her real mother at her side. Then this whole interview wouldn't be necessary.

Across from her, it wasn't truly a Grand Qadia—a great judge—sitting on the floor with her legs folded to her side. Attired in a blue hijab and a plain black abaya, Miss Shayma sniffed the tea and surveyed the trailer with a disapproving eye. The skin was tight across her face, as though she'd stretched and clamped the slack at the back of her neck. She'd plucked and curved her brows into shapes that reminded Lely of tarantula legs.

Miss Shayma had the power to determine Lely's fate. So let her be a Grand Qadia. Lely would have fun with that.

The Grand Qadia gestured toward a mural painted on what had been beige, sleep-inducing wall panels.

"Mrs. Zuabi tells me you are the painter of these hummingbirds." Her voice carried an accusation.

"They are falling leaves, Your Eminence," said Lely, gathering as much piety as she could summon. "To depict a sentient being is *haram*—forbidden."

Mama Amena nearly twisted off her own neck, so sharply did she turn to gape at Lely, who found it difficult to repress a giggle. The Grand Qadia lifted an eyelid a mere millimeter.

"Lely!" Her mouth agape, Mama Amena placed a hand over her stomach, the slight bulge of her pregnancy invisible beneath her abaya. Mama Amena made that gesture whenever she experienced strong emotion, as though a four-month-old fetus could serve as a stress ball.

"Then what about all the murals on the Za'atari trailers and walls?" The Grand Qadia set out her bait.

"*Haram.* Animals. Birds. Humans."

"They're not realistic!" protested Mama Amena. "No one is trying to be Allah, most gracious and merciful."

"You're fourteen, Lely, yes?"

"Yes, Your Eminence."

"Lely, stop it! *Your Eminence* indeed. Pardon us, but Lely's ... we've grown used to her antics, but this is too much."

"Quite the contrary. It's endearing. Her spirit has value." The Grand Qadia set her tea on the floor and glanced toward the other side of the trailer where Mr. Zuabi sat observing.

"Let's get on with it, shall we? You remember your friend Amal? She's thriving. She loves living with us high up in a tall building in a city called Seattle. When she looks out her window, she sees ocean water sheltered by islands full of green trees. Beyond them, mountains raise sharp peaks covered in snow. She likes her new sisters, but she misses your friendship. Because of that, my American family wishes for you to join us."

Lely's jaw stiffened. This was entirely too soon. How should a penitent respond to the Grand Qadia's pronouncement? For once, Lely could not find the words.

"Ah, you see? We have surprises for you, too, Lely."

"As well as for me," said Mama Amena. "This feels so sudden. I thought it would take longer to arrange. We've ... we've gotten used to her."

The Grand Qadia shifted her legs.

"It may take a week or two. Our transportation won't be ready right away. And we hope to adopt three more girls of high school age."

Mama Zuabi took the kettle off the hotplate and poured more tea for the Grand Qadia. She gestured toward Lely's mural. "The color you see on these walls—it's like wherever she walks, she paints the air the same way. And such sad times. We'll miss her."

"She'll have such wonderful experiences. It won't all be school. She'll go to gigantic shopping malls. She'll watch movies on huge screens."

"I thought America had closed the door to people like us." Mama Zuabi returned the kettle.

"So they have. But when a family has money, exceptions are made." The Grand Qadia reached over and clasped Lely's hand. "We'll have great fun."

Lely glanced at Mama Amena, whose eyes watered with tears, then down the distance of the trailer to Mr. Zuabi, who had opened a news magazine.

"What about my cousin?" She pulled her hand back.

"After you told me about him yesterday, I contacted the United Nations. The officials there were kind enough to examine their records. He and his family seem to have disappeared shortly after crossing into Turkey. Someone in one of the camps said they tried to make it to Europe, but none of those nations have a record of their entry."

Constriction spread from her jaws down her neck and into her heart. *Ya rabbih.* So many swallowed by the Mediterranean Sea—surely not her cousin!

"They're dead." The words burst from Lely's gut, stamping certainty into her mind.

"Most likely we've only lost track of them," said the Grand Qadia. "Maybe they're back in Syria. I'll continue working with the United Nations. If we can find them before we leave, and they express a capacity to care for Lely, she could join them instead. But under the circumstances …"

Lely looked down at the floor. "I'd be a burden."

Like she was now, even if Mama Amena, new life growing in her womb, never showed it. At the other end of the trailer, Mr. Zuabi turned a page of the magazine. Three months ago a helicopter dropped barrel bombs on an apartment building where Lely's family was visiting friends. Residents in the same apartment, Mr. and Mrs. Zuabi had ventured outside, he in search of food and she in search of water. They had left their girl, a year younger than Lely, inside.

Many graves were dug that day. Before Lely could grieve on the ground that held her family, the Zuabis, may Allah reward them, grabbed her and began a four-day trek from the hell they still called Syria. And although they never made her feel like a burden, she felt the space and the weight of her presence.

"I'll go," she said.

"Lely." Mama Amena's hand gripped hers.

"You're wonderful, oh so wonderful," Lely assured her, and she rose to punctuate the sentiment with a movie-ending hug. "I will write you and never forget you," she murmured to this surrogate mama, and because there are only a limited number of departures a mother can withstand, Mama Amena shook with tears for the impending loss of her substitute daughter.

Lely pulled away and smiled at the dampening eyes and cheeks of Mama Amena.

"It's America. I shall be rich. I'll be educated. And when I am wealthy, I will send for you wherever you are, and we'll live in a big house."

And maybe it was absurd but the idea of it brought a smile to Mama Amena's face, and that made it worth the spinning pain that roiled inside Lely's chest.

"Mama Amena," she said. "My dear Mama Amena." And they embraced again.

CHAPTER FIVE

Boyd rang a buzzer outside the Plexiglass window of the Yukon Inn, a single-story L-shaped motel from the 1960s station wagon era. Perhaps it had been painted since those days, but he wouldn't bet on it.

If that girl hadn't ended up dead outside the Elliott Bay Hotel and Condominiums, he and the joint task force would have already carried out this operation. Every day that went by without putting the Yukon Inn out of business, trafficked girls were victimized many times over. He'd have carried out the sting a month ago, but Roshan and Sherman insisted they gather more evidence and game more scenarios.

Rain clattered on the overhead awning and poured onto the asphalt behind him. He pushed the purple *Dawgs* cap down over his forehead and silently cursed the bureau's techies. If they could figure out how to hide a surveillance camera in a hat, why couldn't they make the damn thing have an adjustable fit?

A scrawny man with thinning gray hair and a turquoise bolo tie walked through a doorway and sat on a stool inside the check-in room. He peered beyond Boyd at the nearly vacant parking lot before bringing his attention to the business at hand.

"A pleasant evening to you," said Boyd. "I'd like a deluxe room and I'd love to have a visitor."

The clerk's gaze paused at the scar next to Boyd's ear. "You know what you're asking for?"

Boyd nodded.

The clerk slid a clipboard through a slot at the bottom of the glass. "Fill this out."

"How much for the room?"

"Seventy-eight dollars twenty-three cents."

"So I pay the rest later?"

The clerk said nothing.

"I'm not going to pay seventy-eight bucks and that's all there is to it. I'll go home and sleep in my own bed. Do *you* know what I'm asking for?"

The clerk waited.

"If I don't have a visitor within half an hour, I'm going to come back here and you're going to give me my damn money back. Is that clear?"

The clerk nodded. "Seventy-eight dollars twenty-three cents."

Boyd clamped a hundred-dollar bill onto the clipboard and slid it, form unfilled, back through the slot. "Keep it. Call it a finder's fee."

The clerk slid back a key to room seven.

Boyd answered with a half wave of his hand. "Nice talking to you, Mr. Loquacious."

In the twenty feet between the lobby and the Chevy Silverado he'd chosen from the FBI garage, a waterfall of rain soaked through his cap, drenched his hair and face. If the mike embedded in the hat could survive this deluge, it could endure anything except maybe a volcano. He drove the truck away from the cottage, glimpsed Sherman sitting in the driver's seat of a white van at the adjacent Taco Bell and parked in front of Room 7.

"You catch that interaction?" he asked.

"We've got it," she said.

He picked up a duffle bag and an empty Starbucks cup and went inside. A queen-size bed with a thin brown quilt occupied four-fifths of the room. A small television leaned down from a bracket high on the wall. Beneath it, a mirror reflected the empty bed. On the other side of the bed, a sink, toilet, and shower crammed a small bathroom.

Boyd put the coffee cup on a microwave and powered up the camera on the lid. He activated the digital voice recording pen in the outside pocket of the duffle bag before placing it next to the only pillow.

After he examined the smoke detector, overhead light, electric outlets, and light switches and found nothing hidden, he sat on the edge of the bed and waited. Excitement and dread raced through his body. He relished the shock of the daddies when they realized they'd been busted; he grieved for the girls. Three months ago, a fourteen-year-old Guatemalan went hysterical—not because of him or the cops, but at the sight of the pimp lying face down on the floor with cuffs around his wrists. A bilingual cop who participated in the bust told him afterward that the girl was screaming she didn't tell, she didn't want the police, she was sorry, she was sorry.

That same girl attended Chief Sealth International High School now. She was struggling and needed special help, but she told Roshan and Boyd during a follow-up visit that she wanted to run track in the spring and was thinking someday she might be a chef.

More such girls, Chinese this time, were locked into a two-room unit diagonally across the lot from Boyd.

Ten minutes ticked by. Had he done something to spook these people?

He found a remote on the nightstand and flipped through television stations. He left it on a channel where some linebacker-type was hauling ass down an alley, two blues on his tail, an unseen camera bobbing behind them.

"Are you watching *Cops*?" Sherman asked.

"No, that's me. I'm practicing my sound effects."

The bad guy leaped and grasped the top of a wooden fence, swung his legs high, hovered, shouted a bleep. He dropped back, faced the cops, followed their command to lie down on the ground.

"How do you like my large dog impersonation?" asked Boyd.

"You'd do better to switch to a creepy john," said Sherman. "Our target's walking your way with a girl."

On the television, the cops rolled the handcuffed suspect to a sitting position, his back against the fence. It sounded as though the dog would bust through the wood any second.

A loud knock rapped from outside. Boyd muted the program and opened the door.

The Chinese girl wore shorts the length of a washrag and a tank top the size of a tea towel. Rainwater streamed off her pixie-cut black hair, and goosebumps peppered her arms. Plastic pink sandals did nothing to protect her feet.

Boyd stepped aside. "Hey, little girl. Get yourself inside."

The pimp, attired in a green parka with a fleece-lined hood, stepped in behind her. He had a blond Fu Manchu moustache and a shaved head. His arms were half flesh and half steroids. It looked like he knocked the stuffing out of medicine balls for recreation.

The girl sat at the edge of the bed and folded her hands together over her lap. She might have been either side of eighteen years old.

"You could use some warming up," he said to the girl.

"Oh yeah," crowed the pimp. "She'll warm you to bursting. You'll be like a hot stove. She'll put you in the broiler."

"How much?"

"Depends."

"An hour."

"Hundred fifty."

"Whatever kind of sex I want."

"I expect her to be in one piece when you're done."

"It's not nice to hurt the ones you love. She'll be fine." Boyd took a roll of bills from his pocket, pulled out seven twenties and a ten, and placed it on the bed next to the wet and shivering girl.

"That's right, bro." The man grabbed the money and glanced at the television. "I think I seen that one. Fuckin' dogs, man."

Boyd put the rest of the money back in his pocket. "It's a dumb show. The bad guys never get away."

"Yeah, they do. I seen it."

The pimp opened the door to leave but froze when a flashlight from outside lit his head aglow.

"Not this time," said Boyd.

The pimp slowly raised both hands.

Boyd let out a breath. Taut coils loosened in his body.

The pimp slammed the door shut and locked it in one motion.

Adrenalin instantly jacked up every molecule in Boyd's body. He darted to the far side of the bed, at the same time taking his pistol from its holster beneath his shirt.

"Stay put!" he shouted. The pimp glared at him and shook his head. From outside, a battering ram smashed into the door, splintering wood but failing to pop it open. The pimp ignored the noise and took a step forward.

From the foot of the bed, the girl lunged at Boyd, clawing like a feral cat. One hand smacked the pistol. Another raked from his forehead over an eye and down his cheek. She clung to his arm as the pimp moved toward him and another thunderous bang crashed into the door.

Time slowed. His brain processed several simultaneous events as though they were separate and sequential—the door popping open but held in place by the metal door guard; Sherman's voice bellowing commands; the girl digging her nails into the flesh of his forearm; the pimp sweeping his arm up, now holding an open blade.

He shoved the girl loose, leaped across the queen-sized bed and spun to face the pimp before the man could even turn around. He put a bead on the pimp's chest and yelled at him to freeze.

One more slam of the battering ram blasted open the door.

The pimp moved his arms away from his sides and dropped the knife. "All right all right all right!" he called.

* * *

Minutes later, Roshan stood with Boyd beneath an awning that failed to prevent the rain from showering them at an angle. A few feet away, six cops stood over the handcuffed pimp lying face down on the cement outside the room.

"You're bleeding, Boyd," said Roshan. "What the fuck happened?"

"I could handle the pimp," he said, "but the girl jumped me and held on like a tiger. I had a hell of a time pushing her off me."

Roshan couldn't stop herself from chuckling.

"You try taking her on," said Boyd. "That girl's a textbook example of the Stockholm Syndrome."

"Sure, she is," said Roshan. "It's just … oh, man." She looked down the sidewalk. "Hey, Sherman, come over here and check out Boyd."

Sherman strolled over and appraised the wound. "She got you good."

"What do you mean?" said Roshan. "It's a work of art! If I had a mirror … Oh, hey, step back in the room."

"I don't want to see it," said Boyd.

"C'mon, Boyd, have a little appreciation. Get in there and take a look."

He could see Roshan wouldn't let up until he complied. Sherman helped her steer him past the demolished doorway into Room Seven, where he positioned himself in front of the mirror on the wall at the foot of the bed. Four rake marks, as though produced by the tines of a sharpened fork, etched perfectly parallel red streaks into his cheek at an angle, with the scar near his ear exactly at the midpoint of the outmost line.

"Shit, that's pretty good," he said. "Think it'll leave another scar?"

"Nah, you're not that lucky," said Roshan.

* * *

While Sherman and another Seattle PD detective went to the cottage to interrogate the clerk, Boyd and Roshan walked through the diminishing downpour to the double-room unit where the girls were housed. A victim counselor, an interpreter, and two uniformed cops were waiting.

Four girls in flimsy attire occupied a brown Naugahyde couch, while two sat on the floor in front of them. Their arms were thin and their faces pale. Although the storm blew cold air beneath the door, a heating system cranked to a bonfire setting broiled the room. It smelled like bologna and mustard, sweat and cigarettes.

Eyes downcast, the girls were mute, as though their emotions had been strangled.

"Tell them they're not in trouble," Roshan said to the interpreter. "Tell them this isn't their fault."

Two girls raised their heads enough to peek at Roshan before lowering their eyes again. One of the girls on the floor, who didn't look at all Chinese, opened and closed her fist. Her hair, wavy and acorn brown, fell past her shoulders. There was a bruise around her right eye.

As the interpreter explained what would be happening, she was the only girl who showed no signs of comprehension. She could have been from a thousand different places, but Boyd had a feeling about her. He knelt in front of her.

"Alarabiah?" he asked. *Arabic?*

Her eyes widened.

"Esmee Asayad Boyd." *I am Mr. Boyd.*

She hesitated, as though between fear and thirst for a mother's hug.

"Ma esmouki?" *What's your name?*

"Hafa," she said.

* * *

Mid-morning the next day Abboud sat next to Hafa Jandali on a pearl-white chenille sofa, while Boyd, Sherman, and Roshan occupied armchairs of the same material. Mozart played softly from a portable speaker. The FBI designed this room for occasions when they wanted to put subjects at ease.

Abboud had brought green tea from her office, and she put a pinch of cardamom in everyone's cup. It gave the brew a different flavor, citrusy and spicy. Boyd couldn't decide if he liked it or wanted to spit it out.

The new setting did nothing to loosen Hafa's demeanor. She shrank into herself, eyes downcast, voice monotone.

"She says she was at this place for two weeks and two days," said Abboud. "She was brought there on her eighteenth birthday."

Boyd leaned toward the sofa. He couldn't understand Hafa's words, but he wanted to mine the emotions behind them.

"Where was she before that?" asked Roshan.

Abboud translated the question and Hafa answered.

"She does not know. She cannot read the English words, but it was much more lavish than where she was last night."

"A goat pen is more lavish," said Sherman. "Ask her to tell us how she got from where she was to where we found her."

Abboud stayed quiet and took notes while Hafa spoke. Twice, she asked the young woman a short question, and afterward she retold the girl's story.

Hafa had been brought to the Yukon Inn because she'd upset the man in charge where she was before. She didn't show enough enthusiasm for the customers. The boss warned her she had to improve or else they'd sell her to someplace bad, but no matter how much she tried, she couldn't summon the smiles.

Abboud took a sip of tea. "They wanted her to … to act like she enjoyed the attentions of the customers. One night after another customer gave her a bad review, the boss became irate. He told his assistants to bring her to a place where they would beat her until she smiled, where they would make her be with lots of men, where the food was bad. That was how she came to be at the hotel last night."

Hafa wiped tears from both cheeks. A quiet rage seethed inside Boyd's chest.

Abboud pushed a strand of mahogany-colored hair from her forehead back beneath her lavender hijab. Her face was smooth, but her eyes were dark like the woods at dawn.

"Can she describe the place where she was before they moved her?" asked Roshan.

Abboud questioned the young woman, who stared at the floor when she gave her answer. "It was next to the water," said Abboud. "The outside walls were windows. She could see big ships."

Sherman squeezed the arms of her chair. "No way," she said.

Anticipation sent a jolt through Boyd's body.

Roshan put down her cup and took out her smartphone. "Let's find out," she said.

She found the photo she wanted and handed it to Boyd to hand to Abboud. It was an outside shot from ground level, with the words "Elliott Bay Hotel and Condominiums" in white lettering above a smoky glass entrance. Hafa stared at it, shook her head, spoke to Abboud.

Abboud passed the phone back to Boyd. "She said she never saw the building from the outside. They kept her in a big apartment, like a house. She knows it was high off the ground. In all the time she was there, she was never allowed to leave the apartment."

Roshan found an inside shot of the penthouse. A half dozen cocktail tables were situated in front of a small bar of polished wood.

Hafa's eyes went wide. She looked away from the phone, as though she'd glimpsed a room from hell.

Boyd's heartbeat quickened.

Roshan moved to the sofa to show Hafa more photos. Boyd joined Sherman, who'd gone behind the sofa to watch.

Hafa knew the first names of the girls that the surveillance cameras had captured. Ayisha. Dima. Amelia. Riham. She did not recognize the deceased girl who'd worn the Syrian eagle earrings, but she knew the woman who brought the girls to the ninth-floor condo, as well as the two men who occasionally did the same: Shayma, Jack, and Majd. She didn't know much about the other girls' lives before they were brought to America, except for what they had in common. They all came from families whose parents had died during the war. They were orphans.

And they all came from Za'atari Refugee Camp.

Abboud kept her voice more even than had been the case when she'd interviewed Mrs. Al-Salek, but Boyd sensed her pain, nonetheless.

"You told us you lived at Za'atari," he said.

Abboud nodded. "I am also an orphan. And a widow, too."

CHAPTER SIX

They sat on white plastic chairs, Auntie Dinar across from Lely at a white plastic table under the slate gray sky. Near them on the other side of a rope, crowds of people strolled or bicycled both directions on the main commercial avenue—funny that everyone called it the Champ-Elysees. It was Za'atari, after all. At this new city in the Jordanian desert, proprietors used propane stoves to cook food within three-sided booths constructed of particle board. The customers ate al-fresco.

But, oh, what food! Fresh falafels deep-fried, piquant with onion and pepper, pungent and smoky with coriander and cumin. Beneath the falafels, hummus, thick and lemony, and on top, toum sauce, creamy white and potent with garlic. Served with plastic forks on a double-layer of paper plates.

"Save some room," said Auntie Dinar. "We're going to have harisi cake afterward. There is a place two blocks ahead. Nobody makes harisi in Seattle." She closed her eyes, leaned back her head, and placed both hands over her stomach. She wore no hijab to cover her hair, so silvery blonde that she had to have colored it. Her eyebrows were curved and narrow, her lips glossy pink, and she had a mark halfway up her right jaw like a piece of skin from a tiny red grape.

No other Syrian women at Za'atari resembled her. Did all the women who found refuge in America crave the same appearance? Did they have a wallet as full as hers? Auntie Dinar—that might as well be her name—it fit her better than Shayma.

No matter how much money they had in America, they would not convince Lely to remove her hijab in public. On the other hand, she might try to color her hair, make it a darker, richer brown, and she would like to have some lipstick, not glossy, but some tint of red.

She used a plastic knife to cut a falafel in half, then a fork to scoop it up with hummus and toum, felt the warmth and the spices tingle in her mouth as she slowly chewed. She would eat it all, and she would have that cake and baklava, too, whatever she could talk Auntie into buying, and she didn't care if she had a stomachache for a week.

"I brought a letter from Amal," said Auntie, reaching into her purse. Her meal, half uneaten, tempted Lely, but she held back. Auntie mustn't think of her as a pig. That could influence her decision about whether to let Lely join her family. Auntie withdrew the letter.

"It's typed," she said, "because everyone uses computers in America. She's excited that you might join her. Shall I read it while you eat?"

"Please and thank-you, Auntie Din ... I mean, Shayma," said Lely, still chewing.

She thought she ought to drop the whole *Auntie Dinar* business—she almost said it aloud! Perhaps this woman might not appreciate the humor. She might close her wallet before they'd eaten cake.

"Dearest Lely," began Shayma.

Dearest. Strange—she and Amal weren't that close as friends. But maybe that's how everyone talked in America.

The letter described the rain and the greenness, tall, needled trees filling mountains and lining the roads, grocery stores with dozens of different cereals, fruits and vegetables without bruise or blemish, friendly people, tall and cute men.

"Wait a minute," said Lely, down to her last half dozen bites. "*Tall and cute men?* This is from Amal?"

Shayma looked up over the top of the letter. "Why? You think she does not notice men?"

"Boys, maybe, sometimes. That would be ... no, I've never heard that from Amal."

"It *is* America, Lely. Boys and girls and men and women spend a lot of time together, and nobody thinks anything about it. Have you seen their movies?"

"Some. But the *cute* part. I mean, that's how I talk, I admit it, when I'm with my friends, but Amal, she was always so serious. We could be checking out the guys and she wouldn't say anything. We used to tease her and, wow, did she blush."

"So you like looking at guys?" Shayma put a tease into her voice and raised her brows.

Lely diverted her attention to her plate and scraped up a fork of hummus.

"Don't be embarrassed." Shayma set the letter on the table. "All around the world girls your age look at guys. And guys check out the girls. Remember, I am your mentor. More than that, your friend. You can tell me anything or ask me anything and I will listen and help you fit in with the Americans."

"Okay. So I have heard ... *sometimes* some Americans will treat you meanly if they see you wearing a hijab."

Shayma leaned back and paused before answering. "Ninety-nine percent would never do that. They'll say you look lovely. Chances are, you'll never run into one of those uglier ones who say things like that. And if you do, others will defend you, and you'll have all your new sisters to support you."

"I've missed a lot of school."

"The schools there will help you, but you don't have to go to school if you don't want to."

"But I *do* want to. I miss it. When I write to Amal I'm going to ask her about the schools. It's funny for her not to mention them. She cares a lot about her education, more than I do if you want to know the truth."

Lely felt Shayma's eyes studying her for a moment.

"There's more than one kind of education, as I'm sure you know. More important ways than school. For example, the kind of knowing that raises you up from a girl to a woman."

Lely took the bite of hummus. No way was Auntie Dinar going to lure her into talking about *that*. She set her fork on the almost-empty plate.

"I haven't had harisi cake in ages," she said.

CHAPTER SEVEN

Boyd zoomed out one click on the satellite map. From above, the Port of Beirut took the shape of a Gila monster with three stubby legs. Container ships anchored along the length of its body for over two miles. It would be easy to sneak a few girls up the gangplank of one of the ships, as long as certain dockworkers and sailors were happy with their remuneration. Hafa, the young woman extricated from Fu Manchu's two-bit trafficking operation, wouldn't have known about the bribes, but she did know she'd departed the Middle East from Beirut.

Holding a Dr. Who travel mug, Roshan stepped into the entry of Boyd's cubicle. "Fisk wants us," she said.

Boyd picked up his iPad and crunched the Necco in his mouth. "What the hell for?"

"He didn't say."

. . .

A phone to his ear, Fisk waved them into the office. They waited on chairs in front of his desk while he spoke with someone about flight schedules. He ended the call and appraised them for a moment, his mouth locked into its characteristic scowl.

"I'm sending you two to Jordan," he announced.

Boyd's jaw tightened. Avoiding that region had been a big reason why he hadn't reenlisted three years ago.

"What do you have in mind?" asked Roshan. Her voice and posture made it seem as though all Fisk wanted them to do was order lunch—and she had a husband and two kids.

"I want you to find out how someone's smuggling those girls out of Za'atari Refugee Camp. Like I told you, this is a security issue. That report about the Syrian woman you pulled out of the hotel? It went all the way to Washington, and they bounced it right back to us. They want you two to go to Za'atari with Nawar Abboud. Have her talk to people, show photographs of the woman you rescued and a prettied-up version of the girl who biffed it on the sidewalk. Someone's going to recognize one of them, and you follow the lead wherever it takes you."

"What if Abboud doesn't want to go?" asked Roshan.

"Appeal to her nobility. These are her people. And let her know she'll get twenty-five percent for hazardous duty on top of her regular contractual rate. Same for the both of you, by the way."

Roshan put a hand on the edge of Fisk's desk. "She's very capable. But suppose we agitate the wrong people. She's not trained. She's not an agent."

"She's trained well enough." Fisk turned toward his computer. He fidgeted with the mouse, clicked a few times, and turned the screen so that it faced Boyd and Roshan.

In the full-screen photo, six soldiers wearing green camouflage sat on a curb, a blasted-out building and a ruble of bricks behind them. Black balaclavas covered their heads and faces, and they held a mishmash of rifles, including two AK-47s. Their hands were bare and slender, and they wore sneakers instead of combat boots.

Fisk stood and leaned over the screen. He pointed at the second soldier from the right, one of the two who wielded an assault rifle.

"Nawar Abboud," he said.

Boyd's jaw dropped.

"Interesting," said Roshan.

"Who's she with?" asked Boyd.

"The Sawt-al-Haq Battalion," said Fisk. "Part of the Free Syrian Army, Aleppo."

Fisk turned the screen back. "An all-female battalion. Ms. Abboud never tried to hide that. Not during her UN intake, the background checks for refugee status in the United States, her interviews to work with us. She and her sister soldiers wanted what we want. Democracy. Equality. You ask me, I'd say we let them down."

He rolled his chair away from the desk. "She's admitted she had another motivation. Revenge against Assad. Something else you should know—she's a taekwondo first-degree black belt. Studied under South Korean volunteers at Za'atari."

Boyd tried to envision Abboud kicking the hell out of someone or putting a bullet in a soldier's chest. The picture didn't jive with the woman he thought he knew.

"Abboud knows how to handle herself," continued Fisk. "You'll be video-conferencing with Dr. Daniel Bergeson, a United Nations security officer assigned to Za'atari. Law enforcement jurisdiction falls to the Jordanian Army. Any arrests to be made, they're the ones to do it."

"Aren't there something like a hundred thousand people in that camp?" asked Roshan.

"Implication being, how the fuck are we going to find these traffickers?" said Fisk. "We've got a lot of front-end planning to do. You're going to need to figure out a cover story and a purpose for why you're there and some innocuous reason for showing the photos. Maybe they're your friends and everything's hunky-dory. Figure something out. Keep in mind there's an eleven-hour time difference between Jordan and Seattle. When Dr. Bergeson is on his lunch break, it's one in the morning here. You'll be working through the night. You've got two weeks."

"Two weeks?" said Roshan.

"I told my boss we'd be there in ten days, two weeks max," said Fisk. "We want this hole plugged. It's not just a Za'atari thing. It only starts there. What's their route to the U.S. and Seattle? Who's bringing them? Do they have any other merchandise, particularly the explosive kind? Job one is to get Abboud on the team. You two comfortable talking to her, or do you want to bring her to me?"

"We'll do it," said Roshan.

. . .

A week later, just before eight o'clock in the morning, Boyd sat at a circular table in Roshan's office. Next to him, Abboud was texting an old friend still residing at the Za'atari Refugee Camp.

Roshan leaned toward her desk and opened a mini-fridge. "How about huckleberry?" She held up a bottle of Torani syrup.

He put a hand over his cup. "You already know the answer."

Roshan poured a shot into her coffee. "So what's your friend say?"

Abboud paused from her typing. "She says our idea will fill a need. There are still many babies born in Za'atari. She has a question, though. What if I will not be allowed to return to the United States?" She looked at Boyd and Roshan. "Is this possible?"

"Not if you're with us," said Boyd. He hoped he was right. He couldn't predict what his own country would do anymore.

"This has happened to others, yes?" persisted Abboud.

"They weren't working for the FBI." He glanced at Roshan.

"That's not going to happen, Abboud," she said. "I guarantee it." Roshan's phone rang. and she turned toward her desk to answer it.

"That was Fisk," she said after the call. "He's approved our cover. We are hereby founding members of Women's Corps International. He said he's putting it at the front of the line at our print shop. He wants a logo printed on t-shirts, jackets, a couple of abayas, stationary, pens, and who knows what else by the end of the week."

"I'll let Dr. Bergeson know." Boyd took a sip of coffee, black, the way he liked it.

"He's probably home by now," said Roshan. "Tell him Fisk says we'll also have a website before the end of the week, and he's assigning a couple of agents to monitor it, reply to inquiries, that sort of stuff." She yawned. "I hope I'll be able to sleep today. It's weird going home at eight in the morning."

"We're getting the jetlag out of the way before we ever board the plane," said Boyd.

He wrote the email, hit *send*, and looked across the table at Abboud.

"Let's carpool. I live five minutes away from you."

Abboud put her phone in her purse. "Do you have your car here now? I was going to take the commuter train home."

. . .

On the north side of Tukwila, Abboud directed Boyd to Amani's Halal Market, situated among a block of continuous storefronts a few miles from SeaTac International Airport. Marine clouds dampened the sidewalks and beaded his pickup with dew.

"Shopping?" he asked.

She picked up her purse. "I live here in an upstairs apartment. Will you come into the store? My uncle makes a fantastic manouche zaatar."

"Manouche?" He turned off the ignition. Was she actually inviting him for breakfast?

"You've heard of it?" she asked.

"It's like a little pizza? I had it once in the suburbs of Baghdad." He hadn't had a meal with a woman since Becky, the Amazon programmer whom he'd met via an online dating service. It had been the day before Mother's Day. Becky had kept hinting—and not so subtly, either—how she wanted to be part of that day's celebration, how her biological clock wasn't getting any younger.

That was more than six months ago.

"It is not Iraqi food," said Abboud. "It is Lebanese, and if you think it is pizza you have never eaten a proper manouche. Now you *must* come in. I cannot have you be ignorant about important matters like this."

She opened her door but paused before stepping out.

"It is only breakfast."

"Of course. Let's call it additional research, with a focus on cuisine." He opened his door partway, just as a city bus barreled by within a foot of his vehicle.

"Be careful," said Abboud. "You cannot eat breakfast if you are squished."

"I'm not going to let a little thing like death disrupt my appetite."

Inside the store, he inhaled deeply, recognized garlic, cayenne, nutmeg and cloves. In the front behind heated glass, lamb meat turned on a spit. The aroma of fresh bread wafted from an unseen oven. Past the cash register, also behind glass, half a dozen manouches lay one atop the other, flatbreads covered in a piquant brown paste with sesame seeds.

His stomach rumbled with hunger.

Behind the front counter, a bald and rotund middle-aged man in a blue blazer sat with his back facing the rest of the store, his arms in rapid motion. He glanced at a security mirror, rose from his chair, and placed a bundle of knitting on a small table.

"Nawar!" he called with enthusiasm while eyeing Boyd uncertainly. Abboud spoke to him in Arabic, and afterward he turned to Boyd.

"You are FBI agent!" He broke into a smile.

Boyd exaggerated looks to the left and right, put a finger to his lips, pantomimed "Shhh."

"My apologies! I will keep your secret."

"He is only joking," said Abboud. She introduced them to each other.

"Ah," said Amani Haddad with a nod. "Mr. Boyd." His gaze flitted on the quarter-sized scar near Boyd's ear before quickly moving away.

"Tell us about your knitting, Uncle," said Abboud.

Haddad retrieved his project and held up a brown misshapen mass. "You like it? A sweater for grandson. Number one birthday is next month."

"It is splendid," said Abboud.

"It looks warm," said Boyd. He'd never have guessed it was a sweater in the making. A cover for a small teapot, perhaps. Or a pouch for collecting strawberries.

"Mr. Boyd lives near here," said Abboud. "He offered to give me transportation. It is called carpooling, except I do not have a car."

"That is very kind," said Haddad. "He can do his shopping here."

"Uncle." Abboud wagged a finger playfully at him. "He is our guest."

Haddad nodded at Boyd. "Well, then, I will give you good prices."

"Uncle Amani, you are hopeless." Abboud stepped through a half-door behind the counter.

"It is the land of capitalism, yes, Mr. Boyd?"

"Some would call it the national religion," he said. "And I would very much enjoy checking out your store."

"Breakfast in five minutes," called Abboud.

In the first aisle, Boyd paused at a collection of small canisters. So this was where Abboud obtained her cardamom. One canister held seeds that looked like chipped pebbles ranging in color from dark brown to charcoal black. Another contained the kind of powder that Abboud kept at the office. Other containers, labeled in English and Arabic, held more familiar spices—anise, marjoram, oregano, turmeric—as well as exotic ones—three kinds of shawarma mixes, Shish Tawook, Ras El Hanouk, and in a larger container, Zaatar. His mind drifted back to the shops and small diners in Baghdad, including one outside the Green Zone which had been a favorite of his until a bomb obliterated it, along with the Iraqis and Westerners who happened to be there at the time.

In the front of the shop a bell rang and in a moment he heard Haddad speaking Arabic with a female customer. Abboud appeared at the front of Boyd's aisle. "Breakfast," she said.

He sat with her at the table where Haddad had left his knitting. The female customer, attired in a dark blue abaya and matching hijab, walked past the counter to an ice cream freezer on the far side of the shop. Haddad positioned himself behind it as the woman peered down through the glass to consider her choices.

"Ice cream and it's forty-two degrees outside?" Boyd mumbled.

"It is Bakdash," said Abboud. "Calling it ice cream is like calling manouche a pizza. You can stretch it like taffy. To prepare it in Damascus, they pound it with wooden pestles."

Boyd stood to watch as Haddad handed the woman what looked like an ordinary ice cream cone coated with some kind of crushed nuts.

"Our Bakdash is not like the real Bakdash from Damascus," said Abboud. "But the refugees from my country come here anyway. While they are eating it, they are consuming memories of a place where they can never return. That is why a woman orders a poor imitation of Bakdash when it is forty-two degrees outside. The Jordanians and Lebanese come here, too. It used to be they could drive to Damascus in a few hours or less."

Boyd finished his manouche. Abboud had topped it not only with the zaatar paste but also sliced tomatoes and cucumbers mixed in yogurt.

"I'd drive a few hours for this," he said.

Their eyes met. A small spark in his chest took him by surprise. Had he gone loony? She was a work colleague, and he was a rookie, and the last thing he needed was complications.

She rose and picked up his plate. "So, is this a fair enough trade? Carpooling for breakfast?"

"Absolutely," he said. "This whole schedule is weird. Normally, after work, if I did anything besides go home, I might go have a beer, watch some football."

Inwardly, he groaned. Why did he have to say that? She was Muslim—and he was an idiot. She couldn't drink a beer.

"So, what do you usually do when you're off work?" he asked.

"Depends on the day." She put the plates in the trash and turned back toward the table. "If it is Tuesday or Thursday, I am at the dojang. The other days, I am here. Sometimes I assist with the store."

"Dojang?"

"Taekwondo. That is what they call the place where we do drills and spar."

"I work out, too," he said. "Lift weights. Run. But this schedule's got me messed up."

She sat at the table. "Would you like some Bakdash?"

"Ice cream in the morning? Why not?"

"Vanilla, chocolate, or caramel?"

"Caramel."

She went to the ice cream case and returned with Bakdash in a paper bowl. She sat next to him and assumed a posture of observation, as though she were a chef watching reactions toward a new recipe.

"What about you?" he asked.

"Not at the moment," she said. "Taste it."

It was cold and creamy, like ice cream, but the flavor was different. Delicate. A subtle evergreen aroma. Crushed pistachios and cashews covered the outside of the scoop.

"This is good," he said.

"The reason that it is not truly Bakdash is the absence of mastic. It is a kind of sap from a tree. That is what also makes the Bakdash have its texture…how do you say it? Stretchy?"

"It's still good."

"It has rose water in it also."

"That's different." He took another bite.

"Now imagine it is summer and the sun is scorching hot."

"In other words, not Seattle."

"Definitely not Seattle."

They arranged for Boyd to pick her up to go to work at 6:30 in the evening. He had almost exited the restaurant when he stopped himself, returned to the coffee section and chose a seven-ounce bag of Najjar Turkish Coffee—without cardamom. He took it to the cash register, and Amani Haddad smiled.

CHAPTER EIGHT

The Hawk puzzled over his menu. He didn't know what the hell the gobbledygook meant, and the English lettering didn't help a damn bit.

From a manila envelope Crabby retrieved a five-by-seven photo and passed it across the table. "I think you'll find her suitable."

The Hawk gazed at her—she had beckoning brown eyes, lips with a slight upturn suggesting mischief, a few strands of coal-black hair brushing across her forehead below a gray hijab.

"Lely," said Crabby. "But for our purposes—a *desert lily.*"

The Hawk brought the hookah's black hose to his mouth, drew a blast of lemon-mint tobacco, released it in a slow exhalation. Fucking saccharine shit. Crabby's sweet tooth extended even to the pipe. The hookah sat on the floor, its rosy glass base and brass stem rising to the height of the table, its little bowl conveniently at arm's length.

"Shayma said she might be too headstrong," he said.

Crabby lifted his own hose to his lips. "You told us you wanted them to have spirit."

"Spirit, yes. Rebellion, no."

He looked past Crabby behind the bar at a midget television airing a soccer match. The Washington Huskies were hosting the UCLA Bruins in a real football game less than ten miles away, but whoever ran the television at the Arabian Nights Hookah Bar and Café didn't have a clue.

"She's agreed to go," said Crabby, setting down the menu. "Never been with a man, verified by a doctor at the camp."

"There are a thousand girls like her. I don't need one who's going to be a problem. What the hell's on this menu, anyway? I'm guessing none of it says *pulled pork*."

Crabby took back the photo. "Our Desert Lely has no living relatives. Za'atari is her home, and we are her family now. You should try the sayadieh. Whitefish with rice. Middle Eastern spices. Pine nuts."

"They don't put any fruit on it?"

Crabby chuckled. "If you ask, they may provide some figs."

He put his menu down. "You tell the waiter. I'll never remember the word. And no fruit."

Crabby drew from the hookah and exhaled three perfect rings of smoke. "I understand you've had a recent setback."

"Nothing we won't recover from. That's if you don't supply us with any more faulty merchandise."

"She was fine when she left. How have you been treating our girls?"

He leaned across the table. If they weren't in a public place, he'd grab Crabby by the shirt.

"Like queens," he said. "Fucking billboard-sized television playing Arabic sitcoms half the day. Fancy clothes, fancy food. They lead a hell of a lot better lives than they would stuck in a tent in the middle of the desert. They win and we win, too."

The waiter came and Crabby ordered for both of them. "Throw in a Bud Light," said The Hawk.

"So what are your circumstances now?" asked Crabby after the waiter left.

"We're on a hiatus while my team's in your neighborhood, but don't you worry. We can take care of your fee."

"Good. While we're on that topic—"

"Fuck you, Crabby. I already know what you're going to say."

"Humanitarian assistance is not inexpensive. The families who care for these girls expect compensation. The same with the Jordanian gendarmes. Your country's FBI has decided to watch the Port of Beirut, so I'll have to send the girls elsewhere. I'm not personally benefiting any more than I already have."

Crabby took a sip of water. "I need funds for the expenses."

"How much?"

"Five thousand each."

"Christ." The Hawk drew from the hookah. "One hundred percent inflation."

"Eighty-five, actually. Perhaps we've done enough business together. It's getting more difficult to arrange the release of these girls."

"Perhaps we have. I can get girls from someone else."

"Can you?"

"I can send my team to Amman. They'll find something."

Their dinners came.

"It would sadden me to see your efforts yield nothing," said Crabby. "Four thousand five hundred and not a penny less."

"Done."

The Hawk took a bite of the sayadieh and grimaced. They'd ruined a perfectly good fish. Crammed it with spices that belonged in a pumpkin pie. He set down the fork, drew from the pipe, twisted his nose.

"C'mon, Crabby, order some real tobacco. Cut this citrus shit."

CHAPTER NINE

Boyd leaned back so that Roshan and Abboud could gaze out the window as the Royal Jordanian Boeing 787 began its descent. Pine forests daubed the Golan Heights green but soon yielded to rock-strewn hills and bare wadis colored beige and pink.

The land flattened. Ribbons of road ran straight and curved, connecting oases of towns within the dry expanse. Abboud pointed at one.

"Za'atari," she said.

Visible from the left side of the jetliner, thousands and thousands of metal-roofed buildings crammed a long oval. It resembled a massive compound of small storage units rather than a city of eighty-five thousand residents. Interspersed within the ocean of trailers were large tents with blue UNHCR letters on top.

Russell looked away from the window, stole a glimpse of Abboud. She had lived there for three years, listened to the impacts of bombs and mortars across the Syrian border less than ten miles away. A widow and an orphan.

Did she have any family left in Syria? He didn't know. She never talked about it, and he knew better than to ask, the same way he didn't want anyone asking about his scar. Though hers might not have been as visible, she probably had scars that made his own seem small as a speck.

"There's the solar farm," said Abboud, pointing at the reflections glimmering off forty thousand solar panels. "I wish we had that when I was there."

The left side of the plane tilted up as they turned south, and the city disappeared. A sense of relief washed over Boyd. Why? Where did that feeling come from? It couldn't have been Za'atari disappearing behind them, for they would be on its streets soon enough.

After a moment, he understood. Had they not turned south, they would have passed Za'atari, continuing east over the Badia desert, skimming the northern edge of Saudi Arabia and at last entering the airspace over Iraq. His brain knew he was not going back to Iraq, but his body hadn't been convinced until the airplane turned south.

* * *

"Looks like we'll be riding in style," said Boyd the next morning when their transportation arrived at the FBI Amman Attaché Office.

A dented Plymouth Opal that years ago may have been blue stopped at the curb. A small placard adhered high on the driver's side of the windshield proclaimed in handwritten English letters *TAXI*.

"I remember this car," said Abboud. "It was the first taxi in Za'atari camp."

A young man with a pimpled forehead, curly black hair, and a Pittsburg Steelers t-shirt stepped out from the driver's seat. He placed each of their backpacks in the trunk. Panting lightly bearing a pained expression, he opened both passenger-side doors.

Abboud spoke Arabic, and the driver replied.

"He does not speak English," said Abboud.

"Why don't you ride shotgun then?" said Roshan.

"Shotgun?"

"That's a slang expression for the front passenger seat," said Boyd.

"Ah. You mean bagsy."

"What?" asked Boyd and Roshan at the same time.

"That is how the British say it. Do not ask me why."

They left the city and joined a freeway through the northern suburbs. On both sides of the road, white limestone buildings of multiple stories climbed the hills. The approaching winter had mostly stripped the deciduous trees, sparing only small clusters of pale green and yellow leaves.

"Were you ever in Amman?" Boyd asked Abboud.

"Before the war, yes. From my home in Dara'a it was less than two hours."

"It's pretty," said Roshan.

They passed from Amman to Russayfah, another city of white limestone, this one ascending a gentle incline west of the freeway. On the east side, land lay barren in hues of brown. Abboud engaged the driver in conversation and translated for Boyd and Roshan. His name was Imad. Before he had fled Syria, he had been a civil engineering student at Arab International University in the Dara'a Governorate. He was married and had a two-year-old boy.

Imad took a sip from a Styrofoam cup. Not for the first time, he wiped his forehead with the crook of his arm. When he wasn't wiping sweat from his face, he kept a flat palm against his stomach.

Boyd thought he heard a soft groan.

"Ask him if he's feeling okay," he said to Abboud.

"He says he felt fine earlier this morning," said Abboud after speaking to him. "He's confident he can get us to Za'atari. "We're about forty minutes away."

Imad offered a weak smile in the rearview mirror.

Behind the driver, Roshan said, "How do you say *barf* in Arabic? No, hold off on that. Let's not give him any ideas."

"You ought to be the one that's sick," said Boyd. "No way I could eat that much baklava and not keel over like a rowboat."

"I only had one." Roshan paused before adding, "Of each kind. How could you resist? Abboud, in the camp do they sell those … you know, those things with the special dough …"

"Kataef," said Abboud.

"Yeah, that stuff."

Abboud looked back at Roshan. "Not when I was there. Who knows now? Syrians have great energy."

"That wouldn't be good for Roshan," said Boyd.

"Perhaps you are jealous," said Abboud.

"Jealous?" Boyd exaggerated an aggrieved tone.

"If you did more exercise, you could eat more balaurieh," said Abboud. "Then you would not have to be jealous."

Roshan leaned forward and high-fived Abboud. "He's lazy and he's whining about it."

"You two are going to gang up on me the whole time we're here?"

"Only when you ask for it," said Abboud.

"Onzor." Still grimacing, Imad gestured toward the window on the passenger side.

Down an embankment fifty yards out on the landscape of rocks and sand, eight beige and brown camels strolled north. One of them stopped and tore loose a mouthful of desiccated grass. A Bedouin wearing a faded red keffiyeh and carrying a staff walked among them.

The scene disappeared as the freeway cut through a hill, embankments rising on both sides.

"How do they survive out there?" asked Boyd.

"People think the camel has water in its hump," said Abboud, "but it is actually fat for energy. They do store a lot of water in their bodies and use it to stay cool."

"Did you ever ride one?" asked Roshan.

A loud groan from Imad interrupted the talk. Suddenly, his body stiffened. His forehead jerked back against the headrest, while his leg jammed down on the throttle. His hand yanked the steering wheel left, and their battered sedan veered across the outside lane toward the center divide.

A cement truck coming right at them loomed large in their windshield. In about two seconds, Boyd was going to die.

"Abboud!" he shouted, bracing for the impact.

Abboud grabbed the wheel, nudged it right as the cement truck swerved away, and the two vehicles passed each other no more than a dinner plate apart.

Sixty-miles-an-hour momentum pushed them back across their own lanes as the freeway curved left, placing an even larger object looming huge in their windshield—a boulder-swollen embankment, and there was no way it was going to swerve out of their path. An instant after avoiding one catastrophe, Boyd saw that he was going to die, anyway.

But Abboud muscled the steering wheel against the grip of the spasming driver. The back of the car slid wildly. Tires squealed. It felt as though they would flip and roll. Centrifugal force shoved Russell against the restraint of his seatbelt.

They smashed sideways against the embankment, the engine revving freeway speed. Bolting forward, metal ground against rock, glass crunched, voices yelled.

Abboud thrust her leg across the center of the car and kicked away Imad's leg. She hit the brakes and the sound of skidding tires added to the jangled cacophony. As they slowed, Boyd let out a breath—they had survived.

But the sedan bounced off the embankment, and the rear end ricocheted back onto the freeway. From behind them a horn blew the instant before another crash sent Boyd's head snapping back. The world turned dark and spinning, like tumbling inside a gyroscope.

They landed upright, the sudden stillness a shock after so much tumult. Somehow closer to him than she was before the crash, Roshan moaned. He noticed her door bent inward. Abboud grasped the keys, turned off the engine, shifted the gear to park. Imad's spasms had reduced to quivers. His breathing carried a loud, phlegmy desperation, as though inhaling and exhaling through a barrier of glue.

Stunned and amped on adrenalin all at once, Boyd gazed out the spider-webbed windshield. His whole body felt like a bruise. They were stopped on the shoulder of the freeway, the embankment rising on their right, cars whizzing by on their left. Ahead, a thin-framed workman in a gray uniform exited the driver's seat of a panel truck with a smashed headlight facing them.

"Shit." Roshan gasped through gritted teeth. "Shit-shitshit."

"I will call an ambulance." Abboud looked at the floorboard. "Where is my purse?"

Boyd scanned his area, finding only Roshan's green daypack on the floorboard next to his door. Something bulky lay wedged against his left hip. He pulled it away and found himself holding Abboud's black leather purse. He handed it to Abboud.

Roshan pressed her hands to the sides of her head and moaned.

He put a hand on her shoulder. "Where does it hurt?"

In the front, Abboud spoke Arabic into her phone.

"My left side," Roshan gasped. "Fucker got me good. Fucking door. Look at it."

Boyd had only a moment to glance at the bashed-in door before the man in the gray uniform pounded on the driver's side window. Abboud turned the key back on and pushed a switch on the door to lower the window, but it wouldn't work. The man grabbed the outside handle and pulled, but the door wouldn't open. He went around the front to Abboud's side. When she opened her window the man bellowed an angry Arabic diatribe.

Boyd's heartrate kicked into an even faster gear. He tried the handle of his door. It opened. As the man turned his attention toward him, Abboud's door swung open. It banged against him, sending him tottering backward. She sprang out before Boyd and spoke in sharp, clipped Arabic. The man hung his head. She kept speaking and his head drooped lower, as though to study his bootlaces.

From outside, Boyd leaned into the front of the car to check on Imad, who'd placed both hands around his throat. His eyes, more white than color, showed confusion and fear. There was a kind of whimper in his fading gasps.

He was choking—but on what? All he had was coffee.

The faces of others who had stopped peered in from the outside of shattered windows.

Boyd grabbed Imad by the shoulders, pulled him across the parking brake and passenger seat before easing him to the ground.

"Ask if he's choking," he said to Abboud, who'd hunched next to him. Abboud spoke to Imad, but the man either could not hear or could not respond. The skin on his face darkened. Had he stopped breathing? Boyd leaned an ear against Imad's mouth, watched to see if the man's chest rose or fell.

Except for quivering, he detected nothing. He didn't have a barrier for mouth-to-mouth, but he figured the hell with it, he'd take his chances. Pushing his thumb into the underside of Imad's chin, he clutched the front of his jaw, pulled to open the mouth. But whatever caused Imad's spasms had also locked his mouth shut, like a dog clamping on a rope. A crowbar wouldn't pry loose the man's gritted teeth, and yet his whole body felt weak, like a wooden post with the shakes.

A crowd gathered. He turned Imad to his side, slapped his palm onto man's back. "C'mon. Spit it out. Spit it out. Abboud, tell him to open his mouth."

Imad remained unresponsive.

Boyd rolled the driver onto his back and began chest compressions—at least he might be able to keep the blood circulating. He counted aloud ... *one two three four five ...*

A bearded middle-aged man wearing gray slacks, a white dress shirt, and a gray suit jacket knelt on the other side of Imad.

"I am doctor," he said. "Give him to me."

Boyd stopped the compressions at fifty and rose to his feet, found himself in the company of a dozen people. He blinked. His mind quivered, and for a moment he was standing at night in a compound and the man on the ground was Sergeant Jones with a hole in his chest and blood darkening his shirt. From the guard tower, a muzzle flashed again and again. Bullets smacked a line in the ground six inches away. *Get down move move move!*

He scanned the faces of the crowd. Where was the Iraqi who'd ambushed them? But the soldier wasn't there. These were just civilians, ordinary people delaying their journeys to gawk or help in whatever way they could. On the compressed dirt outside the car, the doctor moved his ear away from Imad's lips. He shook his head and resumed chest compressions.

Abboud was leaning into the backseat, speaking with Roshan.

Boyd wavered on his feet. Had he hit his head? Or was it the memory? Here he stood, in the Middle East again, and a man on the ground was dying with no warning, for no reason.

CHAPTER TEN

A few steps from the main Za'atari boulevard where it seemed half of Syria strolled one direction or another, Lely walked backwards to face her newest friends. Like she, all three were orphans, eyes numb as hers had been until she decided her mother and father would have wanted her to grab hold of life and live it. Beneath the grief of these friends, there stirred a dormant capacity to smile. Lely was sure of this, and she took it as a dare to bring one to their lips.

As though launched by a rocket, she leaped, oh, she imagined, two hundred meters high, pirouetted a full 360 mid-air, extended both arms, thought she might hover there for a minute or two, but in the end decided to come down.

"*Alhamdulillah!*" she called. "Movie theaters. Real schools with lots of books. Whole forests of trees!"

She spun skyward again, flapping her arms like a bird.

"Look out!" called the one named Qamar, whose long-sleeved turquoise blouse hid the scars on her arms where she'd cut herself during her earliest days at Za'atari. Last night Lely had taken a vow of secrecy before Qamar revealed the thin intersecting marks.

From the corner of her eye, Lely spotted a skinny teenage boy turn a bicycle toward her, his attention distracted. At the apex of her twirling leap, she moved a hand back as the boy reached her. She pushed off his shoulder and landed on all fours on the gravel lane. She could see the boy stop, stand astride his bicycle, cover his mouth with both hands. A boxed pizza was strapped on a rack behind his seat—he was one of the numerous delivery boys who worked for the food vendors. She looked at her wrist. The red and blue bangles her mother had given her were still intact.

Shayma stormed from behind the girls and knelt beside Lely.

"You beetle!" she called to the boy. "Give that bicycle to someone who knows how to ride!" Her shout stopped passersby, who joined the others already gaping at the aftermath of the near-collision.

"Peace be upon you," answered the boy. While she examined scrapes on her hands and felt the one on her left knee, Lely snuck a second glance at him. Wearing a sweat-stained green ballcap, he might have been fifteen, a year older than she, a hard worker, destined to be rich someday.

"Are you hurt?" Shayma, ignoring the boy's apology, brought her eyes to Lely.

Lely sprang to her feet, turned to the crowd, and bowed as though acknowledging applause—which had the effect of calling forth cheering and laughter. The boy remounted his bicycle and continued past them, the audience resumed its saunter, and her friends appeared to be devising ways to disassociate themselves from the embarrassment. Shayma clamped a hand on her shoulder and steered her a half-circle back to the girls.

"Another display! Shall I leave you here?"

"What would you tell my new family?"

"That you were too saucy for their palettes."

Lely searched Shayma's eyes for a twinkle but found magma instead.

"Allah forgive me," she said with as much humility as she could muster.

Shayma shook her head. "You need my protection as much as Allah's. See that you don't lose it."

Yana placed a hand over her mouth. Her body shook, and a giggle broke loose, triggering a giggle from Sara. Shayma pivoted to glare, which served only to open a spillway of laughter. All four girls shielded themselves in a huddle, hands on each other's shoulders, all control lost. Lely chanced a glance at Shayma, who stood outside the circle, her face without expression. Or was it sadness? She'd never understand how some adults lost their sense of humor, but she and Qamar and Sara and Yana—they would be friends.

"Enough, girls," Shayma admonished.

They turned onto a street jammed with pedestrians and bicyclists while a rusting black delivery truck inched through the crowd. A chilly breeze carried dust. Everyone wore jackets—browns and grays for the men, violet, blue, turquoise and black for the women.

Shayma barreled ahead, weaving among the crowd, passing stalls of plywood and corrugated metal, most no bigger than a small bedroom. These shops stretched both sides of the road as far as Lely could see. Outside one, a young man sat on a stool while a barber clipped his hair, the two of them forming a small island in the river of souls. A produce stand displayed lemons, yams, figs, eggplants, apricots, and zucchini, all arrayed in wooden boxes painted black. Another booth featured whole chickens rotating on spits in a gas-flamed oven.

What had all these people done before the war uprooted them? Lely glanced at two men renting wedding dresses and imagined they had been lawyers. The woman specializing in pistachios? She may have worked for a theater group that performed three plays a year. The boy hawking a crate full of cigarettes had been a brilliant student and a promising goalkeeper for a Dara'a youth football team. The man holding out a wallet for sale—why, he had to have been a banker. But the two older women, attired in torn and dusty abayas, who sat next to seven crates of sanitary napkins ... Lely couldn't imagine what their lives had been, nor what they were now.

Three blocks and a couple dozen businesses after they turned, Lely spied her favorite sign in all the camp, one that ironically declared this road as Champ-Elysees, beneath which an arrow pointed northwest and an English word announced Paris—3,305 KM.

"Miss Shayma? How many kilometers to America?" she asked.

Shayma stopped so quickly that Qamar almost collided with her. She turned and faced the girls.

"Many, many more kilometers. And yet, closer than you can imagine." She sighed. "I've been a grouch today. I've been trying to think how to tell you this ... this news that I have."

The weight of a stone fell in Lely's gut. She braced herself for the announcement. They weren't leaving Za'atari—that had to be the news.

"We must leave much sooner than I thought," said Shayma. "There has been a development we did not expect. My assistants are visiting your guardians right now to inform them and to compensate them for the care they've given you."

Lely jaw began to drop, but she composed herself to hide her uneasiness. *Compensation?* Was this the way overseas adoptions worked?

The crowds moved past them in both directions. The girls and Shayma had become an island like the boy on the barber's stool.

"How soon, Miss Shayma?" She did not allow worry into the tone of her question. She had Qamar and Sara and Yana to care for, and they didn't need any more anxiety in their lives.

"Very soon," said Shayma. "The ship will be waiting to take us to America."

"A cruise ship!" Lely raised both hands in a high-five gesture, leaving Yana with no choice but to complete the hand-slaps. "We won't see any icebergs, will we?"

"You might see some cubes, but only if the ice machine is working," said Shayma. "We're going on a container ship, very basic. But when we reach our new home you will have much to appreciate, because Seattle is so beautiful, so green, you have never seen anything like it."

"Nice," said Lely. Grief welled up in her heart. She had left her homeland without her family and now she was leaving her people. Despite its riches, America was still a strange place. And she kept hearing rumors about Syrians not being welcome there.

"This is the day we will gather our supplies," said Shayma. "It will be two days to get to port and after that ten days on the ship. You may as well spend your dinars, because they'll be worthless to you after we leave."

She walked ahead, more slowly this time, and Lely and her friends followed. Two blocks later, Shayma veered off the street to a jewelry shop.

"Here we are." Shayma picked up a pair of earrings with Syrian eagles painted on white resin. "There's something I wish to buy for you before we leave."

CHAPTER ELEVEN

The bruises on Boyd's thighs and arms ached as he and Abboud trudged into the conference room at the Amman attaché office a few hours after the crash. He worried for Agent Roshan, who probably had at least a cracked hip and who'd gone by ambulance to the New Zarqa Governmental Hospital northeast of the capital. He worried for Abboud, although she'd required no medical assistance, and he worried for their mission. It seemed a sure thing that Fisk and the other bureau honchos would be ordering him and Abboud back home, especially with Roshan, the only seasoned agent on the team, sidelined.

"I have coffee, tea, or bottled water," said Special Agent in Charge Jonathan Hussein, who supervised the Amman office. Thin and tall, Hussein moved energetically despite a slight limp. Boyd guessed his age to be mid-forties. He had jet-black hair, probably dyed.

Boyd declined, but Abboud accepted the tea. She had changed from her blue Women's Corps International abaya to a burgundy one without logos or lettering, and she wore a brick-red hijab. She had to have the same kind of bruising that Boyd felt, but she didn't say anything and neither did he. He hadn't eaten since breakfast, but he didn't feel hungry.

He glanced at the large monitor on the wall and the oval-shaped conference table made from a dark wood. Fisk would be on that screen in less than five minutes, as well as some brass from D.C. It would probably be a short conference. Mission aborted. Time to go home.

That's not what he wanted. But what about Abboud? They hadn't had a chance to talk.

Hussein went to the front of the room, tapped some keys on a computer and turned on the monitor. Early as usual, Fisk appeared on the screen, wearing a black tie and a salmon-colored shirt. It was almost one in the morning back in Seattle.

"Greetings from Amman," said Hussein.

"Salam, Agent Hussein," said Fisk. "You've got Boyd and Abboud?"

Boyd hurried to the table. Abboud sat across from him, next to Hussein.

"There you are," said Fisk. "Are you sure you're okay? I saw photos of that wreck."

"A little sore but nothing broken," said Boyd.

"Same with me," said Abboud.

"The thing about this video crap is I can't tell if you two are lying," said Fisk. "If this wreck had happened on my turf, you'd have both gone to the hospital, no questions asked. I don't mean that as a reflection on you, Hussein. These two haven't been in my building for a year yet, and I already know they've got stubborn streaks."

Another image appeared on the screen—a man and a woman sitting side by side at a small table. They introduced themselves as SACs Melody Rangel and Quashawn Wilson. It was nearly four o'clock in D.C., but both individuals were attired as though it were in the afternoon and not the wee hours of the morning. Wilson was bare-headed and thin. Rangel had broad shoulders and wore her light brown hair in a ponytail.

"Let's get down to business," said Fisk. "What's the probability that your driver suffering a sudden seizure had nothing to do with the fact that his passengers were working undercover for the FBI?"

"We talked about that as I drove them back to Amman," said Hussein. "We need more information. I have an investigator for the Jordanian gendarmes who's in contact with the hospital where the driver is now. He's in critical condition. The doctors have not offered an explanation for what happened to him."

Wilson lifted his hand. "We also have a contact, someone who works for the hospital. I'm sorry to have to tell you this, but we received word twenty minutes ago that the driver has died."

Boyd's heart felt as though it had doubled in weight. For all his worry about continuing the mission, an event of far greater impact had occurred. Imad had a wife and a child, and they were already in a refugee camp. What would their lives be now?

"We've obtained and translated the driver's medical records," continued Wilson. "He does have a history of epilepsy, but he hadn't reported any seizures for the past three years. He was continuing to receive medication from a clinic at Za'atari."

"So, possibly a fatal seizure," said Fisk. "That's rare, isn't it?"

"Very rare," said Rangel. "But it does happen. Right before we started this conference, I did some quick research. There's a certain kind of epilepsy for which the mortality rate is rare but not negligible."

"They're planning to do toxicology tests?" said Fisk.

"We've been told no," said Wilson. "The lead physician sees no reason to do so. The police are doing their own follow-ups, but in all probability, before this day is over Imad will have been buried according to Islamic tradition."

Fisk shook his head. "I don't like it."

Abboud leaned forward. "You are asking if someone knows who we are and why we are here."

Boyd looked across the table at her. She didn't take long to get to the point.

"I am doing exactly that," said Fisk. "Do you have any special insights, Abboud?"

"Only that we want to continue our assignment," she said, as though their only setback had been a flat tire.

On the screen, Wilson and Rangel exchanged a glance.

Abboud continued. "You have said we must stop these traffickers, because later they may export terror instead of girls. But I do not wish to see any more of my Syrian sisters smashed on a sidewalk. We have a plan, and we can still implement it. We should not let a car accident stop us."

"If we accept what you're saying, we have a Roshan-sized hole in the plan, Abboud," said Rangel. "You and Roshan are supposed to share a trailer in Za'atari. She's going home via military transport tomorrow. Given today's events, for your safety I do not want you housed by yourself, and the conservative nature of Syrian culture won't allow you and Agent Boyd to room together without attracting a great deal of unwanted attention."

For a moment, nobody said anything. Again, Boyd saw quite plainly that the decision was already made. The roommate problem gave the head honchos a pretext to bring them home when the bigger reason had to be Roshan's injury. Why would they entrust the mission to a rookie agent and an interpreter who one month ago was translating cell phone records?

"Then we will get married," said Abboud.

Boyd fought to keep his mouth from gaping. What the hell? Was she crazy?

"Did I hear you correctly?" asked Fisk.

She took a sip of tea. "I do not mean in actuality. What I mean is we change our story. Agent Boyd and I can say that we are married. There are many jewelry stores in Amman. Surely we can find modest wedding rings."

She turned toward Boyd, pointed at him, and showed a mischievous smile. "Do not get any wrong ideas, Agent Boyd. You will be sleeping on the floor."

Boyd felt everyone's eyes on him. How, they must all have wondered, would he respond to such a nutso idea? He turned to the monitor. "I agree. I should sleep on the floor."

Roshan and Wilson chuckled.

"We can handle this," said Boyd. "And Abboud is a special asset. She knows the camp. She knows the people. I've done plenty of security-type work in the army. I know what to watch for. We're here right now. Let's do this."

"Well, this is interesting," said Fisk. "You want to get your feet wet, Agent Boyd? I like that. Doesn't mean I'll agree, but I like that. We'll take your proposal under consideration. Wilson and Rangel, do you have time for an additional conference to discuss how we should proceed when we're finished with this one?"

They agreed.

He pressed his lips together. It wouldn't take long for them to decide. For a moment, he'd believed that he and Abboud had talked the brass into letting them complete the mission. But that was magical thinking. He and Abboud would soon be on their way home, probably on the same flight as Roshan.

The rest of the session consisted of Boyd and Abboud relating all the events that led to the crash as well as the aftermath. Fisk ended it by directing the two of them to put into writing everything they had just recounted and to send the reports to him and the D. C. agents via secure email. Then it was adios, with a promise to inform him and Abboud of their decision by the next day, whatever that was with the eleven-hour time difference between Amman and Seattle.

Less than an hour later, he received a text from Fisk—authorization to continue the mission was granted. He read it again, thinking he might have skipped the word *not*. But, no, it was real.

"Looks like we're going to get married," he said before showing her the text. She read it and pumped a fist.

"It will be a rather dull and short-lived matrimony," she said.

"That's okay. I mean, I like you as a person, but marriage? It's a bit too soon, wouldn't you say?"

* * *

As he stepped outside the passenger bus near the main gate of Za'atari Refugee Camp, Boyd donned his cap and squinted his eyes. A chilly breeze peppered his face with grit. Diesel and a potpourri of sweat, perfume, and cologne scented the air as he waited for the driver to pull baggage from beneath. Among the passengers bunched around him, he heard Arabic, Korean, French, Dutch, and English.

He claimed two backpacks and as he handed one to Abboud, their hands nearly touched. On each, a gold wedding band glimmered in the pale sunlight.

"Well, Mrs. Abboud, quite the site for a honeymoon, wouldn't you say?"

"Indeed it is." Abboud hoisted her pack. "My friend Katya was married here. She and her husband had their honeymoon inside those walls. There was nowhere else to go. They live in Italy now."

Along with the other passengers, they strolled toward a line of people that extended fifty yards from the gate. A twelve-foot-high concrete wall topped by razor wire enclosed the city. A hundred yards from the gate, an army compound surrounded by chain-link fencing and razor wire emphasized that Za'atari Camp had not been born during a time of peace. Inside the fenced compound, tanks, trucks, and howitzers painted desert camouflage awaited duty.

Bursting out from inside the Za'atari gate, a dozen children, most pushing gray metal wheelbarrows, hurried across the packed dirt toward them. The first to arrive, a boy about ten years old, called "Cee-gar-ettes!" The cuffs of his trousers sagged over his shoes, a white t-shirt hung to his thighs, and a faded black Real Madrid cap flopped loosely over his forehead. He set down a wheelbarrow half-full of Camel cigarettes. The other children arrived, hawking cucumbers, figs, cantaloupes, bottled water, Tootsie-Pops, and more.

Boyd bought a pack of cigarettes.

"I have not seen you smoke," said Abboud.

"That's because I don't."

A flatbed truck bearing a load of dusty refugees rolled past them and stopped between the gate and the army compound. Watched by Jordanian soldiers, young men and women jumped off. Three women handed babies down to individuals on the ground. Half a dozen children lowered themselves out the back. Soldiers directed the whole group to a building outside the camp.

Abboud gazed as they disappeared into the building. "That was how I arrived. Jordanian troops picked us up when we crossed the border. Nine hundred of us in a single day, truck after truck. Our hearts were sore. We had lost everything."

Boyd tried to imagine the scene. How would he feel if the U.S. bombed Washington State, killing everyone dear to him until he fled for Canada with nothing more than what he could carry?

He decided he couldn't possibly know what she felt on the day of her escape. He couldn't know what she must be feeling at this moment, years later, watching the same scene unfold before her eyes.

"I'm sorry." He put a hand on her arm, as a spouse might do, or a friend.

They strolled to the end of the long line. They'd be lucky to reach the gate in less than an hour.

"Mr. and Mrs. Boyd?" A man in his thirties, with sun-leathered skin and wearing a knit cap over his head, stepped away from the camp wall. Someone was supposed to escort them, and this was probably the man, but Boyd felt wary, ready to reach for his gun if need be.

The man was wearing a blue UNHCR vest, but anyone could get hold of one of those.

"Tamir Pierce," said the man, still approaching them. "Executive assistant for Dr. Bergeson, United Nations. I am to escort you to our office. Are you able to walk half a mile? I understand you had a terrible accident two mornings ago."

"We are quite healthy, thanks be to Allah," said Abboud.

"Follow me." Pierce marched purposely toward the wall from which he had come. Boyd and Abboud stepped out of line to follow. Pierce veered toward an office area adjacent to the gate and stopped a few feet from the door.

"You have your letter?" he asked.

Boyd took from his waist pack a special authorization letter that Dr. Bergeson had provided them. Pierce snatched the letter and strode past the office toward the front of the line. He hailed by name a tall Jordanian soldier who wore reflective sunglasses. After perusing the letter, the guard waved them through. Pierce accelerated his gait.

Boyd caught Abboud's eye. "Not exactly exuding warmth, is he?" Pierce had already sped twenty feet ahead of them and would have been swallowed in a crowd of pedestrians and bicyclists if they didn't hurry after him. Half a minute later, Pierce turned onto a wide boulevard even more dense with humanity. Boyd recognized it from their planning sessions as what everyone called the Champs-Elysees, the main commercial street, such as it was in this city of trailers and tents.

Pierce never slowed down, never looked back to see if Boyd and Abboud were still with him. He walked around people who moved slower, and he stormed right through the ranks of those who walked toward them.

Abboud stopped.

"Mr. Pierce," she called.

Their escort slipped past a group of teenage girls and vanished. Boyd turned a circle, watching for eyes watching him—allies might not be allies. A guide might lead them to an ambush. He had learned this the hard way the first time he'd come to the Middle East. From both directions, a stream of humanity passed them. On one side of the boulevard, a sheet metal shack offered scarves and hijabs for sale. On the other side, in front of an open-air booth a teenage boy held up two pairs of shoes, calling out to tempt customers.

"Not good," said Abboud.

"Let's take our packs off," said Boyd. "In case we have to move quickly."

"Ah, there you are." Like a magician returning from a disappearing act, Pierce stood next to them.

"What's the rush, Mr. Pierce?" asked Boyd.

"No rush. I didn't realize you couldn't keep up."

"We do not fancy knocking people off their feet." Abboud's British accent carried a snarl. "Moreover, these packs weigh sixty pounds."

"Would you like me to carry yours?" asked Pierce.

"That's not the point," said Boyd.

"Ah. Well." Without another word, Pierce resumed the jaunt, scarcely reducing his speed.

Abboud didn't move. "Good-bye, Mr. Pierce," she said as he once again disappeared. "I know the general area where the office is. When we get close, people will be able to show us."

"If you see anyone staring at us—"

"People are going to stare at us," said Abboud. "A white man and a Muslim woman wearing backpacks and wedding rings?"

"Anything suspicious."

"I know what you mean."

They moved with the pace of the crowd. Streetlight poles and drooping power lines swayed overhead. On both sides, metal and plywood shacks featured items and services for sale—produce in one shop, spices in another, soccer balls and shirts, stationery, wiring and cable, undergarments. Falafel, flatbread, and eggplant fritters added their tempting aromas. A bicycle repair stand sold an array of hats having nothing to do with bicycles. A beauty salon sold licorice and candied nuts. On a street corner, a business rented wedding gowns.

"Mrs. Abboud," he said, "we don't have any photos of our wedding."

Abboud surveyed the shop. "Your presence in such a photo would do much harm to the institution of marriage."

"In America we call that a zinger. Yours are particularly sharp."

"I'll take that as a compliment." Showing only a hint of a smile, she looked at a street sign. "I think we are a few blocks from our turn."

They resumed walking. Most of the pedestrians and bicyclists carried either nothing or single plastic bags. "They're not buying much," he said.

"The people have little money. When I arrived, none of this was here. Only tents. No electricity. Meals were distributed in packets. Sand blew constantly. One day I held my hand in front of me and I could not see my fingers. Babies died of lung failure."

He recalled storms of similar ferocity in Iraq, but the context was different. Although he had endured them out on the open desert, he did so knowing that his family and his country were safe.

Pierce showed up again, like a specter taking corporeal form. "I thought I'd lost you," he said. "We're almost there."

Their guide veered left onto a residential street. Sixteen-foot-long trailers lined the avenue. Here and there two or three were pushed together. Brightly colored murals adorned occasional units, but most bore siding of plain white metal. Canopies of canvas or plastic tarps flapped on flimsy posts. Laundry hung from thin ropes.

Children kicked soccer balls, chased each other, jumped rope. Adults and teens conversed, some with portable CD players at their feet. A boy trudged toward them, his body tilted left from the weight of a ten-liter plastic cube filled with water. Shortly afterward, they reached an open square with a water tank—a metal cylinder dressed in chipped orange paint held in place by wooden posts. Another line had sprouted here, one of children and younger teens carrying an assortment of containers—ten-liter jugs, large pop bottles, plastic pitchers.

Halfway up the next block, inside an open-doored concrete building, a half dozen women and girls chatted while tending kettles on a communal stove with eight gas burners in a single row. Aromas of coriander, allspice, lentils, and rice floated out the door.

Still moving quickly, Pierce reached a white trailer triple the length of the residences, with blue UNHCR lettering. A Jordanian guard wearing a sidearm opened a gate in the perimeter of a chain-link fence. On the top step of the trailer, Piece turned toward Boyd and Abboud.

"Marhaba," he said—*welcome* in Arabic.

Having earlier redonned his backpack, Boyd had to hunch low to get through the doorway. He and Abboud leaned their packs against a wall.

"Dr. Bergeson will be here soon," said Pierce before retreating behind a reception desk and diverting his attention to a laptop computer.

CHAPTER TWELVE

Lely glanced from her desk to the row on her right two seats up. Qamar had just flipped over her paper, and Lely imagined the satisfied expression on her friend's face.

Which type of energy? demanded question number seven, and as far as Lely could determine, the scenario she'd just read could have been any of the three choices—kinetic, potential, or thermal.

Qamar opened a novel she had brought to class, and a little ache of envy pulsed through Lely's veins.

Where did that feeling come from? Certainly not Qamar's ability to finish science tests faster than she did, or Qamar's slightly higher scores. And Qamar had her own demons—the scars on her wrist were proof enough of that.

Life wasn't simple for Qamar, but maybe it was clearer. Like question number seven—for Qamar, the answers were obvious. Not so for Lely. The easy answer was thermal, because that meant heat. But as the water warmed, well, that was potential energy in the water, wasn't it? And if the water heated enough to create a lot of steam and it was in a sealed pot and the pressure built enough to blow the lid straight up like a rocket into the ceiling and clattering back down to the stove—that was a lot of kinetic energy.

Like the kinetic energy that demolished her whole apartment building, and to this day she didn't know why she wasn't there with older sister Katya and her parents and her other sister and brother when it struck. But the kinetic energy came from another kind of energy science couldn't explain.

Evil.

Evil was a lot more powerful than kinetic, and you could heat it up way past boiling, and you couldn't erase the devastation it left behind. It kept popping into Lely's head, even in science class, and she had to push it away.

Because if it didn't go away, the pressure would build like steam in the pot and when it blew it could leave marks on the wrists of a pretty girl like Qamar.

Seated on a stool at the front of the classroom Mrs. Daoud glanced at her wristwatch, breaking Lely's train of thoughts. She looked back at her quiz, marked *kinetic*, and breezed through the last three questions by forbidding herself to think much about them.

Mrs. Daoud stood up the way she always did before she told them to stop and hand in work. As Lely turned over her paper, one of the student office assistants walked into the classroom with a couple of notes. Mrs. Daoud glanced at them, walked down the aisle to Lely's desk, and picked up the quiz.

"You are to report to the office," she whispered before moving up the row and whispering to Qamar.

Shayma, Yana, and Sara were waiting in the visitor's section of the office.

"Are we leaving?" asked Qamar.

"Not leaving," said Lely. "Arriving. You should ask, 'Is this the start of our arrival?'"

"We'll talk about it outside," said Shayma, her mouth tighter than usual.

"Shouldn't we check out?" asked Qamar. "Let the school know we're—"

Shayma grasped Qamar by the arm and steered her toward the door.

"These school people work with the United Nations," said Shayma once they'd exited the school grounds, which consisted of eight large trailers inside a chain-link fence. She walked up the street toward the area where Yana lived, and so Lely and her friends followed.

"What's wrong with the United Nations?" asked Qamar from behind Shayma.

"Nothing. Except the UN might not let you go," said Shayma, walking quickly.

"But people come and go all the time," said Yana.

"How many of them are going to the United States?" asked Shayma.

"Amal," said Lely. "Amal went to Seattle."

They reached a street corner, such as it was in Za'atari—it was more like a convergence of alleyways. Shayma whirled around.

"Only because The Hawk family rescued her," she said. "No Syrian girl is allowed in America unless she has a sponsor. And because America refuses pay bribes, the United Nations does not want to let any refugees go there."

She shifted her attention to a pair of young men in black t-shirts who appeared suddenly from behind a trailer near the corner. One had an elephant tattoo on an enormous biceps, while from hardened eyes the other man studied the street behind Lely. They strolled up to Shayma and stopped.

"There are forces inside and outside this camp that you do not understand," said Shayma. "Some people do not want you to enjoy the opportunities of America. They do not like the 'Land of the Free.' Two of those individuals, pretending to be a married couple, have entered the camp today, but we will leave before they have a chance to detain you. Once we get out of camp, they won't be able to stop you. They won't be able to turn you over to the United Nations to do to you whatever the UN does simply because America does not pay bribes."

"But who are these men?" asked Qamar, averting her eyes from the black-shirted individuals who had joined them. Lely gave them a fearless gaze. Buzz-cut hair and tough-guy faces—none of that mattered. Their hearts lacked poetry, and that was all she needed to know.

"They work for The Hawk family, the same as I do," said Shayma. "They are here for our security."

She kept her eyes on the girls as she introduced the men, Majd with the tattoo and Jack with the steel eyes. Neither man offered a nod or a smile, and Shayma didn't bother to tell the men Lely's name or the names of any of the other girls.

Afterward, she turned and resumed the walk, as did the men, as did Lely and her friends.

"First is Yana's house," said Shayma.

"I thought we were leaving tomorrow," said Yana.

"Plans have changed," said Shayma.

CHAPTER THIRTEEN

Thirty minutes ticked by while Boyd and Abboud waited for Dr. Bergeson. Pierce hadn't glanced away from his computer even once to acknowledge their presence. Abboud, absorbed in a UN booklet about Za'atari, didn't seem to mind, but Boyd's ire heated up. It wasn't enough for Pierce to ditch them on the way to this office; now he had to treat them as though they were petitioners waiting all day for a word with the emperor.

Boyd stood from his chair, bent at the waist to touch his toes and stretch his muscles, then approached Pierce's desk.

"I sure don't mean to interfere with your valuable work," he said, "but is there some way you can check to see if Dr. Bergeron has been delayed?"

Pierce typed a few more words and peeked up, apparently still incapable of making eye contact. He had shed the cap he'd worn outdoors, revealing a shaven head.

"We're still here," said Boyd. "Good thing, too. We could've left and you might not have noticed."

"What was it you asked?" said Pierce.

"What are you working on?"

"I have to finish a report." Pierce glanced back at the screen, then past Boyd toward where Abboud was sitting.

Boyd took out his phone. "Okay if I take your picture?"

"What?"

"Your picture. I want to take your picture."

Pierce brought his eyes from the screen to Boyd—more precisely, Boyd's chest.

"I'd rather you didn't." said Pierce, just as Boyd took the photo.

"Sorry about that. I'll erase it." He walked past the front of the desk and stopped next to Pierce's chair, held the photo for Pierce to see. The secretary rolled his chair a foot to the side, watching as Boyd erased the photo.

He hoped that Pierce hadn't noticed he'd also taken a shot of the monitor screen. Not that it mattered. He snuck the photo more for his own entertainment than for whatever information it might reveal.

He returned to the front of the desk, noting that Abboud had set the pamphlet on her lap in order to observe the interaction.

"Any idea what's holding up Dr. Bergeron?" he asked. "Is there some way you can find out if he's been delayed?"

"It's not what he told me to do."

"Are you allowed to decide by yourself whether or not to check in with the boss?"

"Well …" Pierce hesitated, as though wrestling with a conundrum. "He didn't tell me I couldn't, but he didn't tell me I could. I didn't ask him."

Outside the trailer door, the sound of footsteps interrupted Pierce's deliberations. He sprang upright and stood at attention as the doorknob turned.

"My God!" Dr. Bergeson noticed Abboud as he stepped inside. "You're here. I wasn't expecting you for another hour."

"Is the bus always that late?" said Boyd, prompting Dr. Bergeson to turn away from Abboud to his secretary's desk.

"Agent Boyd," he said, extending his arm for a handshake. "What do you mean *late*?" He was stockier in person than he had been on video when they'd been strategizing in Seattle. Gray had only begun to fleck his black hair, thick at the top and fading to a buzz around his ears, a younger man's cut but nonetheless fashionable on him. His moustache, too, was thick but neatly trimmed. He wore a white dress shirt with a loose navy blue tie beneath the same kind of UN vest that Pierce wore.

His eyes flicked toward Pierce. "I was told you'd be arriving at two o'clock. Well, never mind that. At least you're here. What an appalling start to your ..." Again, he glanced at Pierce. "*service* here at Za'atari. When I saw the photographs of that crash, I thanked God that you were okay."

"I wish we could say the same for the driver," said Abboud as she joined them in front of Pierce's desk.

Dr. Bergeson lowered his eyes. "Appalling," he murmured. "Do you know he left behind a widow? He had children, two of them, I think. He and his family were in line to be admitted into Norway. My colleagues in the UN are trying to accelerate the process for his family now. Let's bring this discussion to my office. Mr. Pierce, have you offered tea to our guests?"

"They didn't ask," said Pierce.

After a sigh, Dr. Bergeson said, "Bring us some tea, please. Knock on the door when it's ready."

Dr. Bergeson's office was small. He had a wood veneer desk and white folding chairs for guests. He sat with his back to the only window. When a breeze blew, the curtain nearly brushed the top of his head. Three metal file cabinets that may have been manufactured before the UN came into existence stood along the side wall.

"I must apologize for my secretary," said Dr. Bergeson, swiveling his chair at an angle so that he had room to stretch his legs on top of his desk. "He's a bit of a savant. Fluent in seven languages, written and spoken, including Arabic, of course, and absolutely clueless about social niceties. I don't know what kind of life he has when he steps outside this trailer. He won't talk about it. I wish I could supplement him with a decent customer service secretary, but I have no budget for that sort of thing."

"You take care of all these people," said Boyd, sweeping his arm to encompass 180 degrees of the camp.

"We try. Do you know this desk is broken? One of the legs, anyway. You can't see it from where you are, but the only thing holding it up on my right is an old Lawrence Durrell novel."

"*The Alexandria Quartet?*" asked Abboud.

Dr. Bergeson tilted his head and cocked an eyebrow. "You know of it?"

"I have read them. I doubt anyone would publish it today."

Dr. Bergeson took his feet off his desk and opened a drawer. "To answer your question, it's *Prospero's Cell.* A memoir, lovely prose, publishable in any era."

He pushed the drawer shut. "Speaking of budgets, I'm glad you're able to continue your mission, although I do miss the opportunity to meet Agent Roshan in person. You're doing the work I wish I could do, if I had the funding to carry it off. And I understand congratulations are in order."

"For?" asked Boyd.

"Your marriage, of course."

Boyd felt his face flush. "You know it's not—"

"What happens in Za'atari stays in Za'atari," Dr. Bergeson interrupted with the hint of a smile. "It's a famous saying. Perhaps you've heard of it? Where is that tea?" He rose from his chair, squeezed between the desk and the wall, and opened the office door.

Holding a tray with steaming mugs, Pierce stood almost leaning toward their office.

"Mr. Pierce," said Dr. Bergeson. "Didn't I tell you to knock when you were ready?"

Pierce stared at his feet. "I was just about to do that."

"All right, Mr. Pierce. Thank you for the tea. I'll take it from here."

Boyd waited for Dr. Bergeson to hand out the tea before asking the question that had been gnawing at him for two days.

"Is it possible that anyone besides your superior officers knows why we're really here?"

"Not at all," said Dr. Bergeson. He opened the side drawer of his desk again, and this time he extracted a silver flask and held it up. "Begging your pardon, Abboud. I assume your taste for literature does not carry over to alcohol?"

"You assume correctly," she said.

"No thanks," said Boyd. "What about your secretary?"

"Mr. Pierce?"

"Do you have any others?"

"I'm afraid I'm shackled with Mr. Pierce. But except for his impact on public relations, he's quite harmless. He knows nothing of why you're here."

"How can you be sure?" asked Abboud.

The UN officer poured a full shot into his tea. "That's not the way he's put together. He doesn't think that way. What you see is what you get, rough edges and all." He took a sip of tea, swished it like wine. After swallowing it, he added a nip to the cup and put the flask away. He leaned forward in his chair, dropped the casual demeanor, assumed a look of command.

"Now then," he said, "especially because you're one person short, let's review the plan."

CHAPTER FOURTEEN

The Hawk loosened his belt a notch before sitting at the hotel room desk and reexamining the Byzantium Luxury Condominiums brochure. The flooring alone blew his mind. Oregon White Oak. Chevron Parquet. Sustainably sourced wood. When the words "eco-friendly" had rolled off the real estate agent's tongue, he liked the sound of it. He could hear himself adding those details when his clientele marveled at the floor. The whole environmentally-conscious thing exuded Northwest chic.

And it was all one big penthouse, no need for extra condo units to accommodate clients on busy nights. Tight. Self-contained. No worries about hallway surveillance cameras. The girls could conduct business and live their lives 24-7 in one spot.

This would be their last night in a fleabag hotel. Moving day was tomorrow.

His phone beeped—a text from Jordan.

Crabby: They've gone

Hawk: How much gone

Crabby: Out of UN office

Hawk: I need more gone than that

Crabby: Patience

The Hawk glanced again at the brochure. A five-fuck-ing-figure mortgage payment every month. And no in-come without Jack and Majd to run security.

And if those asshole FBI agents stumbled upon the right people, there'd be no income ever. He tapped a reply.

Get them gone.

CHAPTER FIFTEEN

Pierce stopped the white UN passenger van and pointed at a weathered UNHCR tent on the other side of a concrete building whose fetid odor confirmed its function as a public toilet. Boyd and Abboud took their packs from the back of the van and Pierce drove away.

Twenty yards past the tent, an eight-foot-high concrete wall topped with razor wire marked the eastern edge of Za'atari. Lanes of small trailers extended away from the wall on both sides of the tent. Several children chased a small bouncy ball. Wisps of cloud dulled the sky and a breeze blew west.

They walked around the building and stopped in front of the tent's drooping canvas vestibule. Boyd tore loose packaging to extract a Necco—it was white, supposedly cinnamon. He held the pack up to his eyes, hoping there weren't many more of that variety.

"I have never been to this end of camp," said Abboud.

"Why are we so far from the main part? People come and go—there must be vacant trailers and tents scattered all over."

"Perhaps there are waiting lists. Or perhaps Major Bergeson delegated the job of finding our quarters to his secretary. How confident are you that no one else knows why we are here?"

"Bergeson seems a bit naïve. Of course, someone else could know. Looked to me like Pierce was eavesdropping when Bergeson opened the door, and he just swallowed Pierce's explanation without a thought. Makes me wonder if Pierce arranged our transportation a couple of days ago."

"He may have accomplices."

The children had stopped chasing the ball and stood staring at Boyd and Abboud. In a trailer behind the children, someone closed a curtain.

"Did you see—" began Boyd.

"We should go inside the tent," said Abboud.

"Might be that it's furnished." Boyd lifted his pack. "Electricity, running water, a jacuzzi."

"Yes, and we will have housekeeping service in the morning."

Inside, there was a canvas floor and nothing else. Russell leaned his pack against a wall and sat on the floor with his back against the pack. With nothing to do until tomorrow, he took out a book, *Theodore Roosevelt and the River of Doubt*. He was glad he'd brought an actual book, rather than an ebook, because the lack of electricity would make relying on his phone problematic.

Twelve feet away on the other side of the tent, Abboud had unrolled a thin camp pad and sleeping bag. She sat cross-legged, eyeing the vestibule opening.

"Maybe we can buy something we can use for a curtain," said Boyd.

"You know how to look the other way, yes?"

"Of course."

"Without a mirror?"

"Absolutely."

"Yes, we could use a curtain."

"You don't trust me?"

"You are a man."

"So case closed, huh? Automatically guilty. Remember, I'm the one who suggested the curtain. I just want you to be comfortable, that's all. Sure you don't want a Necco?" He held it up for her to see.

"No, thank you."

"I've got a ton of them."

"I am sure you do."

"What's that supposed to mean?"

"There must be a self-help group for someone with your affliction."

"Right. Used to be chewing tobacco. Would you rather I switch back to that?"

"Lip cancer or diabetes. You decide."

"You know, there's such a thing as cardamom addiction, too. Makes your nose turn upside down."

She cocked her head and studied him a moment. "Is it the sugar or the food coloring?"

He knew he shouldn't ask, but he did. "What do you mean?"

"Something has to be impacting your mental capacity."

"No, no. This is as good as you're going to get from me."

The next wafer turned out to be cinnamon again. He hated it when that happened. He read a couple of pages, then noticed from over the top of his book that

Abboud hadn't moved. He hadn't seen her do the *salahs* that Muslims did at certain times of day: the standing, the raising of the hands, crossing the arms, bowing, rising, prostrations. Perhaps she was praying at that exact moment. He recalled from his time in Iraq and Afghanistan that individual Muslims practiced different variations, some devoutly following every precept and others more flexible.

How did she view relationships with non-Muslims?

Not that that was ever going to happen. Not with him, anyway. She was kind and smart and feisty, but his visions of the *right woman* had never included someone wearing a hijab—not that there was anything wrong with a hijab.

He liked to think of himself as open-minded, but was he?

He returned to his book. She was a partner on a mission and nothing more.

Six pages later, she stood and bent down to touch her toes. The tent flapped lightly with the breeze and the children outside had resumed their playing. She rose, placed her hands on her hips, and did a rotation exercise for her waist.

"Is it difficult, in some ways, to come back here?" He didn't know why he asked the question. Was he being intrusive?

She sat back down on her sleeping bag, focused again on the vestibule, so that Russell could watch her only in profile, could not read her eyes in the dim light of the tent.

"I came here ..." She stopped and swallowed.

"You don't have to say anything."

She took a breath. "It was after I killed a man. I shot him from the fourth floor of a building. He was driving a bus with soldiers. He might have been a soldier, too. I did what I was trained to do. Afterward, the Free Syrian Army attacked the bus and killed more soldiers. They deserved to die, doing the bidding of that butcher Bashar. And I thought I would feel satisfied, vengeance for my husband, for my family, my friends, our nation, justice."

She rubbed her lips together and sighed. "But I felt only shame. The next day I left Syria, and I will probably never go back, not unless things change."

Although Boyd was gazing at Abboud, what he saw was a yellow stucco house at 3 a.m. on a winter night in Baghdad. A house whose occupants manufactured death—IEDs and suicide vests.

Pfc. McDonnell blew open the door. Mejia threw a percussion grenade. A dash inside, darting figures, shots. Russell leaped over a downed man, whirled at the door to his assigned room, shouted "Freeze" in Arabic. A motion, the red flash of a muzzle, the certainty of his own death even as his training guided his aim, the squeezing of a trigger, the blur of events ending with a man collapsed and quivering in a corner, with a woman on a bed screaming, screaming.

The whole thing was over in ten seconds. Three of the enemy killed, two wounded, a shitload cache of explosives. A full-body ecstasy—still alive, a damn miracle. He should have felt triumph, the way Abboud thought she might feel, but he didn't, and obviously, neither did she.

"I'm sorry," he said. "I shouldn't have asked."

She turned away from the vestibule and eyed him, no tears, no fear or shame that he could detect. "I ran from my anger, from my thirst for vengeance, perhaps from my thirst to die. But I will not run from the memories. The world must know what has happened to Syria. If somebody asks, I will tell them. I will tell them even if they do not ask."

. . .

Abboud fastened the second end of the beige cloth she had purchased after they'd eaten dinner. It hung nearly to the canvas floor, leaving about a foot of space. Outside, night had fallen. On their walk back to the tent, occasional streetlamps had cast circles of light, but behind the long restroom building none of the outdoor lighting penetrated the walls of the tent. Only a pair of headlamps hanging from straps in the ceiling provided illumination.

"I shall perform my salah now," she said. "It has been a day of travel, so I can combine the Maghrib and Isha, but beginning tomorrow I must do all five."

"Would you like me to leave the tent?" he asked.

"It is fine for you to stay. Whatever you wish."

She disappeared behind the curtain, while Boyd sat cross-legged beneath the headlamp on his side of the tent so that he could read. From the other side of the curtain came the sound of rustling—had Abboud brought a prayer mat, or was she using her sleeping bag? He glanced toward the curtain, caught sight of a pair of bare feet, and looked away. He had not seen her feet before.

Outside the tent, a cricket provided background music to her softly mumbled prayers. Five minutes passed.

Footsteps approaching at a rapid pace interrupted the cricket's song. Boyd reached beneath his shirt and unsnapped his holster.

"Masaa el kheer," called a male voice—*good evening* in Arabic.

Abboud emerged from behind the curtain. "You must be the one who goes out first," she said. "After a minute, I will follow."

Boyd kept his hand on his pistol as he crept to the outside edge of the vestibule and peered at the visitors. Backlit by a streetlight in front of the restroom building, three men stood side by side. Their hands were visible. They carried nothing.

He stepped out into the crisp night air. The man in the middle had a beard the color of soot and appeared to be in his late fifties or early sixties. He wore an aviator cap, a brown hunter's jacket, and black boots beneath blue jeans. The men to his left and right, probably in their mid-twenties, tall and broad-shouldered, wore hoodie sweatshirts, one copper-colored and the other black.

The older man rattled off Arabic, too fast for Boyd to separate out particular words, and offered his hand. Boyd shook it.

"Motasharef," he said—*pleased to meet you.* He placed his right hand to his heart, a gesture Arabs made to enhance the warmth of their greetings.

The man in the middle continued, his tone assertive yet conversant, while the younger ones maintained the postures of bodyguards, quiet and observant.

Boyd shook his head. "Aasef," *Sorry.*

The man stared at him a moment, then nodded his head. Boyd sensed movement from behind him, and Abboud appeared at his side. She spoke to the man and he replied.

"His name is Yusuf Shabat," she said. "He is the leader of this area, District Eight."

"What brings him and his entourage to our tent?" Boyd kept his face affable and his voice even.

After more conversation, Abboud explained.

"A representative from the United Nations security office informed him. He understands I am here to meet with expectant mothers and that you are my husband. He wants us to know that if we encounter any difficulties, we are to go to him and he will assist us. Everyone in this district knows where he lives and they will take us to him if we ask. He will make sure no one disturbs our tent or steals our possessions."

"Tell him we are grateful, if that's the appropriate response."

"It is." Abboud communicated the sentiment, and the man gave a slight nod. Once again, Mr. Shabat offered his hand.

Boyd accepted the gesture. The man's grip was firm but not aggressive. "Shokran," he said. *Thank you.*

"Your Arabic … good," said Mr. Shabat, struggling with the pronunciation of the words.

"Your English … good," returned Boyd.

"No." The man laughed.

Boyd and Abboud waited outside the tent as the man and his companions turned and walked away.

"What do you think of our visitors?" she asked.

"I don't know. Is it normal for a neighborhood to have an informal leader like that?"

"He is a sheik. He was a sheik in Dara'a, and so he remains a sheik at Za'atari."

Boyd snapped his holster and took out a Necco, but he couldn't see the color—was it licorice? He held the pack out for Abboud and this time she pulled loose two wafers.

"Welcome to the rotten teeth club," he said.

"Laa," she said, Arabic for *no*. She squeezed one wafer into each eye socket, squinted, and spoke like a pirate. "Arrr."

"You're wasting processed sugar. Give them back."

"Arrr. Try taking them." She widened her eyes and let the wafers fall to her open hand. He reached for them, but she yanked her hand away and popped the Neccos into her mouth.

"You're tainted now," he said.

"Only because of you." She gave a subtle nod toward where the men had departed, a path next to the outside wall.

Boyd looked the same direction. No one else had entered the path, but two men walked away in the opposite direction from the restroom building. He could not see their faces. One was large and beefy; the other was shorter, wiry. Each wore black hoodies and dark-colored jeans.

"What?" he said quietly.

She shook her head. "Nothing. For a moment there was something familiar about them."

He watched the men move down the lane until they were out of sight. "You're right. Not necessarily about them. But we need to be alert. I think, based on just today, someone knows who we are."

"You mean someone like Mr. Pierce?"

"Yes. And maybe others."

"We should take turns sleeping tonight, yes?"

"Agreed."

"The pistol you brought—will you leave it for me when it is my turn to watch?"

He detected nothing like bravado in her voice, nor anything like anxiety. Just a matter-of-fact request, like please pass the salt. He recalled what Fisk had told him about her.

"You know how to use it, I assume."

"I do."

He nodded. "Okay."

CHAPTER SIXTEEN

Lely didn't need Shayma to tell her. She knew exactly where the taxi had left them, even though it was dark and the lights around the gate glowed four hundred meters in the distance.

"My father used to work here," she whispered. "He drove a forklift and loaded trucks."

Away from the road, plodding without headlamps through the desert, Shayma stopped and whirled at Lely and her companions.

"Shush," she said.

Lely pressed her lips together and bowed her head. Shayma was right. If Lely couldn't keep her mouth shut, she could get them all killed or captured or something bad, because it wasn't the Jordanian-Syrian Industrial Free Zone up ahead anymore. The Jabhat al-Nusra had taken it over, stripped it of all its assets, and if they were still there—*ya Allah,* those fanatics could do any number of cruel things. They might even force her to marry one of them.

Her legs trembled. So why were they sneaking through the desert to get there? Twelve hours ago she'd been taking a science test, and now her whole life was changing, not even close to how she'd envisioned it.

Perhaps she could turn around and start walking back. Shayma might not notice her absence right away, and even if she did, she couldn't stop Lely from leaving. It was raining lightly, but she wouldn't get too wet before she reached the Jaber al-Sarhan Center next to the Jaber Border Crossing. She'd find someone who'd bring her back to Za'atari, to Mama Amena, to her paints and a limitless supply of bare wall canvasses. She glanced left and right to her companions Qamar and Yana and Sara, and she saw in their eyes not only the reflections of the distant lights but also the same fear that set her legs shaking.

She couldn't abandon them. They needed her.

And so she bent her elbows out on both sides and flapped her arms like a chicken behind Shayma's back, but she did it quietly. Yana shot a hand up over her mouth. She made a spitting noise trying to hold back a giggle, prompting another shushing whirl from their stern-faced chaperone.

Wearing daypacks that held everything they owned, the girls followed Shayma on a diagonal line away from the gate toward the cement wall that surrounded the facility. Lely strained her eyes to discern details in the night as they grew closer and yet could see nothing like a gate. What would they do when they reached the wall? Surely the phrase *Open Sesame* would do them no good without Ali Baba to pronounce it. And even if it could work, no magical cave of wonders awaited them on the other side.

Shayma did not shift left or right but kept them pointed at a certain spot along the wall, a location that fronted leafless trees on the industrial side. When they reached that spot, Shayma turned her back toward the distant gate, turned on her phone's penlight, and studied the wall. She crept forward, Lely and the girls behind her, until she found a head-high blue circle ten centimeters in diameter. At that point it wasn't an enchanted word that she called to gain them admission. It was a three-toned whistle. A mysterious opening did not appear in the wall; instead, a rope ladder flew over it and flopped down in front of them.

Ya Allah—were they supposed to climb that flimsy thing? Shayma turned, pointed at Lely, gestured to the ladder. She felt the watching eyes of the other girls. Would they follow her if she reversed course and marched back to the official border crossing and found a kind person to bring them back to camp?

But this was their only way to America, now that its government had withdrawn the welcome mat from Syrians. Only the rich could get them there—Shayma had warned them that the journey would not be easy. Amal had made it. She was living the good life. Shayma had shown Lely pictures to prove it.

Shayma again gestured with her head toward the ladder, more emphatically this time. Lely thought it would be easier if she tossed her pack over the wall, but where would it land? Maybe it would hit someone. That could be funny—unless it was one of those al-Nusra goons.

Beneath her black abaya, the trembling in her legs grew, even as she forced herself to trudge to the foot of the ladder. She wrapped her hand over the red and blue bangles on her wrist, the only artifacts connecting her to her mother and her family, and she mouthed a prayer—*bismillah*—in the name of Allah. She grasped the ladder and without thought pulled and stepped, pulled and stepped, scrambled to the top, twisted around, felt her way down the rungs on the other side, trusting Allah, fate, Shayma, the goodness of the universe.

Only when her feet touched solid ground did she permit herself to focus beyond the route over the wall. She counted three men, all of them young, perhaps college-aged. It was difficult to see in the dark industrial yard. Two wore baseball caps. All had beards—but the beards were close-trimmed, not long as al-Nusra mandated. They stared at her, openly, brazenly, the way some men would do, and she wanted to admonish them—*what are you looking at, you dogs?* But these were the individuals who had facilitated their entry—to what, she didn't know.

Sara appeared next. She stopped at the top of the wall and whimpered, earning nothing but a sharp hiss by one of the men as well as Shayma on the other side. It took her three times as long to get to the bottom as it had Lely. Shayma went last. The men hesitated, as though expecting more.

"Jack and Majd will come later," Shayma whispered. She began walking. "Take us to the truck."

The man without the cap hustled ahead of Shayma and stopped. "The truck is not here yet," he said, his voice a growl, his eyes those of a predator.

Shayma met his stare. "Jack and Majd will not be happy."

"Too bad," said the man. "We have a place where you will wait." He had ivory-hued hair—Lely was sure it had to have been bleached or colored, and the reason he wasn't wearing a hat in the rain was just so he could show it off.

"Every hour that goes by without a truck reduces your compensation," said Shayma.

The blond-haired man moved ahead, taking a narrow path between two enormous metal buildings. Lely fell in behind Qamar, and the two other men took the rear positions.

"Compensation?" one of them said, close enough behind Lely to evoke a shiver. "There are more kinds of compensation than money."

Shayma stopped and whirled, as though the man had been one of the girls. "What do you mean by that statement?"

The man and his partner laughed.

"Shut up," said the blond man from the front of the line. "Have either of you two clowns had the pleasure of meeting Majd?"

"Don't look like he's here," said one of them.

"He's never far away," said the leader. "And you can't get far away enough from his reach."

"Got rubber arms, has he?"

"No. More like bags of cement."

They crept ahead, the dark silhouettes of looming warehouses forming skinny corridors. Before the war, Lely's father had brought her and the rest of the family to this industrial zone. At night brilliant lights swamped the entire area so that the whole place shone like a spotlight in the desert. She understood why those lights no longer functioned, but she didn't know why the men did not use flashlights or headlamps. Although they apparently were not al-Nusra, perhaps they feared al-Nusra. But they had spoken in normal voices.

Over the next ten minutes, they made so many turns through skinny alleys that she felt like she'd been spun in circles while wearing a blindfold. If suddenly all the lights did come on, she was so dizzy with turns and fright, she'd probably walk straight into a wall. It might be funny to veer a little bit and pretend to collide with a wall. She'd done that with doors to make her friends laugh. Tonight, however, such a move would freak everyone out more than they already were.

Somewhere in this giant complex of buildings, the Syrian-Jordanian border crossed. Lely's father, may Allah have mercy on him, told Lely the line went straight through at least one of the buildings. At last the blond man stopped, unlocked a padlock, and pushed a sliding door to reveal an interior dark as a tomb. Even Shayma refused to cross the threshold. Perhaps there was no floor or ground on the other side, and they'd plunge to the center of the Earth.

"Ya khara," he muttered profanely before stepping in and turning on a light switch. Overhead fluorescent lights blinked on, illuminating a portion of what appeared to be a vast warehouse stripped clean and a concrete floor layered with dust and metal shavings. On the other side of the doorway, two mousetraps each held a dried rodent corpse. A rancid smell tinged with metal pushed through the opening, as though even the air craved escape. The buzzing of the lights echoed in the cavernous space.

Lely nearly jumped when she felt a hand clasp her arm, but she saw that it was only Qamar.

"Go on," said the blond man. "It won't be long."

Shayma shook her head. "No. We'll wait out here."

"Kess ikhtak"—another profanity, a bad one this time. "You're going to get wet out here."

"Well, then, you little cockroach," said Shayma, "you'd best make sure the truck gets here soon."

CHAPTER SEVENTEEN

Beneath a sky of feathery clouds, wind from the west blew dust down the dirt lane almost directly into Boyd's face. It was the afternoon of his second full day at the camp, and Abboud was inside an adjacent trailer, visiting an expectant mother. He wished there was a tree he could shelter behind, but trees were not a feature of the refugee camp, except for scrawny potted things that a few residents nurtured with scarce water. Instead, he pulled down the visor of his Women's Corps International cap and squinted. Fifty yards away, two men with newspapers sat against the fence of a Mercy Corps playground.

Eighteen minutes had passed since either one of them had turned a page. They had quit bothering to pretend.

Earlier, while walking toward an appointment, he'd had a funny feeling, like an itch between his shoulder blades. He whirled a one-eighty, and there were the two men, each carrying a rolled-up newspaper, a block behind Abboud and him.

Their height and builds reminded him of the two men who'd used the public toilet outside the tent at least twice the night before, and once that he knew of on their first night. It was hard to discern physical details while the wind pushed grit at his eyes, but one of them had a sinewy build and blond hair. The other one was stocky with thick arms and a head shaved as shiny as Pierce's.

When the wind offered a pause, he took out his phone and retrieved the grainy mug shots the FBI had gathered from surveillance video at the Elliott Bay Hotel and Condominiums. The two men watching him here at Za'atari could have been the two younger men who came and went from the penthouse entry, except that the blond hair didn't match. But it was easy to color one's hair.

He switched the phone to camera mode, fingered the screen to zoom. If they weren't going to pretend, then neither would he. But before he could raise the camera to photograph the men, the wind resumed its dominance, cluttering the air and any chance of a clear shot. After a minute, the wind ebbed, and he took a shot.

"We have something." Abboud's words startled him—the sound of her leaving the trailer must have been blunted by the wind. He turned and saw that Mrs. Zureiq, whose bowling-ball belly protruded beneath a black abaya, had also exited the trailer. A little girl with tightly curled hair had one hand placed within Mrs. Zureiq's hand and her other arm wrapped around the woman's leg.

"What do you mean?" He glimpsed back toward the men.

When he returned his gaze to Abboud, he saw her take a peek past his shoulder. "Mrs. Zureiq knows Amal Nasri," she said, "our friend who works at the Elliott Bay Hotel and Condominiums. She knows the family Amal was staying with before she left for America. She will bring us to them now."

He willed a care-free smile to his face. "That's wonderful."

Amal. Amal Nasri. So that was the name of the dead teenage girl. And now they were going to find out more.

He glanced back again. Both men had risen, newspapers rolled in their hands. Blondie was speaking into a cell phone, while Bald Guy stared straight at Russell.

CHAPTER EIGHTEEN

The Hawk stood from his desk overlooking Lake Washington, paced to the other side of the penthouse office, then returned to the window wall. Outside, rain dribbled noiselessly down the darkly tinted glass, while to the south, only a few headlights and taillights glimmered at 4 a.m. on the floating bridge.

He couldn't believe his lousy luck. The F-fucking-BI agent and his interpreter had found Amal's Za'atari family.

Russell Boyd and that Abboud woman shouldn't have even been there. They should have been dead, victims of a tragic automobile crash. But that had been Crabby's scheme. Crabby was too damn worried about getting his hands dirty. Hell, if The Hawk had been running the show over there, he'd have arranged a little terrorist attack, maybe blown up the whole damn FBI building before they could get their sorry asses out of Amman. He'd told Crabby two days ago to finish them off, told him he could leave it to Jack to figure out, but, no, Crabby had insisted he'd finesse another unfortunate event.

Yeah, so when, Crabby? After they bust your ass? From a jail cell, huh?

He wanted to call Crabby and fling that question at him, but he was finished with Crabby. He was finished with the whole Za'atari operation. Get those four girls with Shayma over to his eco-friendly Byzantium Penthouse, add them to the four already here, and he'd have enough. He just needed Jack and Majd to do a little cleanup work before they left.

He glanced at his phone on the desk—yeah, sure, looking at it was going to make it ring sooner. Maybe, while he was waiting, he could test the fucking windows in this joint and see if they were strong enough to keep a fist from punching through. Maybe pick up a trash can and pound on the window … bam, bam, bam—see how long it would hold together.

He shook his head. Anger would only make him stupid.

He walked back to his desk, his hands jumpy, his feet, too. He glanced at the notepad and the number he'd circled over and over and over.

Five thousand dollars every damn day.

Thanks to that Amal debacle, that's how much money he was losing while he played nanny to four idle girls who'd spent yet another day chewing gum and watching Arab soap operas. Normally he'd have sent only Jack with Shayma to retrieve the new girls, but thanks to Amal and the FBI jumping into it, he sent Majd, too. If he had kept Majd they could do some limited business, but he didn't dare risk it with only Darsi, who was getting advanced in age and a bit soft with the girls.

He deserved better. He was one of the good guys. Just last week he'd read about a multi-agency task force busting some asshole known by the name of Puget Paul, who ran a so-called "luxury" operation. This Double-P character forced his girls—he went for the Chinese variety—to work twelve hours a day, seven days a week. Set up an "exclusive" customer club, charged $300 per encounter.

Wrong on so many levels. Sure, maybe Double-P raked in the dough, but where was he now? Jail, the dumb fuck. Too many customers, too much internet presence, too many ways to get busted. And that was a shitty way to work his girls.

The Hawk girls worked six-hour shifts five days a week, and they cost $500 per, thank you very much. Special arrangements for special customers. The whole night? Three G's. Be the first she ever had? Four were on the way. He'd wait to see who produced the highest bids.

Add to that a swank location and a girl with a little more enthusiasm—or else, on that last part. He wouldn't tolerate anything less, considering how sweet he'd made their working conditions. Six men a day maximum, usually not that many.

So: pay more, get more. Take care of your people. And don't tolerate fuckups.

He sat back in his chair and stared at the spreadsheet. Twelve thousand dollars a month for the penthouse. Forty-five hundred per girl on the container ship. Salaries for Shayma, Majd, Jack, and Darsi. A lot of one-time bribes to get those girls here. Food, clothing, bling.

Income so far this month? Nada.

Finally, his phone vibrated.

"They are walking in the direction where Amal lived," said Jack. "Majd is watching them."

The Hawk drew another circle around his lost daily income. "We can't wait any more."

There was a pause. "O … K…" Jack spoke the word slowly.

"They need to disappear. Boom. Gone. No trace. Can you do it?"

"I could have done it yesterday. I could have done it the day before."

"What about today? Is it nighttime over there yet?"

"Not yet. And, yes, I have an idea that should work. There are only two of them. I've spoken with our assets."

"Not Crabby?"

"No, not him."

"Good. Put him on the list, too. He's not an asset any-more. You understand?"

"The ground is hard over here. I expect a bonus."

"Fuck it. Fine, I don't care. I'll take care of you. Get the job done. Today."

CHAPTER NINETEEN

On the way to Amal's old residence, Boyd purposely trailed Abboud, Mrs. Zureiq, and the little girl. Twice, he walked back half a block, scanning the yards of trailers as well as narrow alleyways, after which he strode double-time to catch the women.

The two men appeared to have abandoned them, but that didn't put his mind at ease. He'd need to report this development to Fisk and Hussein. Most likely, somebody knew the real reason why he and Abboud were walking along this street. If so, that meant the taxi crash wasn't an accident. They were in danger. More specifically, Abboud was in danger, and it was his job to protect her.

They were so close to making a breakthrough. *Amal.* Maybe there would be justice for her, after all, and for Hafa and who knew how many other girls?

Except he and Abboud would almost certainly be pulled away and sent home.

Mrs. Zureiq pointed at a trailer with a half-dozen

peonies growing in flowerpots spread across the front. Sheets of green-painted scrap metal fenced a side yard and entryway, within which two raised-bed gardens bore kale, chard, and leeks.

The woman who had cared for Amal met them at the door, giving Mrs. Zureiq and her daughter warm embraces before stepping back to allow her friend to introduce Boyd and Abboud. Attired in a light blue hijab and a navy blue abaya with white polka dots, her name was Mrs. al-Rasheed. Abboud gestured toward the garden and spoke enthusiastically. Smiling in response, their hostess ushered everyone inside.

They sat on mats across from a kitchen area with portable shelving screened by tangerine-colored skirting. On the top shelf, four feet off the floor, a fan rotated back and forth. Next to it, a miniature refrigerator hummed. An aroma of spices reminded Boyd of Amani's Market. A curtain patterned with a combination of red roses and paisley shapes separated this small space from the rest of the trailer.

While Mrs. Zureiq's daughter played jacks on the floor next to her mother, the adults drank tea. Boyd found himself welcoming the addition of the cardamom, its resinous scent and hint of green apples—he'd grown to associate it with Abboud.

An imperative repeated itself in his mind. He needed to protect her.

According to Abboud, the women's conversation focused mostly on changes at Za'atari since she had lived there. In addition to the solar energy farm completed earlier in the year, there were new football pitches, additional water stations, and an employment office offering work opportunities outside the camp in Jordan.

After a few minutes, Mrs. Zureiq touched Mrs. al-Rasheed's forearm, and Boyd heard her speak the name Amal. Mrs. al-Rasheed pressed a hand to the middle of her chest and gasped. Her eyes grew wide, and she bit on her lower lip.

With her eyes focused on Abboud, she spoke in a quiet voice. When she paused, Abboud held up a hand and turned to Boyd.

"Mrs. al-Rasheed has not heard a word from Amal in over two months, since the day Amal departed Za'atari," said Abboud. "The woman named Shayma who was to bring her to America has a phone, and the plan was for Amal to send regular text messages. Mrs. al-Rasheed says she has been worried sick, and she is greatly relieved to know Amal is safe in America and that we have spoken to her. But she is confused about why she herself has not heard from Amal. She tried calling Shayma, but all she heard was a recording in English. She had a friend who knows English try the phone number. Her friend said the number was no longer in service."

Boyd smiled at Mrs. al-Rasheed. If he did it right, his smile communicated his pleasure in being able to assure her that they had seen Amal, and that all was well. If he did it right, the guilt he felt in his stomach for lying showed nowhere in that smile.

"Tell her it's been a while since we saw her," he said, choosing one of the lines they had rehearsed. "We noticed she had earrings with the Syrian eagle on them, and we asked her if she was Syrian. We care a lot about what is happening in Syria. A month after that, when we learned we were going to volunteer at Za'atari, we decided to search for the family she stayed with. We're curious to know about the steps that Amal had to take in order to get to the United States."

While Abboud translated Boyd's reply, Mrs. Zureiq kept a comforting hand on their hostess's arm. Mrs. al-Rasheed followed with more questions.

"She wants to know more about Amal," said Abboud. "Where did we see her? Did she seem happy? Who was she with? When was the last time we saw her?"

"Which story do you think we should use?" he asked.

"The one about meeting her at a park along the waterfront," said Abboud. "It's the happiest one."

Boyd agreed. It was a story that included a picnic of Ivar's clam chowder and croissants from Three Girls Bakery at Pike Place Market, followed by a ride on the Seattle Great Wheel.

None of the details brought the hint of a smile to Mrs. Rasheed. Her head down and her face grim, she kept both hands pressed together against her chest. When Abboud finished the story, Mrs. al-Rasheed shared her thoughts.

"When we return," said Abboud, "she wants us to find Amal and tell her that her foster mother from Za'atari wants to hear from her. She will give us her phone number. Perhaps Amal forgot it, and that is why there has been no communication."

Abboud and Mrs. al-Rasheed continued conversing. Mrs. Zureiq interjected her own thoughts, the tone of which made Boyd think she was trying to reassure. When there was a pause, Boyd added his own observations.

"We had this sense that Amal was a bright girl who cared about others," he said. "She was sad about Syria, sad for her family, confused about America. She must have forgotten your phone number, perhaps in the confusion of the trip. She didn't strike us as the type to stop communicating with someone as kind as you have been to her."

After Abboud's translation, a tear flowed down Mrs. al-Rasheed's right cheek. She wiped it away and asked if anyone wanted more tea. Boyd and Abboud accepted, but Mrs. Zureiq used the invitation to announce she and her daughter needed to return home. After the good-byes, Mrs. al-Rasheed appeared to have pushed the sorrow back inside herself. She served more tea and sat next to Abboud.

"So," said Boyd, "if we wanted to adopt a girl like Amal, what would we have to do?"

"She says she does not know," Abboud explained after listening to Mrs. al-Rasheed's response. "She did nothing for Amal to be adopted. A woman named Shayma came to her. This Shayma is from an adoption agency named A Better Future. She brought brochures and forms to fill out."

"Does Mrs. al-Rasheed still have the brochure? Does she have any other materials that the woman left?"

Mrs. al-Rasheed had only a brochure. She rose to retrieve it, departing through the rose-and-paisley curtain.

"There's almost no chance the traffickers put anything on that brochure to help us to find them," said Boyd.

"But you still want it," said Abboud.

"You never know. Maybe there will be something in the wording. Maybe the printers put their logo at the bottom."

Mrs. al-Rasheed returned with a colorful brochure all in Arabic with numerous photos of families with multi-racial children of all ages, smiling and joyful.

Abboud perused the half-pages twice. "No printer's logo, no address, no phone number. But there is an email address." She spoke with Mrs. al-Rasheed.

"She says that after some days of not hearing from Amal, she wrote to the email address, but no one responded. She has written three more times. She tried searching the internet, and there was a website, but it had no contact information on it."

Mrs. al-Rasheed touched Abboud's shoulder and spoke animatedly.

"She thought she saw this woman Shayma two days ago in the market area," said Abboud. "It was from a distance, so she was not sure. She hurried to get a closer look, but she could not find her. She told her husband about it, and he said that the next time he sees this Shayma, she should tackle the woman and drag her by her feet to the Jordanian police. She and her husband have been worried that something bad happened to Amal. Amal would have texted them. She had become like a daughter."

The heaviness in Boyd's heart grew, but they had a plan and needed to stick with it. When they returned to the U.S., someone from the Bureau would write a letter of condolence to Mrs. al-Rasheed, and she would know the truth.

He withdrew a Women's Corps International Arabic business card from his shirt pocket and gave it to Abboud. "Let's give her this. Ask her to call us if she ever sees Shayma again. And ask for her number or a way to contact her. We'd like to help find Amal, too."

Mrs. al-Rasheed accepted the card, and Boyd rose and put a hand to his chest. "Shokran," he said. *Thank you.*

Just as he and Abboud were about to exit the trailer, Mrs. al-Rasheed thought of something else. After listening, Abboud asked her to write something on another of their business cards.

"She says she knows another woman who was taking care of a girl, and that girl also left with Shayma," said Abboud. "This woman is in Amman today, but she is supposed to return tomorrow. We have her address now."

"Shokran jazeelan," said Boyd. *Thank you very much.*

At the edge of Mrs. al-Rasheed's yard, he stopped and scanned left and right on the narrow street. The wind had diminished, but the temperature had dropped. Dusk was probably an hour away. Three residences down, two boys sat in the shade of a trailer, playing with what looked like tiny toy cars. In the opposite direction, at the home next door, a gray cat eyed him with indifference. There was no sign of the two men.

Halfway down the next block, he stopped to peer behind them. Although the men were nowhere visible, he couldn't shake the feeling that they were somewhere nearby, watching him and Abboud.

CHAPTER TWENTY

Dusk had tinted the sky pale orange when Boyd and Abboud arrived at Dr. Bergeson's UN trailer. A chill continued to lower the temperature, and the wind had woken from its siesta. He wished he hadn't left his jacket in their tent.

Pierce stood at his desk when they entered, an uncharacteristic courtesy. "Precisely on time," he said. He gave only fleeting eye contact before returning his focus to the computer screen.

Boyd took out his phone and stepped in front of the secretary's desk. "Do you recognize these two men?" He showed the photograph he'd taken from Mrs. Zureiq's residence, a shot that he had since zoomed to enlarge the men. The result was grainy but distinct.

Pierce glanced at the photo before peering downward again. "No. Is there a reason that I should?"

"We thought they might be friends of yours," said Abboud.

"Why would you think that?" Pierce was either genuinely confused or a fine actor.

"Just a hunch," said Boyd. "They seemed interested in our work."

"Assisting pregnant wives?"

"Odd, isn't it? That's what we thought." Boyd stepped back and pocketed the phone.

From the hallway beyond the reception area, Dr. Bergeson cleared his throat before entering. His moustache was symmetrical and trimmed, as it had been when they met three days ago, but his graying hair was mussed. He extricated a cough drop from its wrapper and placed it in his mouth. "Sorry," he said, a tightness evident in his voice. "Please come to my office. Will you have tea?"

After declining, Boyd and Abboud took seats in Dr. Bergeson's office. Like Pierce, the UN official did not recognize the two men in the photograph.

"Sorry," he said. "Please send me the photo. I will have my officers look for them." He reached into the back of a lower drawer and withdrew his flask. He poured a modest shot into an empty coffee cup. "You reached your supervisor?"

"Yes, and also Agent Hussein in Amman," said Boyd. "Hussein is pulling another agent off an assignment in Lebanon. He should be here by morning."

Dr. Bergeson nodded his head. "I wish I could … Maybe I can. I have a security officer I can spare. Officer Renault. She's new here, but she's not new with UN security. I'm told she knows how to be discreet."

He returned the flask. "Cocktail hour. I'm off shift in fifteen minutes. There's absolutely no question but that you two will be staying in different quarters tonight. I was amazed when I found out Mr. Pierce had ensconced you in a tent in the farthest corner of our camp. You have my profound apologies."

"He did arrange for us to be watched," said Abboud. "A Mr. Yusuf Shabat."

"He's a fine man," said Dr. Bergeson. "At least Mr. Pierce got that right."

"Why is that okay?" said Boyd. "It isn't part of the arrangements we made."

"Standard practice. Whenever we bring in a new NCO, I make sure my neighborhood leaders know about it. Had we not reached out to Mr. Shabat, *that* would have been unusual."

Boyd nodded. Perhaps the arrangement was legit. Perhaps Pierce was legit. But he wouldn't bet his or Abboud's life on it. "About your secretary. What—"

Dr. Bergeson waved his hand. "As I told you before, he's as innocent as they come. I trust him absolutely. Well, maybe not with the social niceties, but as for discretion and integrity you won't find a better man." He sipped from the cup. "So then. You've learned something."

"We spoke with Mrs. Ghaaliya al-Rasheed in District Twelve," said Boyd. "That's the woman with whom the deceased girl had lived. There's another woman named Shayma who lured the girl away, promised her she was going to be adopted. We know the girl's name now—Amal."

"That's real progress." Dr. Bergeson looked at Abboud. "It must be a big asset for you to be assisting with this case. So many talented individuals have spent time in this camp. And tomorrow you're going to talk to someone else? What's the name of that woman?"

"Rahiq Rezk," she said.

"Ah. Interesting." The cough drop clicked against Dr. Bergeson's teeth. Boyd wondered if the cocktail hour had begun earlier in the day. How much help was this man going to be able to provide?

"Let's talk some more about Pierce," said Boyd. "I know you trust him. But do you have any other idea why two men are tailing us? It's not because they care about pregnant women, is it? And if they know why we're really here, how is it that they know? You said you coordinate your operations with the Jordanian military. Whom have you told?"

"No one. That's what we arranged, and I've kept my end of it. This doesn't have to fall on me. It could be that word leaked out in the States, maybe through your own office. Don't assume it had to have come from here."

"I don't assume anything, including the innocence of your secretary. He's treated us like shit from the moment we arrived. That might be just the way he is, but even you admit you're surprised about where he placed us in the camp. Where would you position a couple of investigators if you wanted them as far away from the action as you could put them?"

A cough seized Dr. Bergeson. After recovering, he asked, "Would you like me to bring him in here? Do you want to interrogate him?"

"And alert his friends?" said Abboud.

"She's right," said Boyd. "I might already have given him a scare just now in the reception room. I showed him the photo of those two men. He claimed he'd never seen them."

Dr. Bergeson nodded. "Mr. Pierce does not tell lies."

"As far as you know," said Abboud.

The UN officer sighed. "I'll tell you what I'll do. I'll stay late after Mr. Pierce leaves, tell him I've got a report that needs more work. Then I'll check his computer, see if there's anything suspicious."

"If Pierce is connected to the traffickers," said Boyd, "do you really think he'd conduct that business on a UN computer?"

"If encrypted, he might. Think about what you're suggesting. My personal secretary is the point person for connecting sex traffickers to vulnerable teenage girls? Mr. Pierce underwent a vigorous background check before I hired him, as do all individuals who work at this level for United Nations Security."

"Our question still applies." Boyd leaned onto Dr. Bergeson's desk, close enough to smell the whiskey in the cup and in the man's breath. "Why did he house us at the farthest corner of the camp?"

"Think about it." Annoyance entered Bergeson's voice. "He *doesn't* know why you're here. Why should two volunteers from an NGO no one has ever heard of get a special spot near services and commercial enterprises? Mr. Pierce has done nothing out of the ordinary in regard to you two. You're being followed. That's concerning, especially considering the horrific crash you experienced before you arrived here. It appears you're in real danger, even as you're finding some of the information you're looking for. But there has to be another explanation besides my secretary."

"I'm not saying that Pierce is this or that," said Boyd. "We just shouldn't automatically eliminate him from consideration. That's all I mean. There could be a dozen other explanations."

"Well, then." Dr. Bergeson took a tiny sip and held it in his mouth before swallowing. "I am glad to hear you are considering other possibilities."

"Do you have any other ideas, Dr. Bergeson?" asked Abboud.

"If someone knows, they know either through you or through me. I believe there are actually more individuals on your side of the ledger who know of your endeavors here. I don't mean to cast suspicion upon any of your colleagues, but as you say, how else could anyone know?"

Boyd thought for a moment. Who would it be? Fisk? That didn't make sense. Roshan? She'd already been a victim. Abboud? Maybe not purposefully, but she might have revealed just enough detail to the Za'atari contact with whom she'd been in communication. But Abboud's judgment had proved to be solid, and she was strongly committed to catching the traffickers.

Could someone in the bureau's printshop or a techie who created their bogus website have blabbed to the wrong person? But no one in those support services would know the details of the mission.

"We appreciate your willingness to watch Pierce more closely," said Boyd. "Please give me a call after you've checked his computer. And thank you for bringing in an additional security officer. Let's confer tomorrow on how we want to coordinate your officer and our agent as surveillance. We'll want to visit Mrs. ..." He looked at Abboud.

"Rezk," she said.

"... Mrs. Rezk and learn whatever she can tell us. Maybe she knows more about the woman named Shayma. But we won't want to make it obvious that we've got extra security."

"Right," said Bergeson. "Give me a call at nine and we'll work out the particulars. Meanwhile ..." He opened a wide drawer in front of him and took out a key. "Here's a key to your new residence. I myself have chosen it. It's five blocks from here. At least you can lock the door to a trailer. The address is on the little tab on the keychain.

You'll be going to the tent to gather your belongings, yes? I'd offer Pierce to drive you there, but I suspect you'd rather rely on someone else."

Abboud looked at Boyd. "Shall we walk? It's the only way we're getting any exercise here."

Boyd had watched dusk give way to night through the window behind Bergeson. He liked walks—they helped him sort through problems, to think of new ideas. On the other hand …

"We might meet our two friends," he said.

"We can invite them for tea," said Abboud. "Perhaps we're mistaken. They might be members of our fan club."

CHAPTER TWENTY-ONE

Shortly after they left Dr. Bergeson, the wind turned menacing, assaulting them at an angle. Boyd and Abboud leaned forward against what felt like an invisible hand shoving them backward and grinding sand across their faces. Power lines swayed and streetlights blinked on and off. On both sides of the lane, flapping tarps of canvas and plastic combined with the frenzy of wind chimes to play a staccato symphonic din. The whine of the wind itself added an eerie chorale. He could no more carry on a conversation with Abboud than if they'd occupied a closed garage with a dozen power tools blaring.

He stopped at an intersection to make certain they hadn't strayed from the route to their tent. Amid the roar and the flying grit, he and Abboud studied a map on her phone.

"Still in District Nine," she said, shouting her words.

He nodded, and they continued. If those two men were tailing them, they'd need to be doing so at an intimate distance, for even when the streetlights blinked on, he could see at most eight feet ahead. Combined with the cold, the possibility that their trackers might still be sneaking behind them in the near-blind conditions created a constant chill up and down his spine. For about the hundredth time, he wished he'd brought his jacket.

Abboud tapped his arm and pointed toward a dimly lit communal kitchen of concrete blocks. The doors were closed, and the lights were off. She veered off the path and he followed her to the lee side of the building. She unzipped her fanny pack and pulled from it a bandanna that she tied around her face. Boyd did the same, checking behind them to see if their pals had emerged like ghosts from the blowing cloud of nighttime grit. Seeing nothing, he slid on a pair of goggles while Abboud did the same.

Before they'd left for Jordan, she had warned him about the wind, but he hadn't needed the reminder. He'd dealt with it plenty during his stints in Iraq, sometimes so extreme that it shut down both ISIS and coalition forces.

"Not conditions to visit anyone tomorrow," she said, not quite as loudly as when they'd been on the street.

"No," he agreed. "It's hunker-down time."

"Hunker?"

"Like staying in shelter."

"As we should be doing now?"

"Exactly."

They took sips of water and ended their respite. Boyd felt as though he were burrowing forward more than walking. Jawad Street turned to Al Zahraa, marking their entry into District Eight. A particularly fierce gust stood them up and vanquished the streetlights for good. They flipped on their headlamps and continued. He'd been through worse. He recalled Abboud telling him she'd barely been able to see her hand in front of her face during a storm the first year she'd resided in this camp. They could press forward. At least on the return trip, the wind would be mostly at their backs.

Dim glows from trailer windows, the outputs of candles and lanterns, glimmered from an alternate universe. Droplets mixed with the blowing detritus of the desert. Boyd wasn't sure if the moisture came from clouds; for all he knew, it could have originated from a man urinating half a mile away. Near their tent, he pulled Abboud out of the wind to the sheltered side of a mosque.

"They know where we live," he said.

"It is a fine night for an ambush." Her words gave him pause, not because of the threat she identified, but because of the matter-of-fact tone in her voice. If he'd had any doubt about her experience, that tone erased it.

"Our headlamps will give us away," he said.

They turned them off. "We should move off the street, close to the caravans," she said.

"Exactly." Damn, she was smart. How much combat had she seen? Hers would have been asymmetrical, she on the stealthy side, a guerrilla soldier against the Syrian government, while in the next-door nation, he had been on a government's side—and yet, they had both fought for the same ideals.

The forces arrayed against Abboud had been overwhelming and heartless, and the stakes were deeply personal. Death had been the most likely outcome. He had been aligned with the dominant force. Death and maiming shadowed him everywhere, but the most likely outcome for him had been a flight home after his tour was finished.

Sure, he had experienced war and all its hell. But she had lived there.

"If they want a piece of us, they'll be waiting inside our tent," he said. "Let's get right up to it. We'll wait and we'll listen, maybe a half hour. When I'm ready to go in, I'll tap your shoulder, and you get yourself to the other side of the bathroom building. What I'll do is crawl into the vestibule, and when I go in it'll be fast as hell, and I'll be ready to shoot. Most likely it'll be a bunch of fuss for no reason, and I'll come get you after I verify it's all clear. We'll get our sleeping bags and our packs and get the hell out of here."

She didn't answer for a moment. He had a feeling that she didn't like the idea of him taking the risk all on his own. "If I have to shoot, I don't want you in the path of a stray bullet," he said.

She nodded. She grabbed his forearm, gave it a little squeeze. He thought she was trying to tell him something, trying to tell him she cared. They were a unit now, a unit of two.

The usual bathroom smell did not greet them as they approached the building and their tent, for the wind carried the odor southwest, away from them. When they passed the last trailer before their tent, it quickly became apparent that there would be no reason to wait outside their tent. Vivid in the void of storm created by the wall, a pair of pencil-tip orange glows angled down in an arc next to the bathroom building.

Each holding a cigarette, two figures rose from where they'd been sitting. They stood at most thirty feet away. Boyd retrieved his gun, but he kept the muzzle pointed down. He flipped on his headlamp.

It was them.

The din of flapping canvas was diminished here at the edge of Za'atari, but not altogether gone. The whistling voice of the wind took the louder role, while droplets spat at a more downward angle.

Abboud switched on her headlamp and pointed it directly into the men's eyes. They squinted. The larger of the two raised his arm to shield his eyes, then lowered it, apparently not wishing to show a weakness. Each wore dark pants and black sweatshirts with the hoods up. Had Boyd encountered them in the direct wind, he'd have discerned no details about them at all, except for the outline of their forms.

"No need for a gun, Agent Boyd," called the smaller man. *Agent* Boyd—so he knew. What was his accent—French? He had a nose that belonged on a bigger face, but that was all Boyd could see, despite the spotlight gleam of his and Abboud's headlamps. "We are no threat to you. We actually want to help."

Boyd thought he could use some help. Who was this Shayma who'd lured the girls away? Surely, she must have had accomplices. How did she know which homes to visit, which substitute parents to target? Maybe he'd been wrong about the men. Why else would they allow themselves to be caught out in the open?

He removed his goggles and pulled down the bandanna. "Exactly how are you going to help?" he demanded.

"You are looking for a woman."

His beefy companion was silent—perhaps he didn't speak English.

"Maybe," said Boyd.

"Have you learned her name yet?"

"Maybe."

"Do you know how to find her?"

"Stop being cute. If you're going to help us, tell us how."

"Oh, believe me, Agent Boyd, help is on the way."

"What do—"

Belting out a warrior's guttural cry, Abboud spun half a turn. From the corner of his eye, Boyd caught the image of another man in the glow of her headlamp at the very instant the base of her hand smashed into his nose. Bellowing, the man staggered. By the time Boyd finished his own half turn, a second man had reached him, his arm mid-swing and his hand gripping a machete. It would have been the last split second of his life except that Abboud, with incredible speed, whirled with a kick to the side of the assailant's knee, toppling him onto wet dirt.

Shocked that he still breathed, Boyd raised his pistol. The man on the ground groaned but couldn't rise. The first man's nose gushed blood, but he'd recovered enough to brandish a knife, pointing it toward Abboud, who crouched in readiness.

Something solid slammed the back of Boyd's head, like he'd been hit by a truck. Agonizing pain seized his consciousness. His legs buckled, and he fell backward with the weight of a mountain hastening the fall. His eyes barely functioned, but he could see it was that large silent man. A fist rocketed down like a pile driver and a new pain screamed out from his nose.

In a single second, his faltering awareness flashed multiple directions—grunts and cries somewhere to his left … Abboud.

Stunned, like a bird that had crashed into a window, he couldn't move. The brute on top of him cocked his arm, his hand straight as a board. Boyd saw the aim, knew what the trajectory would be … down, down at his throat, a meaty guillotine. More pain, perhaps death.

What shame, what irony just when they were close to answers. He never thought it would end like this.

In a disembodied way, he saw that his arms and hands rose—where was his gun?—just as the brute swung down. The guillotine blasted past his hands, struck his neck, perhaps not quite so hard as it would have been, not so accurate. Excruciating pain. No breath. Gasping. Choking. As though in a dark tunnel, his headlamp illuminated the same blade of a hand rising again.

Bright lights lit the night at the same time a leg and a foot swung round and caught Boyd's assailant flush on the side of his neck.

The world went dark.

When his eyes opened, Abboud's face filled his view. Her hijab hung loose around her neck. Her dark hair brushed against his ear. She was breathing hard. There had been a fight and she was still alive. Her mouth opened. Her hand stroked his hair.

The big bright light still illuminated, giving her face an unnatural glow. Wind whistled across the ground … the ground … that's where he lay. He had been in a fight and he wasn't feeling well at all.

Another glowing face appeared, and for a moment, given the circumstances, he thought it might be Jesus or St. Peter, but it turned out to be Pierce.

Tamir Pierce.

CHAPTER
TWENTY-TWO

Below deck on the fancy boat, where Lely and her friends had been stuck for two days at the Tripoli Marina, Shayma opened the door at the top of the steps and stuck her head out into the bright lights. She glanced down through the opening at her phone and scowled. It had to have been the billionth time in the past half hour that their chaperone had peeked outside, but Lely decided to keep the count to herself.

Next to her on the beige leather sofa that curved around a small wooden table, Qamar studied her feet, like she always did when she spoke to Shayma. "If those two men do not arrive, will we go back to Za'atari?"

"We cannot go back," said Shayma, facing what Lely thought would be the shore. It was hard to remember. When they had arrived, the truckdriver had slid open the container door, injecting a shock of floodlights into what had seemed like an immense metal crypt.

"Third slip on your left," he had said. "Brown hull, white deck." Lely's trip from the back of the truck to the belly of the boat turned out to be the only opportunity to scan her surroundings, which wasn't much, considering how the bright lights and wee-hour grogginess washed everything to a blur.

Now she felt just as antsy as Shayma to get out in the open, to start moving again. She wanted to spring loose from her seat and launch like a rocket up those stairs, poof, right past Shayma ten feet into the air and float back down like a rose petal, and then, boom, burst off at a fast pace any direction at all. It didn't matter, as long as her feet kept moving. Her toes twitched at the thought.

Shayma stepped down and closed the hatch.

"Those dogs," she said. "Medical appointment, my ass. At nine o'clock at night? More likely, they're drunk."

Yana, attired in a black abaya and hijab like everyone else, put a hand to her mouth.

"Oh, don't look so shocked," said Shayma. "You'll be drinking, too, when you get to America. Your sisters there already do. I can't imagine the Prophet objecting to wine. Fruit of the vine, all around the world. Get used to it."

Lely wouldn't stare at her feet. She'd never do that, even though Shayma's scowls grew tighter every time she came down the steps without a sighting or a message from Jack and Majd.

"Put on your coats and pick up your packs," said Shayma. "The ship will not wait for us. America will not wait for us. We're leaving now. Don't be looking around, don't act nervous, keep your heads pointed forward, and follow me. You're lucky you have me to protect you. The men who work at the docks are not always kind to girls like you."

Lely climbed out the hatch after Shayma. Awash in light, the marina appeared the same as it had the night of her arrival. Seawater and fancy boats extended left and right, while city lights and tall buildings rose on the land in front of her. A cool wind blew from the sea. She smelled salt and diesel and the cedar-scented perfume she'd dabbed on her neck. The white deck where they gathered in front of the cabin dipped and rose in the lapping gurgle of water, prompting Lely to grab the rail to keep her balance.

"No chit-chat," said Shayma. "Nothing to bring attention to us."

Their chaperone grasped the rail, marched through the narrow passage between the cabin and the side of the boat, and descended a couple of stairs. She hopped from the stern to the dock. Lely kept pace, refusing to be frightened by the gap of water beneath her when she jumped to the dock. Within a minute, they'd reached a long sidewalk that formed a barrier between the marina and the open sea. Moving toward the city, Shayma picked up her pace so much that if she were moving faster, they'd be running. She reached a corner and turned left onto another sidewalk, this one on solid land, not lit nearly as much as the marina.

Almost immediately, they reached two big freighter ships, their near-empty decks bright under lights, but somehow Shayma knew these were not the right ones and she kept going. In front of them lay warehouse buildings on their right and open water on their left. The voices of men, boisterous and punctuated with guffaws, echoed between buildings somewhere ahead. Shayma marched forward. Lely and Qamar gripped each other's hands and followed.

In a gap between warehouses, the shadow of firelight reflected on a wall. In another step, the men came into view, but Shayma kept moving, giving them not so much as a glance. From her peripheral vision Lely noted that the fire burned from a barrel, the men standing around it, but she, too, did not look their way. She had nearly traversed the twenty-meter gap when one of the men shouted, "Hey, hey, stop!"

In the distance ahead, a ship horn let loose a long, low-pitched blast.

Shayma did not stop.

"Hey! I said stop!"

Shayma did not slow or increase her pace. The sound of footsteps at a trot thumped on the pavement behind them, closing the distance fast. A single man wearing a ballcap and an orange jacket trotted past them, whirled, and stopped five meters in front of Shayma.

Shayma stopped.

She reached into the pocket of her abaya, flicked her wrist, and a knife blade glinted beneath the floodlights of the warehouse. Behind them, so close that the back of Lely's neck prickled, multiple men cried out what sounded like a mocking *whoa*.

"We're not going to hurt you," said the man, close enough so that Lely could see his slightly rounded belly and pencil-thin moustache.

"Then get out of my way," said Shayma.

"You're not supposed to be here. Didn't you see the signs?"

Lely hadn't seen any signs, but she'd had her eyes locked onto Shayma's back the whole time.

"We are on our way to the *Asian Rose*," said Shayma. "We have tickets."

"The *Asian Rose*?" called a man behind them. "That's at least a kilometer from here."

"We know that," said Shayma, though she had earlier told the girls she didn't know where it was.

"So have a safe journey," said the man in front. "You should have entered through the main entrance. This area is off limits."

"We came from the marina," said Shayma.

"I don't care where you came from," said the man. "This area is off limits unless you work here."

He hesitated. They were in a standoff. What if this man wouldn't let them pass? Or he was lying to them and he meant them harm? What if they didn't get to their ship on time? Her legs wobbled with tension, just like they had at the border crossing.

"This is a dangerous area," said the man. "There can be lots of activity. Cranes. Forklifts. Trucks. I'm going to lead you to your boat. You can keep your knife open if it makes you feel safer."

"We're expecting some men to join us," said Shayma. "They're late and we don't have time. Lead on, but if you try something, I will cut off your testicles."

A chorus of *whoas* erupted behind them. Part of Lely wished she had a knife, too, but another part of her wished she were ten kilometers from the nearest knife.

"Hey, you knuckleheads," said the man. "Break time's over. Go back to work."

"Our boss is going to be a eunuch," said one of the men, but there was a sound of shuffling shoes and footsteps moving away.

Within minutes after resuming the fast-paced trek, they encountered a pair of forklifts zipping back and forth on the pathway, and an enormous crane lifted a truck-sized container as though it were a toy. The man with the cap turned right and led them through a series of turns until they emerged back on the sidewalk, with all the commotion behind them.

In another ten minutes they stopped at a gigantic ship with English and Asian lettering on a moss green hull as high as …

She didn't like the comparison that popped into her head. Her old apartment building, the one that used to be five stories high, before … She let go of Qamar's hand and turned toward the wall of the ship and let the portrait photo of her family, which was the only way she had to remember them, linger a moment in her mind's eye. What would her father and her mother think if they could see her now in this place about to board this ship, to leave her homeland perhaps forever? She shuddered for a moment and thought she might cry, but she pushed down the emotions.

"Tawak kalto ul Allah," she whispered. *I put my trust in Allah.*

CHAPTER TWENTY-THREE

Dressed in underwear and a paper hospital gown, Boyd eased himself off an examination table at the Saudi Medical Clinic in Za'atari's District Five. His legs worked. He wasn't sure about the rest of his body.

He couldn't move his neck, so he had to turn his whole body to find his damp and dirty sweatshirt and trousers draped onto a chair next to his wife Abboud—that's how they identified her to Doctor Abdul, who'd moved on to the next patient. Boyd wore a neck brace, a wrist brace, and a plastic half-mask. Beneath it, his nose was bent off-center, even after Doctor Abdul had wrenched it back in place. That had been a lot of fun, almost as much as the original punch.

Abboud stood up, her eyes sympathetic. The only evidence that she'd been in a fight consisted of a small rip and streaks of dried mud on her abaya. She had repositioned her hijab on the way to the clinic. Dr. Abdul had banished her to the waiting area until he'd finished working over Boyd a few minutes ago.

"May I hug you?" she asked.

"A light one," he said. His voice sounded like a chain-smoking old man. It hurt to swallow.

She put her arms around his waist, leaned the side of her head against his chest. Yeah, he could use one of those every day. Quite a few times. She'd saved his ass, and now she was all feminine. She stepped back and studied him. There was something more than professional regard in her eyes.

"I thought …" She took a breath, pressed her lips together. "When you were lying there, I thought—"

"That I was a goner? I thought you might have been an angel."

She gave a quiet half-chuckle.

"I still do," he said. "An avenging angel. You kicked their asses."

"It was not as though I had a choice, was it? And anyway, the fight was not over. They retreated when Pierce arrived."

He leaned down to pick up his trousers. A sharp pain in the back of his neck told him that was a mistake. He gritted his teeth and gasped.

"Let me help you," she said, picking up the trousers.

"No, I can do it." He stood ramrod straight, reached out a hand, and Abboud gave him the trousers.

The holster was missing from the belt. "My gun. That big brute—he knocked it out of my hand. You didn't happen to—"

Abboud patted a big pocket at the right hip of her abaya.

"Oh, you're more than an angel. I'll take it now."

"If we need to use it, who between us is most physically capable at this moment?"

"I can handle it," he insisted. She gave him the gun and he fastened it inside the holster. He lifted a leg to put on the pants and tottered.

Abboud grasped his arm to keep him from falling. His mind swam in dizziness. When his head cleared, he unsnapped the holster and returned the pistol to her.

Somehow, he managed to get the pants on and tighten his belt. She untied the strings on the back of the gown. He pulled it off his shoulders and let it drop to the floor. He contemplated the Women's Corps International sweatshirt after she handed it to him.

There was no way he could get that thing over his neck.

"Will you?" he asked.

It hurt when she pulled it down over his head, but he repressed any expression of it. The dampness made him shiver. The shiver hurt his neck.

"We have your coat," she said.

"Where is it?"

"It is in Pierce's car. We picked up everything from the tent."

"What about you?" he asked.

"What do you mean?"

"Are you okay? Are you hurt anywhere?"

"I have a scrape on my leg."

"And I thought I was protecting you."

"You were. You did."

In disagreement, he tried to shake his head. He couldn't do that, either.

* * *

It was near 10:30 when Boyd and Abboud left the examination room and entered a large waiting area where a dozen individuals of all ages wore stoic faces, enduring not just whatever afflicted them but also a squalling toddler. Wearing the same olive-green stocking cap he'd had on the day they'd met outside the Za'atari gate, Pierce sat near the hospital entrance. He was fingering his cellphone, oblivious as always.

Boyd stopped, touching Abboud's arm for her to do the same. How was it that Pierce showed up at their tent in the middle of a windstorm while he and Abboud were under attack? Did he have anything to do with those men or the assault?

"What do you think of him?" he asked in a quiet, croaky voice.

"I do not know," said Abboud. "He told me he was worried about us because of the storm."

"Do you believe that?"

"No. There is something more, something he has not revealed. But he helped us."

Pierce glanced up, noticed Boyd and Abboud, and stood from his chair. Even from across the room, Boyd could see the man needed a shave.

When Boyd and Abboud reached him, the secretary, who'd previously shown himself incapable of eye contact for more than a second, stared at him open-mouthed.

"Yeah, they put a bunch of crap on me," said Boyd, "but I'll get rid of it. You know anybody who'd like this mask, a cat burglar or someone in a related field of work?"

Pierce looked aside. "Hardly," he said.

"It's good of you to have waited for us," said Boyd. "We should talk. I've got questions, and I'm sure you do, too. Have you contacted Dr. Bergeson?"

Pierce blinked, showing confusion. "Mrs. Boyd asked me not to. She asked me not to contact the police, either."

Boyd would have glanced at Abboud for confirmation, but he could not turn his head.

"We have some tasks to finish first," she said.

"I agree," said Boyd. Someone didn't want Abboud and him visiting Mrs. Rahiq Rezk tomorrow morning. Although the wind might delay their encounter, he wasn't going to let a band of thugs stop him. Plus, he'd have reinforcement, that extra agent Hussein was prying loose and maybe that UN cop Bergeson was summoning.

"Where can we go?" he asked. "Is it still windy outside?"

"Not nearly as much," said Pierce. "Half an hour ago, I saw stars among the clouds."

Boyd glanced at the toddler, who was sniffling between squalls. "I hope that kid's okay. Let's go."

Outside, the wind still blew, but without its earlier ferocity. Dark rags of cloud slid across a starry backdrop. Generators rumbled nearby. Boyd scanned ahead, pivoted left and pivoted right. He hoped Pierce didn't notice that he couldn't turn his head. Of course, any potential assailant would have Abboud to deal with. But if their opponents decided to abandon close-quarter combat, she wouldn't be able to stop a bullet—probably.

"Where's your car, Tamir?" he asked.

"It's the blue Peugeot, over there." He pointed to the left. It was a small, unremarkable sedan. "Your packs are in the trunk."

"It's cold out here. You mind if we get in and figure out what we're going to do?"

"We should drive somewhere," said Abboud. "Let me choose. I want to know if we are being followed."

"Good thinking," said Boyd.

It hurt his neck to get in the back seat, but he did it quickly. Abboud waited until he was seated, then went around the front of the car and took the spot next to him. The painkillers he'd ingested were beginning to take effect. The throbbing was less acute, but at the same time he felt a small slippage in his mind. He decided not to take any more of the medicine.

"You followed us," he said.

"No, I didn't," said Pierce. "I finished my shift. It was almost five o'clock when you left. I started for the gate—I live in Mafraq. But the storm was bad. I worried about you."

"Worried?" said Boyd. "For our well-being? That didn't seem to be the case on the day we arrived."

"That was—" Pierce peeked at the rearview mirror. He caught Boyd's eye and looked away.

"That was what?" said Boyd.

"I … I shouldn't say."

"We were just attacked," said Boyd. "Now's not the time to hold anything back. You've got information to share—share it."

Pierce took a long breath. "It's about Dr. Bergeson."

"What about him?"

"He's my boss."

"That's not exactly news."

"It's just … if I do tell you, you must promise not to tell him what I've said. I will lose my job. He'll dismiss me."

"That depends, Tamir. If you've committed a crime, that's not a secret we can keep."

"No. No crime. It's about him."

"Okay. This conversation is confidential."

"We should drive," said Abboud. "It may not be safe

to stay in this spot. Mr. Pierce, are you willing to drive where I tell you to go?"

Pierce rubbed his chin before answering. "This is … highly unusual. You are volunteers for an NGO. Why would anyone attack you? And now you want me to drive you around."

"It is unusual," said Boyd. "I'd like to know some answers, too. Abboud lived here for three years. I trust her to know her way around. Wouldn't you like to know if someone's watching us right now and if that someone's going to follow us?"

Pierce nodded. He started the engine. Abboud had him turn right out of the parking lot, the only way he could turn in order to leave. They moved north in District Five, toward the outside wall. As the hospital faded into the distance behind them, they traversed an entirely residential area. Now that the windstorm had eased and electricity had been restored, teenagers ventured outside. Attired in abayas and jackets, the girls clustered in groups, while the boys wore ball caps and swaggered as they strolled in threes and fours.

There were no headlights behind them.

"Okay, Tamir," said Boyd. "Talk to us about your boss."

Pierce kept his eyes on the lane. "On that first day you were here, he told me to give you a cold shoulder. He said you were both nuisances, that you've been badgering him before you even left the United States. He didn't want you to feel like you could visit the security office whenever you felt like it. He's the one who chose your tent. He told me to get Mr. Shabat to keep an eye on you. He wanted to be informed if Mrs. Boyd started talking to people in trailers where nobody was pregnant."

It hadn't occurred to Boyd that Bergeson could be suspect. Fisk had worked with the D.C. office, which had identified Bergeson as a suitable ally. Over a period of two weeks, the security official had participated in six video planning sessions. Despite his predilection for hidden flasks, he'd seemed helpful, genuinely concerned. He'd been defensive about Pierce, and now here Pierce was badmouthing him in return.

But why had Pierce helped them? If he were aligned with the criminals, wouldn't he have shown up at the scene of the ambush with a few weapons of his own? Certainly Boyd had been vulnerable. Pierce could have taken out a pistol and executed both of them—though he would have had to take out Abboud from a distance to keep her from disarming him.

But if the unlikely were in fact true, that Bergeson had gone rogue, why did he keep defending Pierce? Wouldn't it have been to his advantage to keep suspicions directed toward his secretary?

"I didn't know why he wanted me to treat you that way, and I still don't," said Pierce after Boyd's silence. "But … there is something that I was not honest to you about."

"And that is …" prompted Boyd.

"The photograph of the two men who were following you, the ones Abboud said had set up the ambush—I have seen them. I don't know who they are. But I have seen Dr. Bergeson in their company. Twice. Both times in a café sharing a shisha pipe."

Boyd's brain swirled. He didn't know if it was the drugs or a concussion or if it was what Pierce was saying about Bergeson. Probably it was all three.

They stopped at a tee-intersection. Across from them lay an empty lot in front of the outside wall. To their left and right, small trailers crammed together haphazardly. Isolated drops spotted the dusty windshield, and yet stars were still visible.

"Which way?" Pierce asked.

"Left," said Abboud. "At the next intersection there is a school the Kuwaitis have sponsored. Park outside the fence."

They drove in silence for a couple of minutes before reaching the school. Outside lights illuminated lines of trailers with narrow paths between them.

"It's my turn for a question," said Pierce. "What is it that you're really doing here?"

"We are assisting pregnant women," said Abboud. "That is why we cannot understand what is happening to us."

"I saw you kick a man in the face. He was beating up Mr. Boyd. Another man could barely walk. A third man was rolling on the ground with his hands covering his face."

"She has a taekwondo black belt," said Boyd. "I'm an accountant. Who's going to kick ass?"

"An accountant with a gun? I saw Abboud pick up a pistol where you were attacked."

"I'm an American. We all have guns. We have more guns than people."

Pierce shook his head. "I think you are CIA. And you have something to do with Dr. Bergeson. Maybe he is stealing money and the United Nations has asked for your help."

"What makes you think he'd be stealing money?"

Pierce put both hands up to his chin. He flicked his eyes at the rearview mirror.

"Go ahead," said Boyd. "You didn't make up that accusation out of thin air. What's he doing?"

"Okay. I will say. But it's only because I think you are CIA. I know you cannot tell me this. And you have told me you will not tell Dr. Bergeson anything I am saying."

"As long as it does not involve a crime," said Boyd.

"Oh."

Boyd could sense Pierce freezing like a popsicle. "Don't worry. If he's done something wrong, we'll protect you. We have ways of doing that."

"Like you protected yourself earlier this evening?"

"Better than that."

Pierce took a long breath. "I began working for Dr. Bergeson three years ago. He used to spend a lot of time out of the office, going to the various districts, talking to people. I went with him, of course. He needed an interpreter. Besides that, I took notes. Built a database, including details about different refugees, particularly if the war had harmed them in an especially acute way. We knew who had lost wives or husbands, parents or children. That has changed recently. Maybe about a year ago, I think."

"Wait a moment," said Abboud. "You said you knew who had lost parents. Does that mean you know which children are orphans?" Boyd felt her hand touch his arm, but he couldn't see it, not with a strained neck and a brace around it like a straitjacket.

"Yes. We know all these things."

"Do you have the records at your office?" asked Boyd.

"Of course."

"So what changed?"

"Perhaps Mr. Pierce can tell us at his office," said Abboud.

"Oh, I don't think so," said Pierce.

"And why's that?" asked Boyd.

"Well ... what if he shows up?"

"Is that the kind of thing he does? Show up at the office around midnight?"

"I don't know. I'm always home then."

"If he arrives for some reason while we are there," said Abboud, "he will see my husband and it will be impossible to hide what happened to us."

"Maybe he already knows," said Pierce.

"What makes you think that?" asked Boyd.

"He can tell us on the way to the office," said Abboud.

"I know what you want," said Pierce. "You want me to show you the records. But they are confidential. Don't you have to have a warrant?"

Boyd paused. Pierce had him on that one. If Bergeson was guilty—which still seemed crazy—and part of how they discovered that guilt was snooping around without a warrant, boom, their case would go right down the tubes. And so would Boyd's job.

But, on the other hand …

"What if *you* decide to show us?" he asked the secretary. "I'm not asking you for anything. You're the one who suggested we want to look at records. We didn't say that. Are you offering us access from your own free will?"

Three times, Pierce's eyes flitted to the mirror and back to the steering wheel. Either he was damn nervous or a damn good actor.

"Okay," he said.

"Okay what?"

"I would like to share some records with you."

"You understand that if there is a crime, you may have to testify?"

"And you will protect me?"

"We will protect you."

Pierce restarted the engine.

* * *

Except for exterior lighting, the United Nations security office was dark. The guard who'd been there during the day was gone. Boyd and Abboud took their packs from the trunk and leaned them on the porch. It would be only a five-minute walk to the trailer where they'd be staying for the night, however much time would be left of it whenever they finished.

The air inside the trailer smelled a little sour, as though the windows had been closed for too long. Pierce went straight to his desk and opened the laptop.

"You said that Dr. Bergeson may already know about the assault," said Boyd while they waited for the computer to boot up. "Why?"

"What else would he be discussing in a café with the two men who were waiting at your tent?" said Pierce.

"He didn't seem to recognize them when we visited him earlier today … or, I should say, yesterday at this point. But neither did you." Boyd wondered if the names *Amal Nasri* and *Hafa Jandali* would be in a special category in the database. There would be other names there. Too many. The war had created a lot of orphans. What kind of government gassed its own citizens?

But some of those names might lead them to people who might lead them to the traffickers.

"You also wondered if Dr. Bergeson might be stealing money," said Abboud. "Why did you think that?"

Pierce kept his eyes on the computer. "He started taking vacations. A week in Abu Dhabi. A week at Monte Carlo."

"Casinos?" guessed Boyd.

"Yes. He said he won big. He couldn't believe his luck. The thing is, he never talked about gambling or casinos for two years, and then all of a sudden he did."

Pierce's expression changed. "What the …?" He moved his mouse, clicked, moved it some more and clicked again. Open-mouthed, he gawked at Boyd and Abboud. "The file is gone."

Boyd took a long breath. Of course, it would be gone. He and Abboud had come too close. Or did Pierce know the whole time that the file would not be there? "Don't you have a backup?" he asked.

"Yes. There's a portable hard drive. We don't keep these records in the cloud. They're too sensitive." Pierce took a moment to access the hard drive, then shook his head.

"Gone," he whispered.

"What about his office?" asked Boyd. "Doesn't Dr. Bergeson keep the files, too? Does he print them out, leave them in a file cabinet?"

"He always keeps his door locked."

"Let's try it anyway."

Boyd led Abboud and Pierce into the short hallway off which Bergeson's door opened. The sour smell grew stronger, and so did the throbbing in his head. Dr. Abdul had told him he should be resting. He wondered when he'd get around to that.

Bergeson's doorknob turned easily. Boyd opened the door only a crack when something putrid assaulted his senses. For a moment he wondered if Bergeson had taken a crap into his garbage can and left it there.

But when he opened the door the rest of the way and flipped on the light, the source of the smell was obvious. Dr. Bergeson sat motionless in a chair behind his desk. His neck was slashed deep and wide. Dried blood discolored his white dress shirt. It had spattered his desk, a file folder, a ballpoint pen, and his flask. His eyes were wide open and the skin on his face had lost its color. His arms dangled limply. Flies buzzed on the open wound.

Pierce cried out. He tottered into the hall, and a moment afterward Boyd heard retching.

Abboud's face was grim. "Rahimullah," she said—*may Allah have mercy on him.*

CHAPTER TWENTY-FOUR

Boyd stepped back and looked at Abboud. "I have a small kit I need to get from my pack before anyone enters this room. Are you okay waiting here while I get it?"

"Of course."

"We can't avoid contacting the Jordanian police this time. But first I'd like ten or so minutes to look around."

Boyd found Pierce in the conference room hunched over a garbage can. There was nothing in it. Apparently, Pierce hadn't eaten in a while.

From his backpack Boyd retrieved a small crime scene kit, an item he didn't expect to need on this trip. Back inside the trailer, he gave shoe coverings and gloves to Abboud. He put on gloves but needed her help to get the shoe coverings in place. He turned to the secretary, who'd joined them in the hall.

"Tamir, I want you to wait outside in this hallway. Don't go anywhere. And I want your phone."

Pierce glared back. "I don't have to do that. You have no jurisdiction over me."

"You were wrong about my being CIA. I'm with the FBI. Would you like to see my badge?"

"You could show me your belly button for all I care. You're not getting my phone."

Boyd stared at him. Who was the real Pierce?

"I bailed you out of trouble," continued Pierce. "I brought you to the hospital and waited three hours. I've driven you around the camp. I brought you to the office. And this is how the United States government expresses its appreciation?"

Boyd wanted to shake his head at Pierce, but he couldn't physically do it, and he'd look like an idiot trying to mimic the gesture with his whole body. The truth was, he didn't have a lot of leverage. He figured any sort of tough talk would be negated by the braces around his neck and wrist and the stupid half-mask on his face. He was already going to step out of bounds the moment he passed the threshold into Bergeson's office. The Jordanians would not be pleased.

"All right, Tamir," he said. "Keep the phone in your pocket. You can give it to the Jordanian police when they get here. And I don't want you to think I don't appreciate what you've done for us tonight. I'm sure none of it has been easy. Just wait here, okay?"

Pierce said nothing, but the anger left his face. "I'll bet it was those two men," he said. "What if they try to get in? What if they have a gun and shoot through the walls?"

"If they wanted to do that, they would already have done so, yes?" said Abboud.

"You don't know that," said Pierce.

"They are most likely a long way from here," said Abboud. "Calm yourself down now and wait. It is going to be a long night." She gestured toward the conference room. "Will you sit on one of those chairs in the hall?"

"I'll wait right here."

Abboud glanced at Boyd. "All right," he said.

Before he entered Bergeson's office, Boyd stood in the doorway and surveyed the room. On the desk, a bare rectangle absent of blood and dust marked where the laptop had been. A black plastic organizer containing pens, highlighters, and paper clips remained upright. Next to the desk, a garbage can stood undisturbed. Files lay stacked on top of cabinets. Over the window behind the desk, a pair of curtains hung motionless.

Quietly, so that Pierce would not be able to hear, he murmured to Abboud. "It appears that the killer positioned himself behind Bergeson, maybe pretending to look outside. There is no sign of a struggle."

"Which means Dr. Bergeson knew his killer."

"Exactly." Boyd put his phone in camera mode and took a photo. He had Abboud wait at the doorway, entered the room, and took several more photographs from different angles.

"Okay." He motioned for Abboud to enter. She hadn't even gasped when they first saw Bergeson's body. Her eyes were set and her face was stoic. Clearly, she had seen more than her share of death.

He pointed toward a corner of the office. "Go through that file cabinet over there and see if you can find anything interesting. Don't take anything out and leave everything exactly the way it is now."

Boyd put the phone back in his pocket and positioned himself behind Bergeson. A space of about four feet between the chair and the window would have given the killer plenty of room to operate. Bergeson would not have known of his peril until the blade had already traversed the width of his throat. The assailant probably held him in place as blood drained and life gurgled away.

"It is locked," said Abboud, standing next to the file cabinet.

"Maybe he's got the keys." Unable to bend at the waist without suffering a wave of pain, Boyd squatted down and opened the wide drawer in front of Bergeson—pens, pencils, a box of thumbtacks, paper clips, but no keys. He tried a side drawer, but it, too, was locked. He stood and considered Bergeson's corpse. "Sorry, old chap," he said. He put a hand on the chest to hold the body in place, then snaked his other hand into Bergeson's trouser pocket, darkened where he had urinated as terror and death overtook him. The trousers felt stiff, as though the moisture had dried, but it was hard to tell for sure while wearing the gloves. The reek of excrement triggered a gagging reaction, but he pushed it back, didn't make a sound. He removed two sets of keys.

"Try these," he said, tossing the ring of smaller keys to Abboud.

He turned around again and examined the curtains. There were probably fingerprints on them. He wished he had more time.

One of the keys worked. Abboud sifted through files from an open cabinet drawer.

"Toss me the keys," he said.

The second one he tried opened the top side drawer, which in turn enabled him to open the larger bottom drawer. In the top drawer Bergeson kept a bottle of Tums, a roll of mints, a box of granola bars. He had a digital voice recorder, a cell phone box without a cell phone, a rolled-up necktie, and a letter opener.

"Anything?" he called to Abboud.

"UN documents, statistical reports, Za'atari district maps, budgets, resumes, and interview notes."

"Keep looking."

One of the flies buzzed him, then hovered inches from his mouth. Instinctively, he grabbed it out of the air and crushed it. The damn thing had probably been consuming Bergeson's blood and who knew what else for … how long? Several hours? Boyd didn't have the forensic tools to enable him to estimate more specifically than that.

He put on a fresh pair of gloves and reminded himself not to squish any more flies.

The back of the bottom drawer still contained Bergeson's flask. The front of it held a set of multi-colored hanging files, half of which were empty. Several contained copies of recent police reports—vandalism, theft, burglary, domestic violence.

The fifth file was red, and it held manila envelopes with handwritten dates on the outside. Fortunately, they were not sealed. He opened the first one, dated a little more than a year ago. There were photographs inside, and what he dreaded was what he found—three eight-by-ten headshots of teenage girls, all of them wearing hijabs. One of them was Hafa. The second envelope, dated a couple of months ago, held two portraits, one of which was Amal. There was a third envelope with four more photographs—it was dated two days ago.

Four more girls had been lured out of Za'atari while he and Abboud were there. He reminded himself that this was a city of over 80,000 residents, that one agent and an interpreter in any town that size could not control everything that happened. But he couldn't shake off the feeling of responsibility.

For a moment he wanted to slap the corpse's face, hope that even in death Bergeson would feel it. This so-called security official had gotten what he deserved.

But what if someone had planted the folder in Bergeson's desk? The same individual who'd killed him?

Someone like Pierce.

How long had Bergeson been dead? Could his murder have taken place before Pierce "intervened" at their tent and brought them to the hospital?

An automobile engine started outside the trailer.

Boyd rose sharply. Withering pain pulsed like a tsunami from his neck to his feet, followed by a wave of dizziness that nearly toppled him. At the same time, Abboud sprang out of the office.

"He has gone!" she called from the hallway. Boyd tottered out of the office as she rushed into the reception area and flung open the front door.

"Our packs are still here," she said, "but he has driven off."

Boyd moved next to her and peered into the night. Powerlines still swayed and the wind blew in a low-pitched whistle.

"Either he's a part of all this, or he's freaking out. It's time to call the police, see if we can stop him before he gets out the gate."

"At this time of night, he is probably already gone."

Boyd nodded. "Let's call them anyway. Tell them Pierce has fled the scene of a murder. And then come back to Bergeson's office. I have some photographs to show you."

CHAPTER
TWENTY-FIVE

It was nearly eight o'clock in the morning when Boyd and Abboud returned with Agent Hussein to the Amman attaché office. They had exactly six minutes to get ready for a teleconference.

Boyd walked stiffly to the table and lowered his body onto a chair. He'd already stashed the plastic mask in his pack, and now he removed the neck and wrist braces and set them on his lap. His neck felt weak, as though it couldn't hold the weight of his head.

"Why did you take those off?" Abboud sat across from him, wearing an expression of concern.

"Roosevelt never let the camera film him in a wheelchair. He was one of our greatest presidents, you know."

"I know who he was. I also know that he died before finishing his term."

"I'm not going to die anytime soon. Got at least a hundred years to go. I'm going to be the world's oldest human someday."

Hussein opened his computer and pressed a key, bringing the teleconference application into view on the wall monitor.

Boyd fought an urge to close his eyes. If he allowed himself to do that, he'd be instantly asleep. Images from the past twenty hours cycled through his head: Amal's foster mother held a pamphlet next to her heart; two men followed them down a dirt lane bordered by small white trailers; Bergeson poured whiskey from a flask; a bear paw of a fist came smashing down at his throat; flies harvested blood from the slash in Bergeson's neck.

Interviews from Jordanian police. Interviews from United Nations police. Writing a report with one hand for Fisk. A long, quiet, uncomfortable ride back to Amman.

Hussein set the meeting in motion. The opening screen caught Fisk pulling away the hand on which he'd been propping his chin. His tie was crooked and his eyelids drooped. It was nine o'clock at night in Seattle.

"You get hit by a train, Boyd?" said Fisk.

"Something like that."

"You don't sound so good, either. I was sorry to read about the assault. Abboud's report indicated you're supposed to be wearing a neck brace."

Boyd glanced at her. She nodded, then returned her attention to the monitor.

"It's … I will, sir. Right now it's in another room."

"Abboud, what about you? How are you feeling?"

"I am unharmed."

"Good." Fisk sipped from a coffee mug. "Here's what's going on right now. The Jordanians are taking the lead on the investigations, but the UN is involved, too. During your morning over there, maybe even as we speak, they'll be making simultaneous visits to all the adult guardians whose girls ended up leaving camp with the traffickers, or at least the girls whose photographs you found. Later today, the interview teams will all convene and share notes. Maybe we'll have more information than we do now. Agent Hussein, you've been working with the homicide detectives. What have you got?"

"The Jordanians and the UN are investigating both Dr. Bergeson and Tamir Pierce," said Hussein. "They're searching for Pierce as we speak. I've been working primarily with Colonel Aziz from the Jordanian army and Major Jeffrey Stevens from the UN. Neither one has offered up a hypothesis. Either Bergeson and Pierce are both tied to the traffickers or one of them is or none of them are. All three scenarios are possible. You two interacted with both of them. What are your thoughts?"

Abboud looked across at Boyd.

"I think it's best to regard them both as suspects," said Boyd. "Plus, there are the two men who followed us, and a couple of other men who attacked us. According to Abboud, the smaller guy from the two who'd been tracking us didn't participate in the assault. All he did was watch. When Pierce showed up, he gave a loud whistle, and they all got the hell out of there. Have you been able to compare the photo I took earlier that day with the CCTV footage we had from the Elliott Bay?"

"Dead ringers," said Fisk.

"That means they're exactly the same."

"As we thought," Abboud added.

"Looks like they've been flying back and forth from here to there," said Fisk. "Same with that woman, Shayma."

"I do not imagine they will be coming back to the refugee camp," said Abboud.

"There's a positive outcome," said Fisk. "You two have disrupted the pipeline."

"But there are four more girls in it right now," said Abboud.

"In all probability, yes. How about you, Abboud? What's your impression of Bergeson and Pierce?"

"I do not trust either one of them. I never trusted Mr. Pierce, but when he helped us I thought perhaps I had been wrong. Then he fled the scene. What did he have to hide? Or, as Agent Boyd has said, perhaps he was overcome with fright. He did say he was worried that the attackers might shoot at us through the walls of the caravan."

"We'll have to rely on the Jordanians and the UN to sort it out," said Fisk. "Agent Hussein, what's your impression of Colonel Aziz?"

"He's a good man. Competent. Honest. Oversees security at Za'atari. Has the respect of his force. He did make a request of me. He wants Agent Boyd and Abboud to stay put in Amman for a week while he continues his investigation. They are witnesses, after all. I told him I needed to check higher up on the chain of command. What are your thoughts on the colonel's request, sir?"

It was interesting, Boyd thought, how his own opinion on the question was completely irrelevant. Ah, the FBI. Not so different than the military.

"His request is granted," said Fisk. "Agent Boyd, I want you and Abboud out of action from this point, except as the Jordanian and United Nations investigators request. Give them your full cooperation. It's their show now. Agent Hussein, do you have secure accommodations in Amman where they can stay?"

Hussein nodded. "Yes, sir. Anticipating your response, I already arranged it."

"Good. Agent Boyd, I understand you need to follow up on a medical appointment."

Boyd glanced at Abboud, but she ignored him this time. Apparently, her report had been more complete than his. "I do, sir."

"Agent Hussein," continued Fisk. "Make sure Agent Boyd sees a throat specialist while he's there, preferably today or tomorrow at the latest. I want a copy of the medical report."

"Yes, sir."

"Also, Agent Boyd?"

"Sir?"

"Your nose looks a little different than the last time we spoke."

"Well, it's—"

"According to Abboud's report, a doctor repositioned it last night."

He didn't bother to glance her direction this time. "That's correct."

"You're supposed to be wearing a protective mask."

"That's correct."

"Well?"

"I feel fine, sir. You know how doctors are. They'll put a finger cast on a hangnail."

"We'd like to have you back on board with us as soon as possible. It will help if you follow the advice of medical professionals."

"Yes, sir."

"One more thing."

Boyd sighed quietly.

"You and Abboud did fine work. Along with Agent Roshan, you developed a strategy and it worked. Seems like it worked so well that the bad guys got desperate. We'll catch those sons of bitches sooner or later, preferably sooner, in no small part because of what you've done."

Was this a commendation? The hurts on his body and pride diminished their intensity. For a moment.

"And now, Abboud." Fisk smiled—at least, for him, it was a smile. On anyone else it would have been regarded as a twitch.

"Yes, sir?" she said.

"How long until you're a citizen?"

"I … I am not sure."

"We can put you on a fast track. You can't be an agent if you're not a citizen."

"I have not thought about this. I am Syrian. I love my country."

"Keep loving it. You can have dual citizenship."

"I will think about it."

* * *

Agent Hussein parked a black Audi SUV in front of a six-story white limestone building, four blocks inside a gated and guarded community. Abboud carried her backpack and Hussein took Boyd's to the entry, where he entered a code on a keypad and used a card to get inside an exquisitely furnished lobby. They took an elevator to the top floor. Hussein knocked on a door, and a middle-aged woman with a narrow face and prominent cheekbones opened it. She wore a full-length light blue dress and a lilac-colored hijab. Her slender physique reminded Boyd of an ultramarathoner.

"Mr. Hussein." She held out a hand in greeting. "You have brought our guests." She smiled at Boyd and Abboud with no hint of judgment in her eyes, despite his bruised face and crooked nose and the scar next to his ear and the odor of old sweat. "Welcome, Mr. and Mrs. Boyd. I am Sadeen, the housekeeper. I also live here. But Mr. Hussein has probably already told you this. Please come in."

One step inside confirmed they were a long way from Za'atari. Instead of a canvas floor, they stood on soft, spotless carpeting suitable for an opera house. Beyond the entry, a sofa and armchairs with cream-colored cushions faced a super-sized flat screen television. There was a credenza, two polygon-shaped coffee tables, and chest-high bookcase on wheels, all constructed of black wood. A box chandelier with dozens of tiny bulbs filled the room with soft light, and bamboo blinds covered glass walls. From the ceiling, a quiet piano concerto played so vividly that Boyd expected he'd see a Steinway Grand if his neck would have allowed him to look up.

"Mr. Hussein indicated it has been a long while since you two have eaten a meal," said Sadeen. "Our chef is preparing lunch. It should be ready in half an hour. There are two bathrooms adjoining the guest room, so you can each have a shower or a bath beforehand."

"I hope you won't mind," said Boyd, "but I left my tuxedo back home."

Sadeen smiled again, as polished as the furniture, as warm as the ambiance. "I won't mention it to management if you won't." She looked at Hussein. "We'll be fine. We were beginning to be bored. It's good to have guests."

"Thank you, Sadeen," said Hussein. "Let me have a minute with Mr. and Mrs. Boyd, please. I'll show them to their accommodations."

He led them a few steps down a hall. Paintings of Bedouin scenes lined the walls. "This place has only one guest bedroom, though it's as large as some people's apartments," he said. "There's only one bed, but there's also a sofa in a different room. Boyd, I'll have two support staff here tomorrow morning to bring you to the throat specialist. I'll send you a text when I know the time."

He unlocked a door and handed the key to Boyd. "Here you go," he said, leaving back down the hall.

. . .

Boyd's jaw dropped as he stepped through the doorway. Abboud's pack fell to the floor. "Subhanallah," she whispered.

It was a sitting room, suitable for a Saudi prince. Polished wood planks of reddish brown comprised the floor. In the middle, graceful blue herons populated a cream-colored rug. A large burl coffee table in the shape of a conch shell occupied the center of the rug, its top as smooth as glass, the sides gilded with ... it couldn't have been actual gold, could it? A bouquet of yellow lilies and a funnel-shaped bowl that could have been pilfered from a museum of Asian artifacts lay on the table. Their reflections gleamed on a credenza of mirrored glass placed against the wall. A sofa and three chairs featuring blue-hued upholstery surrounded the table.

One door led to a bathroom featuring white granite countertops and the other led to a central room with a king-sized bed on a raised platform. A headboard and footboard of white wood framed with rectangular green trim created an Egyptian feel. Along a side wall, a mini-kitchen consisted of a small range and refrigerator of stainless steel and a pedestal table with two chairs. From this room, a large opening led down two stairs to a living room whose furniture featured gradations of black.

A door between the bedroom/kitchenette and the living room led to the second bathroom.

"I have never been in a place like this," said Abboud.

"That makes two of us," agreed Boyd.

They used their phones to take photos before convening at the kitchenette table.

"I think I'll sleep in that front room," he said. "That way I'll have my bathroom and you'll have yours. You'll have more privacy."

Abboud chuckled. "Men give the women the nicer arrangements. All that is required in return is acquiescence."

"Acquiescence? I could study another language for five years, and I doubt if I could come up with the equivalent of that word. Especially after more than a day without sleep—I'd be limited to *huh, hey* and *oh.*"

"But could you ascertain the cultural divisions between men and women?"

"Ascertain? Whoa. There's another one."

Playfully, she gave a light slap to his wrist—the wrong wrist. It felt like a hand drill twisting up his arm. He couldn't help but wince. Abboud bolted from her chair, swept behind him, hugged around the shoulders. A circular saw chewed into his upper vertebrae.

She bounced back. "I am so sorry!"

"It's okay. A little pain in exchange for a hug. That works for me."

She moved back to face him, standing behind her chair. "You know, when you wear your braces it is not only stabilizing your injuries, but it is also a signal for others about where you are hurting."

"Which is exactly why I don't want to wear them."

"That is another thing about men."

"*Thing?* Is that the best you can come up with? What about *characteristic* or *quirk* or—"

"Aggravation?"

"That sounds about right."

She sighed with what sounded like exasperation.

"Yeah, we're incurable, aren't we? Little boys in men's bodies."

"Sadeen is expecting us. We should take our showers."

"You go ahead. Will you please offer my regrets? I'm starving, but sleep—"

"You cannot refuse lunch. It would be considered rude."

"I don't even know if I can swallow Jell-O."

"You might have to chew more slowly than you are accustomed to."

"Is that a comment about my eating habits?"

"Certainly not. But you might discover different types of food have different flavors."

"I'd laugh, but I don't want to tweak my neck."

"Are you going to shower or not?"

"All right."

. . .

After adjusting the throw pillows several times with no arrangement working exactly right, Boyd settled for only one pillow. He stretched his legs, extending his feet beyond the sofa's opposite arm rest. The neck brace felt totally weird, but he admitted to himself that it alleviated some of the pain.

He hadn't realized just how hungry he'd been until he sat down forty minutes ago to a lunch of tabouli salad, a shrimp and crab baguette, and namoura, a sweet cake made of semolina flour. Apologizing to Sadeen for his inability to tackle the baguette, he nonetheless thoroughly enjoyed the shrimp and crab mixture. Abboud had been right. The injury-enforced requirement to chew slowly magnified the fresh aroma of the seafood and the exquisite creamy curry that held it all together.

But the highlight of the meal had been Abboud's presence. Attired in an apricot-colored abaya and a hijab of yellow roses on slate gray cloth, she exuded sunshine, even though exhaustion swelled the skin beneath her dark and deep-set eyes. He felt himself drawn toward her, and it worried him. The whole admonition about relationships with professional colleagues yammered silently against letting any attraction take root, but he couldn't stop his feelings any more than he could stop his breathing.

Now, lying on the couch, he twisted the wedding band on his ring finger. It felt strange, and yet during these past days he'd gotten used to it, so much so that he often forgot it was there.

Blankets rustled in the adjoining room. Did she think of him the way he thought of her?

Probably not. She was more professional than he, and, besides, she was from a different culture. She wore the hijab and she performed the salah prayers—did that mean she could have eyes only for a Muslim man?

Maybe she adhered to a tolerant strand of her faith. He would have to ask her about that sometime, but how could he do so without creating a great deal of awkwardness?

He thought it best to let these feelings go. He had his career, and she had hers. Their paths had crossed, but it was only temporary.

He closed his eyes and slept.

• • •

"Laa! Laa!"

Someone was shouting. He opened his eyes. Where was he?

"Laa!"

It was a woman—Abboud in the next room, shouting *no* in Arabic. In her voice was terror, grief, despair. A bad dream?

She whimpered, and silence followed. Perhaps the nightmare had passed.

He drifted back into his own dreams.

"Ya kalb! Ya sharmouta!" *You dog. You bitch.*

He rose, wincing when his neck reminded him of its sprain. He didn't know much Arabic, but he'd learned how to curse. Should he wake her?

"Laa!" He heard a sharp movement, and he pictured her yanking herself out of sleep, perhaps swinging that lethal arm of hers.

It was quiet.

"Abboud?" he asked.

"Oh!" She sobbed, her breath heavy and audible. "I hate that dream."

"It's real, isn't it? I know what those dreams are like."

For a long half minute, he heard nothing. Maybe she'd fallen back to sleep. But then: "Yes," she said.

"I'm sorry."

"What time is it?"

He reached for his phone on the nightstand where it was charging. "Seven-thirty."

"Morning or night?"

"I think night."

A lamp went on in her room, its pale light extending out the passageway, spilling tones of gray onto the luxurious sofa where he sat.

"I am going to read for a while," she said.

It had been six hours since he'd gone to sleep. If he lay down again, he'd probably wake up at midnight or three in the morning, and he'd never be able to sleep after that. Besides, in the book where he had left off, Theodore Roosevelt and his companions were lost in the Brazilian jungle, and the ex-president was sicker than he'd ever been in his life. History recorded that Roosevelt survived, but Boyd wanted to know how.

"Shall we read together, or would you like your own space?" he asked.

"Are you dressed? I will join you in the sitting room. Would you like some tea?"

Ten minutes later she brought out a tray with tea, cashews, figs, and crackers. Evidently, the kitchenette was well-stocked. He was grateful for it, especially when he noticed that Sadeen had texted two hours earlier asking for a reply if they would be awake for dinner at six o'clock.

They read for half an hour. Boyd found himself transported to Brazil. Suffering from an infected leg wound, Roosevelt had a high fever and had lost a great amount of weight.

Abboud set down her phone and rubbed her eyes. They'd eaten the snacks, which would have to suffice for their dinner. She stared vacantly toward the door, as though waiting for someone to knock. Perhaps she'd grown tired again.

"You were right," she said.

He put a marker in the book and closed it. "About?"

"The dream was real. It is always real. I want it to go away, but I do not want to forget."

Boyd's nightmare popped into his mind, unbidden. He felt no ambivalence. He, too, wanted it to go away—and he wanted to forget.

"You Americans do not know what happened in Syria. You think it is just a war, rebels on one side and the government on the other."

"All I know is it's a mess. There are more sides than you can count, and the government would have fallen if it weren't for Russia and Iran."

She grew quiet again, her eyes fixed on the door. There was something haunted in her eyes, as though she were reliving some horror. In the gap of silence, blips from his own memory popped into his head.

Night at the academy compound. A little ceremony for the Iraqi soldiers he and his unit had trained. Suddenly: Muzzle flashes. What the fuck? Tat-a-tat-a-tat-a-tat. Whistles from passing bullets. Shouts. Groans. Jones down. Hernandez down. Gripping Jones by the shirt. Diving toward a Humvee, dragging Jones, crawling, move move move. Whap! A bullet like a right cross to the cheek. Jetliner noise in his ear, exploding pain. Keep going keep going got to get to the Humvee. Crazy motherfucker, Crazy motherfucker ...

The memory of the pain radiated from the scar on his face. Fear squeezed at his breath. He pushed the images away. He was okay. He was in a ritzy condo in the fucking Middle East, but it wasn't Iraq. It wasn't Afghanistan.

Abboud was no longer staring at the door. She was looking at him.

"Are you okay?" she asked.

"Yes. Yes, of course."

She took a sip of tea. "If you knew what happened to my husband, you would know what happened to Syria."

"You can tell me," he said, his own voice almost a whisper.

She stared again at the door. "It was in March six years ago, the Arab Spring. My husband carried an olive branch. All of the men carried olive branches. They were protesting the treatment of some teenagers who had been arrested and beaten and were still in jail. I was with the other women, watching from an apartment on the third floor."

A pair of tears trickled down her cheek. Moisture swelled in his own eyes, and a lump formed in his chest.

"The soldiers started shooting. A horrible noise. We were screaming. *Run!* Even though they could not hear us, they ran. We rushed down the stairs to the lobby. They were taking shelter there, some of them shot. Blood was growing like a pond. *Why?* they kept shouting. *It was peaceful. Bashar, you dog! An ambulance! Somebody call an ambulance!*

"I wanted to go out to find my husband. I did not care about the bullets, and anyway, the shooting had stopped. But men who were not wounded prevented me. The soldiers would have shot anyone who came back onto the street."

She wiped her cheeks. "Some men in the lobby died right before our eyes. I never saw my husband again. A month later I was told that he was dead."

She tore her eyes from the door and looked at Boyd. She opened her mouth as though to say something else, but all she did was shake her head.

Boyd rose from the sofa, walked around the fancy coffee table, and hunched next to her. He took both her hands in his, and they remained that way for a while.

Through the only window of their cabin, high above the deck of the ship, Lely stared down at the rectangular towers of metal containers, stacked seven units high and twelve units wide. In her opinion, the stevedores and crane operator who'd loaded this ship lacked imagination. If she had been in charge, she would have stacked the brown containers in the middle, wrapped the reds around them, and placed the blues around the perimeter.

She would require each seaman to spend an hour every day painting scenes from their homelands on the outsides of the containers. When the Americans unloaded the containers, perhaps they would learn to better appreciate other places and peoples, and maybe they would never ever let what happened in Syria happen anywhere else. Her idea would spread. Art would sprout everywhere, in the most unlikely spaces, and everyone would participate, an hour a day, and think of what it would do for their souls. In that kind of a world, how could a man drop chemicals out of the sky onto his fellow human beings?

Lely thought her scheme might work—except for the fog swallowing their ship, as though Earth had snuck away and abandoned them in a gray void. While they rose and fell with the rolling of the waves, condensation soaked every surface, so that no paint could possibly adhere. At breakfast Shayma said they would move past the Straits of Gibraltar and into the Atlantic sometime in the early afternoon, and it seemed a certainty that Lely would miss the sight.

The *Asian Rose* bellowed a mournful horn. Tired of waiting for a gap in the gray, Lely turned away from the window and glanced at the wall clock. It was almost time for the first of their twice-daily walks around the deck.

Sara and Yana sat at the tiny dining table playing a card game, while beyond them Qamar lay on the top bunk where she and Lely squeezed together to sleep at night. Leafing through a magazine, Shayma sat with her back propped against the headboard of the double-bed she reserved for herself. Although not fancy like the little yacht they'd occupied in Tripoli, their cabin was adequate, chairs constructed of brown molded plastic and a sofa covered with brown Naugahyde. A desk of molded plastic was embedded against a wall.

At the chest of drawers in front of the bunks, Lely picked up her black hijab. Inside the cabin, out of the sight of men, none of them covered their heads. Strands of Qamar's curly red hair spilled over the side of her bunk. Yana and Sara each had black hair, though Yana's was longer and darker. Shayma's hair was also dark, but it was feathered, parted at the center, and she had dip-dyed the tips mahogany. Her brows were plucked and shaped into thin dark curves.

In the mirror atop the dresser, Lely glanced at her own hair, the color of coffee. She brushed both hands across the top of her head and down the back. Almost dry, it felt soft and smooth, thanks to the shower she had taken in their tiny bathroom. She was about to wrap the hijab around her head when Shayma put down her magazine.

"Hold off with that," said their chaperone.

"Are we staying inside?" Lely asked. She had to get out of this room, this tiny space, and into the open air. It didn't matter how much the cloud-fog would soak them.

"No, it's something else," said Shayma before turning her attention to the others. "Sara and Yana, put your game on hold. Qamar, come down from the bunk. Let's sit together on the carpet."

The start of a groan escaped Lely's lips, but a glare from Shayma stopped its full expression. The other girls didn't seem to mind these gatherings. In a jiffy they sat cross-legged in a partial circle, and Shayma took her place in front of them.

"In a few minutes Jack and Majd will be waiting outside our door the same as always," said Shayma. "We should count ourselves fortunate that they arrived before we left Tripoli. Without them, I would never permit these walks. We'd be stuck in our cabin and we'd drive each other even more crazy than we already do."

Lely began once more to wrap the hijab, and once again Shayma stopped her, this time by holding up her hand.

"Ah, Lely," said Shayma, "you're demonstrating exactly why I want to gather us before we go outside. Part of my duty as your chaperone will be to teach you the ways of the culture we'll be entering. We'll use this time of traveling to help you see and accept a new way of living. I've already told you we'll be in the Atlantic before nightfall. We'll be that much closer to America. We'll be that much closer to freedom, including ways that you never imagined. I'm not talking about walls, like the one around Za'atari. You're almost free from an even greater barrier—one that surrounds you simply because you happen to be female."

Like a shopkeeper making a sale, she smiled before pressing her lips together and moving her eyes from girl to girl. Her expression was smug, as though she alone were the benefactress delivering this shiny freedom to them. There was some truth in that—she had chosen Lely, had gotten them through a scary journey out of the refugee camp and finally onto this ship. She was entitled to a little pride.

So why did Shayma's smile and voice poke Lely in the chest and freeze the nerves in her back? It hadn't always been that way—only since she started gathering the girls on the carpet for these talks.

"Even the Prophet recognized the special charms Allah has given to women," Shayma said. "In America the woman is allowed to show her beauty with pride, a pride that extends not only to the fact of your bodies but also in your capacity to use them. No shame, no need to hide your necks and arms and hair, no requirement to wear the hijab—you have seen this on American television shows, yes?"

Lely's friends nodded.

A crow—that's what Shayma was. Sticking her beak into their lives, their values, the way they'd been raised, their senses of right and wrong. Always so sure of herself.

Lely put a hand over her mouth and coughed, but it sounded more like a caw.

Shayma's eyes narrowed. Lely's friends turned toward her, surprise and perplexity on their faces.

"Sorry, Miss Shayma," she said, clearing her throat.

Shayma continued. "Let that thought rest in your minds. Your lives can be different. America is a place of freedom and not just for men. Beginning now you do not need to wear the hijab. That is an old way we are leaving behind. Think of it now as a costume for a drama or a comedy or as a fancy outfit for Eid-ul-Adha. Wear it or not, as you choose."

Shayma stood. Still seated, Lely wrapped her head with the hijab. She sensed the other girls watching her and glancing at Shayma at the same time. After a moment they stepped to the dresser and retrieved their hijabs. While they wrapped them, Lely couldn't stop herself from coughing, a rattling hack-hac-caw! As Lely feigned embarrassment, the girls succumbed to giggling. She regained control and snuck a glance at Shayma.

Their chaperone did not look pleased.

CHAPTER
TWENTY-SEVEN

The next afternoon, Boyd's driver took him directly from the throat specialist to Hussein's office. Wearing her clean and untorn Women's Corps International abaya and a matching hijab, Abboud sat at the conference table. Hussein, attired in a pressed white dress shirt with the sleeves rolled, looked up from his gray metal desk.

"Agent Boyd," he said. "I see that they've permitted you to walk among the living. What's the prognosis? Did you bring the medical report? Fisk is going to want it."

Boyd set a manila envelope on Hussein's desk. "A bruised larynx and a grade two neck sprain. I'm clear to resume my professional boxing career."

"And I am free to resume my duties as a brain surgeon," said Abboud.

Ten minutes later, Colonel Aziz from the Jordanian Army and Major Stevens from the United Nations arrived, bringing with them a pair of assistants. Aziz glanced at Boyd and Abboud, and scanned the walls, pausing at the framed photographs. He had a hairline that receded on the left and right, leaving a patch of close-cut dark hair above the center of his forehead. His olive-green uniform shirt featured black epaulettes with gold insignia. Major Stevens had East Asian features. Her hair was pulled back in a bun beneath a sky-blue UN beret and above a matching blue neckerchief. She wore camouflage fatigues.

They gathered at the table. A Jordanian adjunct placed a voice recorder in the middle.

"We have read your reports," said Aziz, using carefully pronounced English. "We have also read the reports of the officers who interviewed you on the night of Dr. Bergeson's murder. It was a sad day." He looked at Boyd. "We feel badly that you have been injured in our country."

"It happens," said Boyd. "Thank you for your concern."

The colonel nodded. "Now, to the point. Please provide for us an account of what happened the tenth of December, beginning when you noticed the two men following you. I have the photographs from your supervisor, Agent Fisk. Major Stevens and I will interrupt you from time to time to seek details and clarification."

It took more than thirty minutes to recount the events, mostly because of all the questions they were asked.

"How many times did you interact with Dr. Bergeson after you arrived at Za'atari?" asked the colonel when they had finished.

"Twice," said Boyd. "In addition to the afternoon of his murder, we met in his office the day we arrived."

"And what was your impression of the man?"

"There was nothing about him to make us think he was anything other than what he appeared to be," said Boyd. "He acted like he wanted to find some answers as much as we did."

The colonel looked down at his phone, which appeared to consist of notes in Arabic script. "What about before you arrived? Did you meet with him in Seattle?"

"No. He was here, and we were there."

"Our interactions were virtual," said Abboud. "Only by computer."

"But he was in Seattle during part of the time you were engaged in planning. He arrived at Seatac International Airport at 18:43 the 28th of November and departed from the same airport for Amman at 7:03 the first of December. And you never saw him? Did he meet with anyone else at your FBI office?"

The information hit Boyd like an electric shock. He glanced at Abboud, who silently mouthed the word *wow*.

"You know this?" said Boyd.

"As of yesterday," said Major Stevens, who spoke with an Australian accent. "We have his flight records. We've made a request for airport surveillance at the appropriate gates and times. We expect to see him in the video."

Boyd drew in a long breath, then exhaled slowly. "Right under our noses."

"If he was not there to work with you," continued Major Stevens, "why else would he have been there?"

"We did hold a planning session with him during that time," said Abboud. "The 30th of November. I remember because it was a Thursday and it prevented me from going to my taekwondo practice. But it was all on computer. He wanted us to think he was in Jordan. He could have been in any city in the world."

Anger pushed aside Boyd's sense of surprise. "That son of a ..." He stopped himself. "He had to have been collaborating with the traffickers. Did you find his secretary, Tamir Pierce? He might be part of this whole operation."

"Soldiers from my unit gained access to his apartment the morning after the murder," said Colonel Aziz. "There were signs of violence. Broken glass. A table and chair overturned. Blood on the floor and a trail of it leading out the door. There was clothing in an open suitcase in the bedroom."

"It sounds as though he was right to be afraid," said Boyd. "But if he's innocent, why would the traffickers bother showing up at his apartment?"

"We have many more questions than answers," said Colonel Aziz.

"What about the foster families of the girls?" asked Abboud. "What have you discovered today?"

"We spoke with six of nine families," said the colonel. "Of the three we could not see, one had returned to Syria. One is said to be in Italy and the other in Germany. For the ones in camp, the pattern is the same. Find an orphan girl. Recruit her and her family with fake brochures and happy talk. Leave behind worthless phone numbers and emails. Then disappear."

He leaned back and tapped a pen on the table. "Except for one individual. The place you would have visited today."

"Rahiq Rezk?" said Abboud.

"Yes, that one. She did not trust this woman Shayma. So Shayma brought a visitor with her to meet Mrs. Rezk. Would you care to guess who that visitor was?"

"Mr. Pierce," said Abboud.

"Try again."

"Dr. Bergeson," said Boyd and Abboud simultaneously.

The colonel nodded. "In full uniform."

Boyd's jaw tensed. "Damn that bastard. That's why he acted nervous. He was about to be exposed. The whole time he was meeting with us, he was planning to have us killed. God, I wish we could have kept him alive. I'd like to see him behind bars."

Abboud's eyes hardened. "I do not mourn his death."

"I have heard your English expression," said the colonel. "Dead men tell no tales."

"If he were alive, he could tell us how to find the other girls," said Abboud. "Were we right about the photographs? Were some girls taken from Za'atari while we were there?"

"Yes," said Major Stevens. "As you might assume, the families of those four girls all still reside in the camp. The women who had served as their mothers are quite distressed."

"We must find them," said Abboud.

"There is no place we are not searching," said Colonel Aziz.

"The Port of Beirut," said Abboud. "That is the place from which the other girls departed."

"We know," said the colonel. "On cargo ships. We must rely on the Lebanese if they are to be found there."

Silence fell upon the room. A feeling of gloom increased the throbbing in Boyd's head. Those poor girls. There was little chance of finding them now. He pictured them on a boat in the high seas. What was happening to them? How long would it take them to get out of the Mediterranean and onto the Atlantic?

"We should know every container ship bound for the United States that leaves from Beirut or any other nearby port," he said. "We can make sure none of them are deprived of a greeting party."

"That's been the subject of some emails earlier this afternoon," said Hussein.

Colonel Aziz turned his focus upon Boyd. "Before we end this meeting, there is one more point that I must discuss. What gave you the right to search Dr. Bergeson's office?"

Boyd's heart beat a little faster. As he had suspected, he now faced a reckoning for his decision. "I have the training to investigate crime scenes, and that was obviously a crime scene."

"I also have training," said the colonel. "Suppose I am in your Seattle now. I gain access to a room. An important man is dead. It is clear he was murdered. So I, a Jordanian military officer, conduct a search. Then I call your police. How will your police feel about my actions?"

"I was looking for critical information. But I apologize."

"We would have found the photographs. We would have understood their significance. We would have shared them with you."

But how long would that have taken? "I understand," said Boyd. "I should have waited."

"Well, now," said Major Stevens. "We all have sensitivities when it comes to our homelands, don't we? You've communicated your point very well, Colonel Aziz."

CHAPTER TWENTY-EIGHT

Ten minutes, thirty seconds per mile—that was no pace at all. Boyd felt like sticking athletic tape over the damn treadmill monitor. The number mocked him. Normally, he whipped out 7:30 miles running up and down hills on roads and trails throughout the Seattle area.

The safehouse exercise room had just about everything—gleaming sets of iron weights, lifting machines, leg presses, a rowing machine, a stationary bicycle, incline boards. All he could do was the treadmill, but at least that was something, a hell of a lot better than languishing in their fancy accommodations, where his biggest exertion the past two days had consisted of lifting a fork.

On the mirrored wall in front of him, Abboud's reflection sat on a bench, curling a small dumbbell. She appeared to value reps more than weight. Closer and therefore larger than her, he beheld a sight even uglier than his lame pace—the spectacle of his own bruised face. His nose had swollen to a puffy lump. Garish shades of purple extended out from it. Perhaps the mask that Dr. Abdul gave him wasn't so much to protect his nose as it was to shield the public from his ugly mug.

"I think I know the *real* reason why the Jordanians want us staying here for a week," he said.

"And that is?" Abboud set the dumbbell down and stood.

"There's no way anyone would let me on an airplane, not with a face like this."

"And all this time I have been thinking your appearance has improved."

"You really know how to make a guy feel better."

"Looks are not everything, you know. Maybe ninety-five percent, but not everything."

After picking up a heavier weight, she did a series of lifts over her head. She wore a tight-fitting Lycra hijab made for workouts, as well as a navy blue shirt with a white stripe along each long sleeve. It hung low over her hips, but not enough to hide the black tights that clung to her legs, outlining sinewy muscles, the shape of a woman who exercised frequently.

He looked away. It wasn't cool to stare. But oh boy, that's where his eyes wanted to dwell.

"We've got to get out of this place," he said.

"Maybe we can wear a disguise."

"Do you think Amman would have a costume store that delivers?"

"The good thing about your nose is that you do not require a disguise. You already look like somebody else."

"I know I shouldn't ask. Who are you thinking about?

"I do not remember his name. But his face resembles a baboon."

Well, now, she was really asking for it. He bellowed like an ape and scratched an armpit. Ignoring his neck, he hop-stepped a lap around the room before settling back onto the treadmill as though nothing had happened.

In the mirror, Abboud showed an indulgent smile. She switched the weight to her other hand. "I will be a butterfly. Open the window, and there would be no need to sneak out the entrance."

"Nice. If baboons could fly, I'd go with you."

She laughed. "I love that image."

In the mirror their eyes intersected for a fraction of a second. He glanced at the monitor and adjusted his speed. When he looked up, she was in the midst of a quadriceps stretch.

"Did you ever sneak away from home when you were a boy?" she asked.

"Yeah. There was one time especially."

"Where did you go?"

"Oh, about three hundred fifty miles. Spokane to a place called Bow on the Puget Sound."

"And you were only a boy?" She rose from her stretch.

"Not exactly. I was fifteen. I took an old pickup my father had set aside for me once I got my driver's license. Only I didn't have my driver's license yet."

"Did you get in trouble?"

"Oh yeah. My dad sold the truck."

"Where did you go?"

"My grandpa's. He's got a ranch north of Seattle. Horse stables for rich people. I thought if I shoveled enough poop he'd let me stay for the summer. I figured my dad would say *no*, so I didn't ask him. My mom was in Europe. My parents were divorced."

"Horses? I love horses. Do you ride?"

"Used to, quite a bit. Not so much now. Too much pavement where we live, not enough hay. Besides that, a horse'll buck a baboon every time."

He turned off the treadmill and moved to the free weight station. He picked up a twenty-kilo dumbbell and tried lifting it up to his armpit. The pain was instantaneous. He put the weight on the floor again.

"Apparently, every muscle in your body is connected to your neck," he said.

Abboud motioned toward a padded bench. "If you will sit here."

"For what?"

"Just do it, okay?"

He obeyed. She stepped behind him and he felt a pair of thumbs on the back of his neck, followed by a light kneading, as though performed by a cat without claws.

"If it is too hard—" she said.

"No. It's heaven."

Apparently, every muscle *did* connect with his neck. His entire body slowly uncoiled. Maybe it was only a few degrees on some imaginary tension scale, but each degree revealed how taut he'd allowed himself to grow, days and weeks and maybe years, so normal he didn't notice.

"So you ride?" he asked.

"Horses?"

"Yes, horses."

"Never. When I was a girl, I used to read horse books. I dreamed about having one. I begged my father, but how could we have a horse? We lived in an apartment."

"When we get back, how about I take you to my grandpa's ranch? I've got two horses there, an Arabian and a quarter horse. I'll teach you to ride."

The thumbs left his neck.

"Really?" she said.

"Sure, why not?"

In the mirror, Abboud jumped straight up. At the apex of her leap, she swung her hands together and clapped. "I had given up on that dream. I never thought it could happen."

"Does that mean *yes*?"

"How long does it take to go there?"

"Depends on traffic. Could be ninety minutes. Could be four hours."

"So we could go there and come back the same day?"

"Easy. But we could stay, too. My grandpa's got a lot of rooms in his house."

"I will think about it." She resumed the massage.

"I'll ask you again when we get back. Don't worry. You can say no. I don't mean anything by it. Just friends. Friends go fishing. They ride horses. I hope that's okay."

His heartrate had increased. His senses were alive to her touch.

"It would not be okay in my country, but we will not be in my country. And so I have decided. My answer is yes."

"That didn't take long."

"Friends go fishing. They ride horses."

CHAPTER TWENTY-NINE

If she could concentrate like Sara, she'd know which cards Yana likely held. Only two remained. Could one of them be a ten?

The ship's horn groaned. Lely jumped up from the game, crossed the small room, and peered out the window. After a two-day respite of sun, the fog had returned, saturating every surface and sealing away the rest of the world. They could be seconds from colliding with another ship, perhaps a lonely yacht with a broken mast and a starving sailor who'd given up hope, or an American aircraft carrier with a jet about to catapult over their heads.

"Lely! It's your turn."

Back on the floor, Lely discarded the three of hearts and picked up the three of clubs. Yana immediately played the ten of clubs.

"Basra," said Yana with a grin. Qamar, Lely's partner, sighed.

Lely sucked in her cheeks like a cartoon guppy. "Sorry," she announced with puckered lips.

How could she concentrate on their ten millionth round of a stupid card game, anyway? Three days remained until they reached America. One moment excitement raced through her veins, and the next moment dread froze her blood.

When her turn came Lely played her last card, and afterward Sara and Qamar totaled the scores. Thirty points for Sara and Yana, plus ten for the basra—forty total, enough to put them over 150 and end the game.

She wished she could get outside, let the gray blanket soak through her skin. Maybe she'd catch pneumonia. She'd be lying on the top bunk, shivering beneath a sweat-damp blanket. If the American aircraft carrier were actually there, Shayma would compel the *Asian Rose* captain to make an emergency contact. A helicopter would lift from the carrier and land on their ship. The helicopter crew would burst into Lely's cabin, carry her out, harness her weakened self in the seat next to the pilot. Their eyes would meet, and they'd fall in love.

At least it wouldn't be boring.

Holding an American celebrity magazine, Shayma joined them on the floor. Lely's neck tightened the way it always did when Shayma entered her space. She didn't know why that happened. Shayma was a grouch, but she cared for them.

Maybe it was because even though she had to be at least ten years older than the girls, Shayma tried to act like she was one of them. She gasped like her body was burning whenever they played the DVD with Saad Lamjarred singing "LM3ALLEM," and it seemed like fifty times a day she interrupted them to point to a magazine page and comment on the makeup some half-naked American actress wore.

"I heard you girls talking about television programs you used to watch," she began. "*Bab Al-Hara. Arabs Got Talent.*"

"I watched *De'ah Da'iah* on YouTube when I was in Za'atari," said Qamar. "It's an old show."

"Different times." Shayma pressed her lips together, and for a moment Lely wondered if their mentor was about to cry. She decided she wouldn't mind if a tear escaped Shayma's eyes. Instead, Shayma gushed a little too loudly, "What about American shows? Did any of your friends have them on their phones?"

"Some clips," said Yana, who brushed her forefinger across her right eyebrow, a habit she'd picked up two days ago after she let Shayma pluck and shape her brows. "*America's Got Talent.* We decided they don't have as much as we do."

"Emanne Beasha!" said Sara. "Did you hear her sing?"

"Eight years old and she gets 500,000 Riyals." Lely tilted her head back and let loose a warbling operatic voice. "La la la la and a big fancy car!"

"Agh." Qamar covered her ears.

"Some friend you are," said Lely. "No more Jordan almonds for you."

Shayma placed a DVD in its player and turned on a small television. "I'm going to tell you about another show that's like a contest," she said. "We don't have anything like it in the Arab world. It's called *The Bachelorette.*"

Lely sighed—a bit too loudly, she realized, when Shayma glared at her.

"I'm trying to help you," said Shayma. "Unless you pay attention to what I'm trying to tell you, you'll be shocked when you get to America. Nothing is taboo there. That can be good, but you will need my protection. Do you understand, Lely?"

"Yes, Miss Shayma."

"Now," Shayma addressed the girls collectively. "Do you remember what I said about American talk shows?"

"They'll talk about anything," said Sara.

"Exactly," said Shayma. "Give me an example."

Lips pressed together, the girls glanced at the floor.

"Oh, we do need practice saying those words, don't we?" Although her lips smiled, her eyes and her voice signified something different—exasperation, perhaps.

"Okay," said Lely.

"Oh, good, Lely. You have an example?"

"An army of paramecia invaded Shabu al-Kook's left nostril."

Qamar, a true friend, giggled, although she kept her eyes pointed down.

"Your flippancy has been noted," said Shayma. "I cannot tell you how much you will regret this, but you will, Lely. You certainly will."

Lely felt a shiver.

"I'm sorry, Miss Shayma. You said *anything,* and that was the first thing I could think. But I won't do that anymore. I'll keep it to myself."

"May Allah grant such a miracle. I see that we're not ready yet for the candid use of particular terms. That's fine. In time you will be able to do this. Now, about *The Bachelorette*—do any of you know what this show is about?"

Lely had never heard of the show, but she could guess. *An unmarried woman says and does shocking things. But nobody cares, because everything is normal in America.*

Otherwise, why would Shayma bother showing them the program?

"A woman who isn't married?" said Yana.

"Exactly," said Shayma, resurrecting her smile. "There's another program called *The Bachelor*, but of course that one features a man."

An unmarried man does anything he wants. But there isn't a question about whether it is shocking or not, because he is a man. Lely also kept this thought to herself. She wondered why she couldn't hold her tongue more often.

"So, in *The Bachelorette*, twenty-five men take turns dating a bachelorette, who, as I'm sure you understand by now, needs no permission to do this. Remember what I said about it being a contest? Whoever attracts her the most, she marries. And it's all on television. After many weeks of dating, the bachelorette narrows the field down to three men. She has to decide which one she's going to marry. That's the point where I'm going to show you one of the programs."

While Shayma started the DVD and found the right program, Lely thought of her father. He had been kind to her and her two brothers and her mother. He would bring them places, like the old city in Damascus, where they would eat Bakdash ice cream. She was eleven years old when the bomb killed him and the rest of her family, and so she would never find out the rules he would have required in regard to a man who wished to marry her. Would he have listened to her own opinions about such a man? Yes, he would have, she was sure of it.

"Here we are," said Shayma. The video showed a gigantic bed with big hearts on the pillows and on the center of a thick duvet. At the foot of the bed was a tray filled with multi-colored grapes and a bottle of champagne. Near the bed in front of a large window, steam rose from a hot tub.

"How do you think this room helps the bachelorette decide which of these three final men she'll marry?" asked Shayma.

"Ya Allah, this is crazy," said Sara, giggling and covering her mouth. Yana joined her. Qamar blushed, and the same flush of warmth spread on Lely's cheeks.

"For all these weeks, a video camera follows the bachelorette on every date with every man. But the camera does not follow her into what they call the *fantasy suite*. One at a time, with each of the three finalists, she spends the night in a suite like this. Afterward, they'll talk about it on camera for all the world to hear. Watch."

Arabic script captions enabled them to understand what was being said. Maybe if Shayma hadn't been in the room, Lely and her friends would have enjoyed watching this bachelorette sitting next to each man while they talked about their night together in the room with the big bed. She and her friends could have laughed and scoffed and maybe evaluated the physiques of the men. Maybe. Because it was completely strange to do something like this.

Even if she were an American, Lely was sure she wouldn't make these three men, who all loved her, compete and bare their souls and apparently everything else and kiss her passionately with the camera close enough to kiss them, too.

"I'm not trying to tell you this is how women in America decide whom they'll marry," said Shayma. "But most women do have sex with more than one man before they decide. It's not like on this show. It's spread out over time. Not everyone is so wealthy. You girls, though—you're going to have fancy bedrooms and a luxurious life. Your beds will be just as nice as the one in the fantasy suite."

"Subhanallah, no more sharing a bunk bed," said Sara. "I like you well enough, Yana, but you almost bumped me to the floor last night."

"And I won't miss you sticking an elbow in my back," said Yana.

Lely shifted from cross-legged to knees bent in front of her. "Will we have to share our beds in America, Miss Shayma?"

"Certainly not." Their chaperone batted her eyes, as though she could do comedy. "Not unless you want to," she added, making her voice husky, suggestive.

"Ya Allah," said Lely. "I don't care if I'm in America. I'm going to wait. I'm going to go to college, and I'm going to be independent."

"You don't have to wait, and you can still go to college and be independent." Shayma looked from side to side and leaned forward, even though there was no one else in their tiny cabin to eavesdrop. "And let me tell you something, girls—it's a lot of fun."

"Do you mean to tell us," said Lely, "that our new parents or guardians or whatever you want to call them won't mind if we bring boys into our rooms?"

"It's America, Lely. Haven't you been listening?"

CHAPTER THIRTY

Boyd pulled a burgundy wingback chair across twenty feet of carpet and parked it close to a gas-lit fireplace in the lobby of their Washington, D.C. hotel.

"Hey, check it out—the invalid is moving furniture."

Abboud pulled another chair next to his. She removed her jacket, still dripping from the downpour outdoors. She pointed toward the other side of the room. "What about that piano? I am thinking it would look better next to the coffee stand. Perhaps you could move it for me?"

"No, you go ahead. Give it one of your taekwondo kicks. Just make sure there's no one in its path."

He settled into the chair, draping his own wet jacket over the back. Almost no heat came from the fireplace, but it was nice to pretend. The outside temperature was thirty-five degrees, and they had at least half an hour of waiting until their rooms—separate rooms—were ready. Finally, after nearly two weeks, he'd have some space to himself. No doubt, Abboud would welcome the privacy, too.

"I don't see the point of that little meeting we just had with Rangel and Wilson," he said. "Rehashing the same events. Nothing new from the Jordanians. No arrests. No Tamir Pierce. No sightings of teenage girls boarding a ship."

"It is unfortunate that those girls are refugees instead of bombs." Abboud stared into the flames.

"How so?"

"If they were bombs, do you think the United States would let any of those ships get as far as the Atlantic Ocean? They stop in Italy, Northern Africa, Spain. Those girls could be anywhere. But they are only refugees. They are not important."

"We care about them. Why else would the FBI assign Agent Roshan and me to those types of crimes?"

"They would not have sent us to Za'atari except for their concern that the traffickers might bring terrorists and bombs. You heard Fisk. That is what he cared about. And you saw Rangel and Wilson this morning. They were happy that we disrupted the network. They did not speak about the girls."

"We'll have agents watching those ships when they arrive at our ports."

"And what is happening to them while they are on the ships? Those ships should have been boarded before they left. What if the traffickers decided to sell the girls in Algeria? Or Gibraltar?"

"I wish we could have searched every boat headed to America. But you know the situation. We can't just barge into another country and swarm onto their ships."

"We are not giving our best effort. You will not allow refugees to enter your nation with dignity, but you will allow them to be brought here as slaves."

"That's ..." He was going to object—she was being unreasonable—but he stopped himself. He cared a lot about the girls. But could he care as much as Abboud did? They were like her sisters, and in Syria they had suffered the same horrors.

"I hope we find them," he said.

Grim-faced, she gazed at the fire and said nothing. She'd been in a funk for several days. At first, Boyd wondered if he'd said something wrong, but the more she talked about the girls, the more he understood how much it crushed her that they failed to find a way to capture the traffickers. *Disrupting the pipeline* wasn't enough. She wanted the girls.

So did he. But he didn't let himself brood. Agent Roshan had warned him about that. Instead, Boyd trained his mind to look forward. Celebrate the wins, learn from the losses. Keep going after it. Be relentless.

It was different for Abboud. This wasn't her job, although the way she handled herself at Za'atari demonstrated that if she were at the FBI Academy forty miles down the road in Quantico, she could go to the head of the class.

She was grieving. Her sorrow seeped into his heart, and a heaviness grew inside.

Maybe a diversion would help.

"After we get checked in, how about I take you to the Smithsonian Museums?" he asked. "I haven't been there since I was in high school. They've got an Apollo spaceship, Judy Garland's ruby slippers, the oldest locomotive in America."

"I do not want to visit a museum. I want to find the girls."

He nodded. She needed some space.

Boyd was answering an email when a receptionist came to tell them that their rooms were ready.

"I'll see you in the morning," he said. "Let's have breakfast before we go to the airport—does that sound okay?"

She agreed.

. . .

At 5:15 p.m., Boyd walked into the hotel bar. Thursday Night Football was about to kick off—his Seahawks against the team he loved to hate the most, the Dallas Cowboys. He expected to see bar patrons half-watching the game, since neither of the D.C. teams were competing, but what he found lifted his damp spirits. Thirty blue-and-gray garbed Seahawks fans crammed together beneath one of the large flatscreens. They wore Wilson jerseys, Wagner jerseys, even one throwback Curt Warner jersey, and they were making noise even before the first play from scrimmage.

He joined them—an instant family. Soon he was drinking the first beer he'd had since leaving Seattle for Jordan.

The Seahawks didn't disappoint, rising to the prime-time moment as they usually did. After two runs netted twelve yards, Wilson hit a deep pass for sixty-three yards and a touchdown. In the whooping and hollering that followed, a tall blonde woman wearing a Beast Mode jersey high-fived him first on the left hand, then the right, then the left again.

"I haven't seen you here," she said. "Where you from?"

She was pretty—oh, she was pretty. Curls the whole length of her hair. Sparkly blue eyes. A smattering of freckles.

"The fabulous apartment mecca otherwise known as…" He did a drumroll … "Tukwila! How about you?"

"I grew up in North Bend. Now I'm a senior at George Washington University. Middle Eastern studies."

"No way."

"Yes way."

"I was just there. Za'atari Refugee Camp in Jordan. This is my first night back."

She picked up a beer from an adjoining table and sat next to him. "No way."

"Yes way."

"And the reason?"

"Secret. It was, anyway. Not so much now."

"So you're military."

"Not anymore."

"CIA."

"Nope."

"State Department."

"Nope."

"NGO."

"Nope."

"What the hell?" She peeked at the television. It was still playing commercials.

"FBI," he said.

"Why's the FBI overseas?"

"Something related to Seattle."

"You mean a crime?"

"Very."

The Cowboys had the ball now. A jet sweep yielded one yard. On the next play, the Dallas running back burst up the middle, cut left, found open field in front of him. A Seahawk linebacker dove at him and ripped the ball loose, but the ball tumbled out of bounds. In five seconds, the Seahawk fans went from groans to cheers to groans, and then more groans after the players cleared away and the same linebacker lay on his side clutching his knee.

Time for a commercial.

Appropriately somber in the aftermath of the linebacker's injury, the curly-headed blonde turned toward him. "My name's Becky. That doesn't sound much like an ambassador. If I reach my goal, someday it will have to be Rebecca."

"Well, Ambassador Rebecca, my name is Russell. My mother named me after the Seahawks quarterback."

"Oh, yeah, sure. I'll bet he wasn't even born then."

"My mother had a premonition. Plus, she's a Seahawks fan."

"Sure, sure."

She drank from her beer. With a big gulp, Boyd followed her cue. This was an unexpected development. He wondered if she had a boyfriend—none of the men in the crowd appeared to be watching.

"I've never met an FBI agent," she said. "Show me your badge."

"Your friends might think I'm taking you in for questioning," he teased. "They might wonder what you've been up to."

"No, no. I have to pass my background checks. I'm squeaky clean." She held out her hand, palm upraised, and flicked her fingers. "C'mon. Out with it."

He took out his wallet and showed her the badge.

She studied it, then tugged at the sleeve of a shorter woman with light brown hair. "Hey, Sharon. Check it out."

Now he felt like an idiot, flashing his badge. He pulled the wallet back, but Becky grasped his wrist. He could have yanked his hand free, but he didn't want to feel like a jerk in addition to being an idiot.

Sharon gave the badge an awestruck gaze—was she spoofing him? "Whoa. What'd you do, Becky?"

"Nothing. Just wanted you to see." Becky let go of his wrist.

"Told you," Boyd said to Becky while putting the wallet back in his pocket.

Sharon raised a hand and assumed a guise of faux solemnity. "I hereby promise I'm over the age of twenty-one. But I don't know about Becky. She just got out of high school."

"Fuck you, Sharon," said Becky.

Sharon laughed.

As the game resumed, the Seahawks linebacker rode a cart to the locker room. The Cowboy drive ended with a field goal, prompting another set of commercials.

Becky turned her near-empty stein in a circle. "Tell me about Za'atari," she said.

The question woke a dull ache in his neck and nose. Ambassador Becky had probably already noticed that his nose didn't appear to have been molded properly. She'd have seen the scar.

"The Syrians are amazing people, at least the ones at Za'atari." He drank from his beer. "They had nothing, just whatever they could carry across the desert. Somehow they've made a city with an economy inside the walls. Every kind of business you could imagine, housed in small trailers or plywood booths. Families live in tiny trailers. Eighty-thousand residents, half of them children. It's rough."

"And Assad's going to get away with it," said Becky, the bitterness in her voice obvious. "Gassing his people. Bombing his people. Torturing and killing political prisoners."

This woman knew what the hell she was talking about. "The people there …" He paused—how to say it? "They've lived a horror show."

He thought of Abboud, holed up in her hotel room with grief her most prominent visitor. There was zero chance she'd walk into this bar and see him interacting with a college woman. If she did, what would it matter? It wasn't as though he and Abboud were in a relationship.

Still, he felt a small sense of unease.

"I want to help," said Becky. "I don't know how. Maybe the UN, maybe an NGO. Oxfam's got a program, Lel Haya, I think they call it. Training refugee women. Helping them find work. I want to help the women especially."

Her eyes were young and earnest. "That's awesome," he said. "They need it."

"You know what else is crazy? We don't let them in. No Syrian refugees allowed. I've read what you told me about Za'atari. That kind of energy, that kind of entrepreneurship—that would help our own economy."

The football game returned to the television. The defenses of both teams stiffened. Punts were exchanged, and the first quarter ended. The waitress came and Becky ordered a glass of chardonnay.

"If I buy some nachos, will you help me eat them?" he asked.

"Sure."

He added jalapeno poppers to the order and the waitress moved on to the others in the group.

When the first half ended, the Cowboys led by six. By then, Boyd and Becky were in their own invisible bubble. The other Seahawks fans belonged to a separate group.

Becky pulled loose a chip laden with avocado and put it in her mouth. She wasn't trying to be sexy. But for some reason, it super-charged him. Maybe it was the second beer, after having gone so long without any alcohol.

He'd gone a lot longer than that without a woman.

Becky grabbed another napkin and wiped her mouth and hands. He wondered how such a gesture could hum with eroticism—it had to be coming from him, not from her.

"How long are you going to be here?" she asked.

Why would she ask that question? "Flight leaves for Seattle at 6:20 tomorrow morning."

She froze for a moment. "Oh. Well, I've really liked meeting you. I think we care about the same things. We just go about it differently. We should be Facebook friends."

"I don't do Facebook. We could text."

Her face brightened and she opened her purse. "What's your number?"

He told her, and she typed a text. *Stay nice*

He wrote back. *U2*

Wish you could stay

Me 2

Maybe?

Her face showed … what was it? Did she want him? Was there an offer in her eyes?

Maybe what?

She rubbed her lips together. Her forefinger hung above the phone before finally tapping a reply.

Maybe you could eat another chip. She picked one up and fed it to him.

That was not the *maybe* she had meant. He knew it. She knew that he knew it. The unspoken words blared louder than the alt-rock music pumping from the bar's speakers. Just how was this evening going to play out?

She excused herself, said she'd be back in five minutes. Her eyes were sparkling. There was a whole half of football to go, but the game was secondary now, at least the game on the screen.

How was Abboud feeling, seven floors above this bar, in a room adjoining his room? What would she think if she happened to step out her door just as he arrived with a woman at his side? What if Becky was the kind of woman who made a lot of noise?

Maybe Becky had a place of her own.

Maybe he had no business being with Becky. Not the way he was beginning to feel about Abboud, except there could never be anything with Abboud.

Just one night. And Becky wasn't a floozy, either. There really was chemistry with her.

She returned, eyes only for him. She ignored the television.

His phone vibrated and he took it from his shirt pocket. It was a text from Senior Special Agent Rangel.

Call me. Now.

CHAPTER
THIRTY-ONE

Lely couldn't sleep. Neither could she toss and turn, for she didn't want to awaken Qamar. Tomorrow during the night they would rise from this tiny bunk, leave the ship, and board a smaller craft near the coast of America. Shayma wouldn't tell them where. Judging from the snow that fell during the afternoon, Lely guessed it had to be to the north.

Once on land, they would go by vehicle all the way across the United States to a new life with a new family. Would they like her? What would happen if they didn't? Could they send her back to Za'atari? Did either of the parents speak Arabic? She wished Shayma had used the precious time on this voyage to teach them English instead of all the other things she talked about.

If only her mind would shut up, maybe she could doze. An itch just below her right shoulder blade demanded a scratch, but she couldn't reach it without disturbing Qamar. Their small quarters still smelled like the chicken and rice they'd eaten for dinner. Perhaps what she looked forward to more than anything else in America was a bigger bed. Her own bed, even for one night.

Somehow sleep must have hushed the yakking in Lely's brain, because in her next moment of awareness someone's hand was shaking her by the shoulder. As her eyes focused, she saw that the hand belonged to Shayma, who stood next to her, illuminated by the ship lights sifting through the curtain of their only window. Holding a finger to her lips to signify silence, Shayma smiled, though it was a Shayma smile, mechanical, more calculated than spontaneous. She rose on an elbow and cocked her head—*for real?* she tried to communicate. Shayma nodded and nudged her shoulder.

Disentangling herself from the blankets and stepping with sock-clad feet onto the floor, she noticed Shayma wore a knee-length coat and a wool cap over her head. She moved toward the closet where they kept their coats, but Shayma tightened the grip on her arm, made the shushing gesture again, smiled. What did their mentor have in mind? A quick word in the little passageway outside their door?

She hadn't done anything to upset Shayma in the last day or so—at least nothing she could remember. She allowed herself to be pulled to the door. The instant she stepped outside the cabin, frigid air penetrated her pajamas, and she was wide awake. She hugged her arms around her chest. Shayma abandoned the smile, yanked her away from the cabin door and pulled her down the skinny corridor.

"Where are we going?" she asked.

In reply, Shayma jerked her close, thrust her face inches from Lely. "Quiet!" she hissed. She spun Lely in front of her, nudged her to the door of a stairway that led down to the deck. Lely hesitated, but Shayma shoved her hard. "Go," she commanded.

Something perilous waited on the other side of that doorway. Her thoughts jumbled too much for her to formulate any kind of resistance. Shayma always said they needed her protection, so maybe it would be more dangerous if she didn't follow her mentor's orders. She opened the door and stepped onto the stairs. The metal steps felt like ice against the bottoms of her socks and the cold air squeezed through her skin into her bones. Perhaps there was some danger, and Shayma would need Lely's help in protecting the other girls. Why else would she be so insistent?

When they reached the bottom, Shayma opened the door and pushed Lely into a wind that stiff-armed her. Two headlamp beams popped into the dark, one from Majd and one from Jack, both in black leather jackets and black knit caps. Majd thrust forward his good arm and smacked a clump of cloth to Lely's mouth. The force of it smashed her lips into her teeth, jolted back her jaw. Like an enormous bear paw, Majd's hand pushed against her face and spun her around. With a single arm, he clamped her to his chest. Blood dribbled onto her tongue and gums.

She thrashed left and right, tried digging down her feet, but her socks slipped on the cold wet deck. While Majd squeezed harder to hold her in place, Jack stepped in front, his headlamp blinding her except for the slab of his face. He uncoiled a backhand across her temple, twisting the tendons in her neck. A siren screamed in her head.

"Enough," Shayma shouted from behind.

Majd held her firmly. Still tense, still ready to bolt, Lely paused her resistance. Her breath came in gasps.

She couldn't stop herself from whimpering. She tasted the blood in her mouth.

Shayma moved in front of them. "Follow me," she said.

Lely fought enough to make herself a nuisance as Majd kept his arm locked tightly around her while they marched down a length of containers stacked far above their heads. She saved what she could of her waning strength so that she could break free if the chance arose.

Where were they taking her? Why were they treating her like this?

At the end of the row of containers Majd yanked her starboard to a darker place lit only by stars, next to the glinting steel of the rail and the whooshing waves below it.

A'uzo billah. One fling and she'd be falling over a precipice, her only net the dark ocean. A wetness trickled down her legs. She had lost control of her bladder. She threw the last of her breath into a tornado twist, but Majd used the momentum of it to slam her down on her back as though she were a heifer or a ewe, and she lay crushed by his body a foot from the edge of the deck, swaying up and down in ceaseless waves, her mouth muffled by cloth and blood.

Shayma squatted down to study her.

"Do you know how easy it would be to disappear into the ocean?" She enunciated the question slowly, above the noise of the wind and the waves and the panting of breaths heavy from exertion. "A single solitary girl like you? A refugee and an orphan no one would miss?"

Shayma let the words percolate a dozen beats of Lely's pounding heart.

"I am the only person to keep you safe. Your life belongs to me."

The photograph of the Seattle family flashed in Lely's mind—and it seemed that Shayma saw it, too.

"Yes, a family waits, but they can wait for another girl. There are many like you, many the ocean has already claimed."

Perhaps Allah would grant her a reunion in the afterlife with her mother and her father, her two sisters, both sets of grandparents, her uncle, her cousins.

No God but God.

"Lely, I can keep you alive tonight. I offer you a good life, hope, with friends just like you."

From her hands and knees she leaned down until her head was inches above Lely's face. She stroked her cheek. She caressed her hair. Lely froze in place.

"I need to trust you, and you need to trust me. If you scream, we will have to say *what a foolish girl.* She jumped in the ocean only one day from America. How sad. Lely, you won't scream, will you? Because I'd like to tell Majd to take the cloth off your mouth. Lely, can I trust you? Nod your head if you want me to trust you."

Perhaps it would be best to die. After the cold and sinking and choking there would be peace.

"If you do not answer, I will interpret that as a *no,* that I cannot trust you. It would be sad for you to die. How would Qamar feel?"

Majd still pressed his body against her, but he had eased the push of cloth against her mouth. The thought of no breath, the panic of no air, the sealing off of life overruled reunions with her deceased family.

"If you scream …" Shayma slowly shook her head. "… I cannot protect you, and you will die. Are you ready for Majd to remove the cloth?"

Lely nodded her head.

"Good." Shayma rose to her feet and Majd moved the cloth away.

"Majd, let her stand. You see, Lely, I will protect you only as long as I can trust you. You must show respect. If you disrespect your American family, they will reject you. Americans want obedient girls. Will you be an obedient girl, Lely?"

A different kind of wave swept over Lely, washed through every corpuscle head to toe. The wave saturated her, then burst out in the form of a gasping sob, and another and another, and she stood spasming with tears and quivering with cold. There was no one to hold her, no one to hold onto. They stood quietly while the spell shook her, and when it subsided Shayma reached out a hand and tenderly wiped a tear from below Lely's eye. Inside Lely something clicked shut, and a burst of gratitude sent her staggering into Shayma, who put her jacket-cloaked arms around her and embraced her, infusing her with physical warmth against the cold.

"Will you be an obedient girl?" Shayma spoke almost like a mother, her mouth inches from Lely's ear.

"Y-yes," she shivered the word.

"Oh, I am so glad. I almost lost you."

She kissed Lely's forehead.

"Let's talk about what happened tonight. You had a bad dream. We found you outside in all this cold, crazy with fear. You tried to run, but fortunately Majd was faster. He tackled you before you could jump into the ocean. Tell me now ..." Shayma took a step back, her hands still holding Lely close. "What happened tonight?"

Three gasping words at a time, Lely repeated the story.

"Good. Let's get you to the main lounge. Majd and Jack will protect you while I get you some warm clothes. Lely, if any of us ever hears some wild story about us dragging you out of bed, that would be a lie, and you will have lost my trust. Do you want to lose my trust?"

No.

No no no no no no. No forever as long as there was air to breathe.

CHAPTER THIRTY-TWO

It was nearly midnight when Boyd grabbed his daypack and stepped out from an FBI sedan into a bone-freezing rain at Joint Base Andrews. The last ten minutes of the drive had been like going through a carwash, and now he was out in it, instantly drenched. The driver dashed around the front, unfolding an umbrella, which he held over Abboud's head as she emerged from the backseat. All three sprinted twenty puddled yards to an office adjoining a large gray hanger.

With her brown hair pulled back in a ponytail and wrinkles bracketing her nose and mouth, Senior Special Agent Rangel was waiting for them. She led them through the reception area into an office with cheap vanilla-hued wall panels. Four agents, all men, sat at a rectangular table. Rangel introduced them as agents Musgrove, Sanchez, Polkinghorn, and Jarlson.

"It took six days, but we finally pried loose some CCTV footage from the Lebanese, covering both the

Port of Beirut and the Port of Tripoli," said Rangel as she took a seat at the head of the table. Near shivering in his wet trousers, Boyd draped a sopping jacket on the back of a chair and sat across from Abboud.

"I've had agents blurry-eyed examining footage from seventy-six different cameras," continued Rangel. "Two hours ago, we found the woman named Shayma with females who appear to be teenagers walking up a gangplank."

"Yes!" whispered Boyd, allowing himself to show a chest-high fist pump. Abboud brought both her hands up in fists.

"That's right," said Rangel. "We have every intention of rescuing those girls. On the same camera, the two men who ambushed these two"—she gestured at Boyd and Abboud—"board the ship almost five hours later. Abboud, you might be interested in knowing that the big guy was wearing an arm cast."

A sense of pride surged in Boyd. It meant something that Rangel referred to Abboud by her last name. That signified she was more like an agent than an interpreter, no matter what her formal title was. *Nawar Abboud.* His partner. Mess with her at your own peril.

"After a bit of digging," continued Rangel, "we found out the ship they boarded is the *Asian Rose*, currently four hours from entering United States territorial waters off the coast of Maine. She's four-point-five hours away from entering Canadian waters on her way to the Port of St. John. So you see our window. We've got a United States Coast Guard cutter standing by in Jonesport, Maine. The cutter will be intercepting the *Asian Rose* before it enters Canadian waters. Its crew will secure the ship and separate the girls from their captors. Guess who else is going to be on that cutter, waiting to speak to the girls?"

"I figured you had a good reason for pulling me from a Seahawks game," said Boyd.

"Bingo," said Rangel. "You and Abboud are going to accompany Senior Special Agent Polkinghorn's team in boarding the vessel. He and his team were briefed on background before you two arrived. They'll interview the traffickers. The two of you will be responsible for questioning the girls. Abboud, we're going to need you to reassure them that their nightmare is over. We'll want to know if Shayma or those two men or anyone else has mistreated any of them."

Abboud nodded.

"I've got a Pilatus turboprop warming up thirty yards from here," said Rangel. "Despite the nasty weather out there, it ought to be able to get you to the Machias Valley Airport in about two and a half hours. From there, a Coast Guard Huey will fly you twelve miles to Jonesport. Abboud, may I assume you'll be okay on a helicopter?"

"I will be fine."

"That's good," said Rangel, "because you'll be able to board the cutter on time if you leave here in …" She looked at her phone. "Ten minutes."

. . .

On a brightly lit cement pad at the U.S. Coast Guard Jonesport Station on the northern coast of Maine, the Huey helicopter touched down softly, despite the storm outside. The pilot idled the engine, diminishing its high-pitched din as well as the speed of the rotary blades. Two Coast Guard seamen hurried to the helo and opened the doors. A whirl of sleet, stirred by the blades, peppered Boyd and Abboud as they and the other agents stepped out. Boyd felt doubly grateful for the heavy FBI jackets with gold lettering that Rangel had procured from a storage room before they left Andrews.

The seamen ushered them a short distance to the dock and onto the deck of a gleaming white 210-foot cutter. The heavy sleet and bright lights blinded Boyd's view beyond the ship's bow, but he didn't have more than a moment to look. Their escorts quickly directed them off the deck and down a narrow flight of steel stairs amidships to the mess, where the four senior agents claimed a cafeteria table and Boyd and Abboud took one adjacent to them.

"Won't be much to see on deck anyway," said a man with a weight-lifter's physique and minimal neck who introduced himself as Seaman Vincent. "The waters will be fairly calm while we navigate around the islands, but once we hit open water, the carnival ride begins, no admission charged. If you need to upchuck or just use a toilet, the heads are down those stairs and to your left. Seaman Bailey and I will be hanging with you until we intercept the container ship. After it's secure, we'll escort you on board and we'll make available whoever you want to talk to."

He pointed toward the galley. "In the meantime, help yourself to some coffee and granola bars. You have any questions or concerns, that's where Seaman Bailey and I will be." The two men walked to a table closer to the galley. The rumble of engines grew louder, and the cutter crept away from its moorage.

Despite the lack of sleep and a dinner of nachos, poppers, and beer, adrenalin roared like a waterfall through Boyd. His team had not only planned and executed the disruption of a supply chain of vulnerable girls, it was now on the verge of rescuing four of those victims. The opportunity to do what he would do this night was exactly why he'd joined the FBI.

CHAPTER
THIRTY-THREE

"Up up." Shayma tapped Lely's shoulder.

Already in her shoes, a thick abaya and hijab, and a jacket over that, Lely sprang out of bed.

She would demonstrate how obedient she could be. Her sass had put them in danger, but she repented her sins before Allah. She and her friends grabbed daypacks and filed out the door into the seesawing cold passageway atop the stairs. Those two men were waiting, the chill of their presence enough to freeze all motion. She bit down on her lip. She'd done nothing wrong. She stole a glance at Shayma.

"You are doing well, girls," said their mentor. "That includes you, Lely."

Lely suppressed a sob of relief. Alhamdulillah, what a privilege to wear a jacket against the cold. Not like last night when she had that bad dream and they found her clad only in pajamas.

After they descended the stairs, they stepped out a door onto the deck. Dazzling white, nearly blinding in the ship's lights, sleet angled downward, pecking Lely's cheeks. Beyond the perimeter of ship, only blackness lay. Lely moved as though tethered to Shayma while they weaved among containers until one of those men opened another door and motioned them down a different set of stairs.

They turned a corner, descended more stairs, repeated the turning and descending twice again. They stopped near a sealed door with three windowed portholes revealing black rolling waves—her grave, had they not tackled her last night. Even here, sheltered behind this wall, she wanted to bolt from the sight, but she pushed against the impulse. She leaned into Shayma, who wrapped a reassuring arm around her.

Swaying with the sea, a passenger boat crept into view, its white and red paint shadowy in the container ship's dim lighting. A man secured both ends to the ship and nodded his head. Majd opened the door, admitting a gush of sleet. Lely wrapped her arms around Shayma, who smiled in return, gently pried loose one of her hands, and guided her across the edge of the ramp onto the waiting boat. There Shayma unlatched Lely and nodded toward an open door in the boat's passenger cabin.

"Go with Majd," she said.

At the bottom of a short set of stairs, Lely entered a cabin almost dark except for two dim overhead lights, one in front and one in back. She and her friends sat on cushioned bench seats. Outside the windows, a barrage of sleet angled downward in muted lighting. The boat rocked much more than the larger ship.

A minute later, Shayma came into the cabin and stood over the girls. Lely probed for Qamar's hand and clasped it when they touched.

"Well done, girls," said Shayma. "It will be three hours before we dock, and it will still be dark. Lie down now and go to sleep."

Lie down meant lie down. Lely obeyed, curling onto the seat with Qamar at her feet while Sara and Yana disappeared behind the seat in front of her. Although she tried to sleep, she could not. On the seat behind her, Shayma and those two men whispered, even after the cabin lights went black and the boat's engine roared to life.

CHAPTER THIRTY-FOUR

"Looks like coffee's the only choice," Boyd said to Abboud as the cutter picked up speed and the room swayed up and down, like a giant cradle rocked by a drunk ogre. "Can I get you a cup?"

"I will stay with water, thank you." She took out her phone and thumbed the screen.

Bracing his legs against the rising and falling, Boyd filled two-thirds of a paper cup with black coffee and returned to the table. The first sip burned his tongue and lips.

"Been a while since I rode a helicopter," he said. "Not since I got out of the army."

Abboud nodded, her eyes locked on her phone.

"We mostly rode Chinooks. Two rotors. Stubby body, like a chopped off airplane fuselage. We could hook up a tank beneath it and carry it a hundred miles. Fast as hell. Beasts."

Abboud looked up. "In Syria nobody wants to see a helicopter."

The rush of Boyd's nostalgia slowed. It hadn't occurred to him that Abboud would have a whole different way of regarding helicopters, but the reason was obvious. Syrian helicopters dealt death to its own citizens, wherever they congregated—schools, hospitals, apartment buildings. "Oh hell," he said. "That makes sense. I'm sorry."

"It is fine. You were trying to protect people. We would have welcomed *your* helicopters."

"But they never came. I wish we could have been there."

"I know it is complicated. Assad has the Russians to protect him. You do not want a war with Russia."

Boyd drank from the coffee, still scalding hot. It was strong and bitter, as though it had been brewed a month ago. "Maybe we can be the good guys tonight."

Abboud nodded.

He turned his attention to the adjacent table, where there had been a break in the chatter. Agent Polking-horn, a middle-aged man tall enough to have been a forward in the NBA, drummed his fingers on the table. He wore a black stocking cap and a standard FBI jacket, and he had eyes so blue that he had to have been wear-ing contact lenses.

"You know they pulled me from my seat tonight?" he said. "Sent me a text right before halftime."

"You should bill the bureau for those tickets," said Sanchez, whose height wouldn't have reached Polking-horn's shoulders had the two of them been standing.

"Au contraire. I should send Rangel a thank you card," said Polkinghorn. "They were getting their asses kicked, per usual. Fuckin' Wizards. I don't know why I bother."

"Maybe you could take medical leave after this gig," said Jarlson, a man whose brick red hair harbored strands of gray. "You're paying money to watch the Wizards? You need to have your head examined."

Boyd jumped in. "Guess I'm eligible, too," he said. "I know it's a different sport, but the Seattle Mariners haven't made the playoffs in sixteen years. And our basketball team dumped us for Oklahoma City—how pathetic is that?"

"One less team to break your heart," said Polkinghorn.

"I'm from Detroit," said Sanchez. "Don't talk to me about the Lions."

Abboud set down her phone. "So the question is," she said, "who gets to whine the most?"

Boyd laughed, as did the other agents.

"What about you, Abboud?" asked Polkinghorn. "You got any sports teams you like?"

"You mean among these minor American sports?" she asked.

"Oh, I get it," said Musgrove. "You're a soccer fan."

"Such a strange name, soccer," said Abboud. "You mean football. Real football."

"Now you're talking!" said Sanchez.

"Yeah, sure," said Musgrove. "Like to see one of your players step on the field with one of our players. One hit—boom. It'd be all over."

"That would be a red card," said Abboud. "Your player would be dismissed from the pitch, and for him it would be over."

"And yours would leave on a stretcher."

"Such short careers, your brand of football." Abboud shook her head the way a disapproving mother might. "And then there are the brain diseases. Do you think perhaps some of those ailments extend to their fans?"

Guffaws erupted. After much discussion, Sanchez was awarded the pity prize. The Lions hadn't won a playoff game in twenty-six years, and Detroit lacked a soccer team, too.

The ride grew choppier. Plates and silverware rattled in the galley. The room squeezed in on Boyd. He wished he could be on deck, even if that meant getting pummeled by sleet and snow. What was out there? Were they within sight of an island? Were they closing in on the container ship?

Jarlson spun away from the senior agents' table. His face was pale.

"Down the stairs," snapped Polkinghorn. The two seamen next to the galley craned their necks to watch.

Jarlson tottered out of his chair, thrusting a hand on Boyd's shoulder to keep from falling. Boyd held his breath. Was this man about to puke all over him? Clutching his gut, Jarlson lifted his hand and staggered toward the doorway to the stairs.

At the top of the stairs, he leaned forward, propping himself upright with an arm against the wall on each side of the doorway. He moaned and then he puked.

"Sorry," he croaked before descending onto the first step. He slipped on the vomitus and would have tumbled down the stairs if he hadn't grabbed a rail.

Joining Polkinghorn and the two seamen, Boyd rushed toward the stricken agent, but he stopped himself short of the stairs.

"You okay?" asked Seaman Bailey, who also refrained from an up-close intervention.

"Yeah." It was more of a groan than a reply. Gripping the rail as though it were a life buoy, Jarlson puked again. And again. Apparently, he had eaten a big dinner.

Fifteen minutes later, Jarlson was back in the mess, alone at his own table. Occasionally, one of the Coast Guardsmen scowled in his direction. It had fallen upon them to do the cleanup, but their efforts could not eliminate the aroma of seasickness mixing with the piney smell of the cleanser.

Minutes later, the boat cut its engines. Outside, a loudspeaker at high volume, audible even from the mess, hailed the *Asian Rose* and commanded it to prepare to be boarded.

Seaman Vincent rose from the table near the galley. "That's our cue. Let's get out of here."

They exited the cabin onto the main deck, where bright lights illuminated the cutter like a football stadium. Vincent herded them to a spot near the stern on the starboard side, one deck below a Browning machine gun manned by a seaman wearing a thick pea coat. A bright beacon cut a circle of light through the sleet from the port side of the stern to a large container ship a hundred yards away. At the stern, a jet-propelled interceptor boat with a half-dozen crewmen slid from a ramp into the water. It made a half turn and rocketed toward the ship, bouncing on waves, illuminated by the beacon.

"How you doing, Jarlson?" said Polkinghorn. "Think you can handle that jetboat when it comes back for us?"

"Don't put him in the front," said Sanchez.

"Yeah, yeah, I'm fine," said Jarlson. "But put me in the back."

"If you puke yourself overboard," said Musgrove, "don't expect us to come back and get you."

"Thanks a lot, buddy," said Jarlson. "I knew you had my back."

"Probably kill all the sea life within a hundred miles," said Musgrove.

Vincent and Bailey put life vests and red helmets on Boyd, Abboud, and the other agents. Boyd's adrenalin once again cranked up to fire hydrant volume. A red-eye flight the night before and now this crazy night hadn't tired him enough to stop him from swimming to the container ship if that was the only way he could get there. He felt none of the cold, none of the cutter's motion. He was in line at an amusement park for the most bad-ass ride the place had to offer.

They waited: five minutes, ten, fifteen. In what kind of conditions would those girls be when he and the rest of the team boarded the ship? He remembered the Chinese girl in her pink plastic sandals that his team had rescued at the sleezy hotel back in Seattle. She had been so cold and so wet. He remembered Hafa, with her black eye and cowering demeanor.

Feeling the cold now, he squeezed against the outside wall of the main deck's cabin to elude the brunt of the sleet.

When they finished this case, he and Abboud would find Hafa. They'd tell her that the information she provided helped set in motion a string of events, including this Coast Guard interception, resulting in the rescue of four Syrian girls, and maybe the other girls, too, if the senior agents wrestled enough information out of the traffickers on the container ship.

Finally, over the din of waves and wind, he heard the tinny, high-pitched roar of the interceptor boat before it entered their spotlighted view on the crest of a wave.

"We call them OTHs—Over the Horizon cutters," said Vincent. "Also RIBs—rigid-hulled inflatable boats. Watch how we recover it."

Thirty yards away, the orange-hulled OTH rose and fell. It carried two sailors—four must have remained on the ship. The pilot positioned it behind the cutter, then zipped forward up out of the water onto the steep ramp and into a net, where it stopped cold.

"Let's go," said Vincent. Russell and Abboud went first, but before they could step onto the interceptor, one of the two seamen shook his head.

"There are no females on that ship," he said. "Zilch. Nada. Zero."

CHAPTER THIRTY-FIVE

Two weeks ago, Lely pictured her entry to America—daylight in the harbor of a big city, crowds of people waiting to greet them. It was nothing like the scene unfolding now.

When they had been on the container ship, Shayma told them what to expect when they came to America. Because they were refugees and the UN had a limited budget, they would transfer to a passenger boat that would operate without lights in order to evade gangs lurking in dark coves. If all went well, they would dock at a quiet beach, where a van would be waiting for them.

Lely squinted her eyes. She dared not sleep. If gangsters assaulted their boat, she would resist. She pictured herself kicking and punching and escaping. She'd find a little closet and hide.

She listened intently, just in case the attackers came. Time passed, and despite the rolling motion of the boat, she found she had to fight her eyelids to keep them open.

Shayma and the men stopped whispering—had they allowed themselves to doze?

She was still awake when a radio transmitter sputtered, followed by a beep. In the seat behind her, someone slid away. Despite the absence of light, she recognized Jack walking past her toward the front of the cabin.

"We're dark," Jack said to the radio.

"Keep it that way," said a man at the other end. "We've just been hailed by the United States Coast Guard."

"Keep them with you," said Jack. "It's your necks as well as ours."

What did that mean? Lely closed her eyes. Shayma said she was protecting them—but from what?

Motoring at a low rumble, the passenger boat slowed. Lely wanted to jump up and run to a window, but Shayma might disapprove. She had told them to sleep. Was America visible in the pre-dawn darkness? Ya Allah, it was so hard to be still.

Finally, Qamar rose to a sitting position. Shayma did not rebuke her, and so Lely rose, too. She turned back to meet Shayma's eyes, to try to read in them if sitting was acceptable, but in the dimness of the cabin, her chaperone and those two men were like specters, their faces gray except for the whites of their eyes. She turned forward again. If they were approaching land, no lights were visible from the shore.

Behind her, static crackled. The voice she'd heard earlier came onto the radio.

"They are gone," said the man whose Arabic had some sort of East Asian accent, perhaps Chinese.

"They are never gone," said Jack. "No more communication." The static ceased.

"The man is a blabbermouth," Shayma said.

"We need to get off this boat," said Majd.

Jack switched to English, and an English-speaking voice responded on the radio. "Five minutes," Jack said afterward.

"Up up, girls," said Shayma. "Grab your packs. Yana, put your coat on."

Lely grabbed the backrest of the bench seat in front of her to keep her balance.

"Up the stairs and hold onto the rails," said Shayma.

Outside, Lely couldn't tell if it were sleeting or snowing. On the rocking-horse deck, she struggled to stay upright against the strong wind. A glimmer of dawn tinged the eastern horizon, outlining the silhouettes of trees. They were surrounded by land. The ocean had been reduced to a storm-churned lake.

A pair of yellow parking lights flickered on and off somewhere to her left. In response, someone on the boat turned on all the deck lights. A bright beam wiggled, then settled on a dock thirty meters away. Flakes of snow blew diagonally from the dark sky. A man Lely didn't recognize climbed down a ladder from the pilothouse to the deck, and when their boat bumped the dock, he jumped off and coiled a rope around a post. Majd followed him, pivoted, and reached out his undamaged arm to help Jack to the dock.

"All right, girls," said Shayma. "Let's go. Lely, you first."

Rejecting Majd's hand, Lely brushed by him with a big step onto the dock. A shot of fear jolted her, and she glanced at Shayma. She wished she could have a do-over and accept Majd's assistance, but it was too late now.

A man stepped out of the driver's seat of a white van, spoke with Jack, and got into the passenger seat of a black pickup. Lely and Qamar took the middle seat of the van, while Jack and Majd occupied seats in front and Sara and Yana joined Shayma in the back. With Jack at the wheel, they followed the black pickup out the small dirt lot onto a narrow road whose yellow divider line had faded almost to invisibility. Snow piled a foot on each side of the road, which curved this way and that through a thicket of trees and brush. The van grew warm. Lely leaned her head against the window and allowed herself to sleep.

When she woke, the black pickup was gone. Next to her, Qamar still slumbered, her head resting against Lely's shoulder. Jack drove, while Majd tuned the radio to an American pop music station. The two-lane highway had grown wider and the snow was piled higher. There were cars ahead of them and cars coming the opposite direction. They passed occasional farmhouses as well as snow-covered fields with cattle bunched around bales of hay.

"I'm in America," she murmured.

America.

America.

Something didn't feel right.

They came to a stop sign. Her instinct screamed:

Get out.

Grab the handle of the sliding door, yank it open before anyone could stop her, and run. But then—where would she go? She didn't speak the language. It would be a crazy thing to do. She reminded herself that her mind wasn't working right, hadn't been working right for a long time, and it was getting worse.

Shayma had already told them what would happen if any of the girls became separated from her. Police would find the girl and detain her. She would be thrown into an American jail where the other prisoners hated

Muslims. She would rot in jail for months or years, until finally one day she would be put on an airplane and flown back to Assad and his soldiers, and she would suffer unspeakable abuse.

"I'm in America now," she whispered.

Half an hour later they stopped at a gas station with rows of tractor-trailer trucks parked around half the perimeter. Shayma hurried the girls into the bathroom and out. Lely's stomach growled with hunger as they rushed past aisles of chips and granola bars and crackers, but they never paused until they were back in the van. After fueling the vehicle, Jack parked them on the far side of the lot. He and Majd went into an American-style burger place. When they returned, they gave Lely and each of the girls two chicken-and-egg "burritos" that looked like shawarma but tasted nothing like it. She dearly hoped the chicken had not been cooked on the same surface as pork, but she suspected it was, and Allah would know her sin.

"Better get used to it, girls," said Shayma as they returned to the highway. "This will be our life for the next four days."

An hour later they entered a small town. Multi-colored lights twinkled on streetlamp posts. Painted candy canes, wreaths, Santa Clauses, and reindeer adorned shop windows. But there were no depictions of the prophet Jesus. Christians did not think it *haram* to portray lifelike pictures of their prophet—so why was his visage absent? People in heavy coats and carrying bags crowded the sidewalks. Lely caught herself gaping at Jewish men in skull caps, Arab women in hijabs, and Westerners, despite the cold, in short dresses and high boots.

In the afternoon they passed a green sign with white letters, and Shayma announced from the back seat, "We're in New York now."

"Where are the buildings?" asked Qamar, peering at fallow farmland and forested hills.

"The state," said Shayma, "not the city. Like Syria. There's the city Dara'a and there's the larger governorate with the same name. We're not going to New York City. What would our family in Seattle think if they found out we delayed our trip and accumulated more debts? It's a 200-kilometer detour, and the amount of money we would have to spend just to get inside the city would mean you'd have to work a lot longer to pay those debts."

"What are you talking about?" asked Sara.

"We're not going to the city," said Shayma.

"No," said Sara. "About the debts. No one ever said anything about debts."

"Did you think the United Nations has the money?" She laughed. "It's already too much for the UN to feed the refugees still in camps. Of course you'll have to work. But it won't be too long and you'll be with friends, other girls just like you. And you'll be living with your family in a big high building like the ones in New York City. Out your window you'll see a beautiful lake, and when the sky is clear you'll see pointed mountains that never lose their snow."

"But you said our American family was rich," said Yana.

There was a pause. A creepy feeling wriggled down Lely's spine. She wished she could warn Yana. It was dangerous to challenge their mentor.

Shayma replied slowly, her voice edged like broken glass. "Your American family wants you to learn the value of work."

She called to the front of the van. "Jack, we're in New York! Can't you find some Arab music? I'm sick of this American noise. It all sounds the same."

Jack found a station, and Lely immediately recognized the energetic voice of Balqees Ahmed Fathi in "Yoi Yoi Yoi."

The door that brings the storm—it's best to keep it shut

Ya Allah, were truer words ever sung?

After Balqees, they listened to Saad Lamjarrad, Nancy Ajram, Wael Kfoury. Lely sensed everyone's mood grow lighter, including her own.

Shayma revived her gushy faux teenager voice. "We must get to Seattle before Christmas. There's a man I can't wait to see. What's funny is that people call him Hawk. And so you can say when we reach Seattle, I will sleep with a bird."

She laughed, like it was normal to give her body to a man named after a bird or anything else, and that it was normal to talk about it, no matter that other men were in the same van and all the girls were virgins uncertain about when they would be married.

CHAPTER
THIRTY-SIX

If the sight of an old lady with a pet goose waiting for the walk sign couldn't bring Abboud out of her funk, nothing would. Boyd nudged her arm and nodded toward the odd spectacle across the street, a crowd of Christmas shoppers and this single waist-high goose among them. Abboud displayed a tiny smile before reverting to a dark cloud, her eyes flat as a patient on life support.

Actually, the goose didn't do much for him, either, not after the debriefing they'd just experienced at the Seattle FBI office.

Bottom line: they were both finished with the mission to find and rescue the trafficked refugees. The whole case had been put on hold, "pending additional developments." All that meant was that if out of the blue some law enforcement entity stumbled across a trafficking operation that included Syrian girls, the bureau would devote resources to finding possible connections and making arrests on federal charges. But for now, Boyd and Roshan were reassigned to the multi-agency task force, this time to focus on Asian massage parlors, while Abboud was back to translating intercepted communications.

Sure, Fisk had commended them for their resourcefulness, their poise, their courage. He emphasized the traffickers no longer had a pipeline to Za'atari to procure vulnerable teenagers. But Boyd attributed that outcome to chance. In their snooping around, they happened to stumble across the people they needed to find—no sure thing in a city of 80,000 souls. And before he could figure out the trail led to Dr. Bergeson, the traffickers murdered the UN officer.

The light turned green, and two herds of bundled-up humans navigated past each other, their breaths puffing small fog balloons, their hands full with boxes and bags, only two days until Christmas. In another three blocks, Boyd and Abboud would hit a traffic jam of pedestrians in the Pike Place Market area, but Abboud made a right turn and Boyd went along with her. The market wasn't their destination, anyway. They were headed for the waterfront pathway, guaranteed to be less crowded, where they could walk off their frustrations during their lunch hour.

Abboud moved quickly. Soon they were near the bottom of the steep hill, only a dozen or so people in sight. She turned right again, and Boyd knew where she was headed.

"It's going to hurt," he said. "There's nothing to be gained by going there, but I understand. I kind of want to go there, too."

"I do not care if it hurts. It cannot make me feel worse than I feel now."

After a minute, she stopped. They stood twenty yards from the entrance to the Elliott Bay Hotel and

Condominiums. There were no partitions outside, and the hole in the glass canopy had been repaired. A middle-aged couple holding hands stepped out from the lobby and hailed a taxi. A woman exited the driver's seat of an Audi sedan and handed the keys to a valet.

He couldn't help but peer up at a particular ninth-floor balcony.

"I'm very sorry," he said.

She nodded. "Do we still have time to go to the waterfront?"

"Yes."

They reached the sidewalk along the waterfront and turned south. A half-mile distant, the lights of the Seattle Great Wheel displayed the color and shape of a Christmas tree. Clouds lay thick and torpid, but no rain fell. They sauntered onto a wooden pier and gazed out at the Puget Sound, its waters an undulating gray. Beneath them, it sloshed quietly among the pilings. The air was heavy and moist.

"There are some things I never want to forget," said Abboud. "I will never forget Amal. I will never forget today, how the FBI quit trying to find her killers."

"We haven't quit. You heard Fisk. We've sent photos to police departments and county sheriffs across the country, with special attention to jurisdictions along Interstate 90. And that's even though, as far as we know, those girls could be on a different continent. We've had agents speak to every real estate agency and management company in the Seattle region. Nobody has either sold or leased a luxury condo or apartment to anyone that fits the profile of the traffickers. We're at a dead end, Abboud. What are we supposed to do?"

"I know only what we should not do. And that is quit."

"And I say we haven't. If you were in charge, what would you have me do right now?"

"Arrest the captain of the container ship. We have absolute proof that those girls boarded his ship." She held up a hand. "I know. It is a Panamanian registered ship and the captain is a Malaysian national. But I still say if it had been suicide vests instead of girls on that ship, it would never have gotten as far as it did. You would have sent drones. You would have used your satellites. The captain would not have been able to scratch his butt without you knowing about it."

"First of all, we're not that good. We wish we were, but we aren't. Second of all …" He paused. "Second of all," he repeated, softening his voice, "like I said, I'm sorry. I wish we could do better. I want to bust those bastards, too. I want to see justice. For your sake and theirs. I want to see you happy."

A Victoria Clipper catamaran motored into view, moving slowly north out of the harbor. A handful of passengers stood on the stern deck, pointing their phones at the city skyline. Had Abboud been to Canada yet? A few days respite on Vancouver Island might restore her spirits.

But he couldn't provide that for her. Maybe sometime in the future. Just friends, right?

"They told us at Quantico—that's the FBI Training Academy—that we would fail. They told us that even when we succeeded, some lawyer might find a way to convince a jury to have a doubt. They told us that politicians might smear our reputations. But what I remember, what I hold onto, is that those are things we can't control. We have to focus on what we can control. We have to believe in ourselves and our mission. We have to hold onto our ideals."

He paused to make eye contact with her. "This seems like one of those times."

She nodded, then stared back toward the receding catamaran.

"I did the best I could, and I say you did, too, Abboud. Maybe I learned something about trusting people, like just because someone's got a title and a uniform, it doesn't mean I should automatically trust him. I thought I'd learned that lesson in Iraq. I've got this scar on my face to remind me. But even if we'd suspected Bergeson, would that have changed the outcome? Maybe. Maybe not. Right now there are other girls and boys, men and women, who need our help. To do that, you've got your way, translating all those calls, and I've got mine."

"I understand what you are saying. I agree. But what I am hearing is that you are giving up on the Syrian girls also."

"Never. But that decision is outside of my control."

She closed her eyes, took in a long breath, exhaled. She shivered, and he knew it sprang from more than the cold. He wanted to put an arm around her, but he didn't dare. He berated himself—as much as those girls meant to him, they mattered far more to her. If they were the world to him, they were the universe to Abboud.

"Come on," he said. "Let's keep walking."

They encountered construction barriers, and so they turned up the hill. The climb pulled deeper breaths from them, enough, he hoped, to warm her up. It turned out there was no avoiding Pike Place's crowds, but the line at a pierogi stand was minimal, and so they went there. They ate their pierogis standing up, with no goose in sight.

"What will you do for Christmas?" she asked. "Will you go to Spokane to see your parents?"

"My mother is in California with my sister. I'll see my father, but it will be at my grandpa's ranch."

A spark lit her eyes. "So you will see your horse, too?"

"Both of them."

She pressed her lips together.

"I promised you a riding lesson, didn't I?"

The spark in her eyes brightened. Her lips formed the beginning of a smile. No one needed to take her to Victoria. All she needed was a horse.

And that's all he needed, too. Abboud's sudden hopefulness burrowed through the cold air and into his heart. He'd been wondering what kind of excuse he could cook up for him and Abboud to keep visiting each other. Carpooling wouldn't work anymore. When he began the newest case, his work hours would be unpredictable.

But his father would also arrive at the ranch on Christmas day. He put his pierogi back on the paper plate. How could he explain?

"My father ... he's got some prejudices."

Abboud nodded. "I see. These prejudices—they include Muslims, yes?"

"I don't want to put you through that."

She was quiet.

"The thing that happened to me in Iraq—you know, this scar." He pointed at it. "I think it affected him more than it did me."

"It is fine. Another time, yes? Christmas is a special day. I do not wish to interfere."

For just an instant, Boyd wished he could fling the paper plate and the half-eaten pierogi like a frisbee. Watch it spin out onto the sound until it was long out of sight.

The hell with his father. He wasn't going to let his dad stop him from bringing a Muslim guest to his grandpa's.

"You are *very* welcome. Christmas is a time for guests, too. I'll make my father behave. I would like nothing more than for you to be with us—if it's okay with you."

"Your father probably does not know many Muslims, yes?"

"Not a soul."

"Then this will be a good opportunity for him."

Boyd couldn't help but smile. He took another bite of his lunch. Was there nothing this woman feared?

"You're right," he said while chewing. "But what about you?"

"I will be fine. I am going to ride your horse. This is an acceptable activity on Christmas?"

"Absolutely. I'll call you tonight to make arrangements. This means you'll be spending the night, but like I told you, my grandpa's house has a lot of rooms. You'll have your own bedroom. Is that okay?"

"It is fine." She gave a mischievous smile. "Although I might wish to sleep with the horses."

"That's okay. As long as you don't mind getting pooped on."

"Pooped?"

Boyd laughed. She knew the multisyllabic words, but she hadn't learned all the basics. How was he going to teach her this one?

CHAPTER THIRTY-SEVEN

Not once across more than five thousand kilometers in America had they exited a freeway into a city. Not in Buffalo or Cleveland or Chicago. On the same freeway, they rolled hour after hour amid rows of withered corn stalks and fallow farmlands blotched with snow. Farther west, they passed flat land and rolling lands bearing nothing but stones and yellowed grass. Lely never trod upon any of these places. Her shoes had known only the asphalt and cement of isolated rest stops and cinderblock hotels.

Now, surrounded by the mountains of Montana, they left as they always did, in the dark. Conifers drooped under heavy burdens of snow, more than Lely had ever seen. Patchy ice and gravel covered the freeway. When dawn came, pale sky expelled granules of snow in lonely arcs, none of it sticking. The road surface cleared and they drove faster. Near noon they descended onto a plateau of trees that reminded Lely of Aleppo pines.

"Washington," called out Shayma as they sped past a green sign with white English lettering. "Six more hours. We're almost home."

Home. What a strange word.

They passed a small city, Spokane. The pines thinned, then surrendered the land to sage, reminding Lely of the Badiyat al-Sham region in her homeland. She half-expected to spot a Bedouin herding goats or sheep.

At a rest stop, she and her friends stepped into a brisk wind that tugged at their black hijabs. A small child gaped at her, until her mother grabbed her hand and pulled her away. Lely did not mind—rarely did she spot anyone with a hijab at one of these rest stops. She felt her strangeness in this new land. Sometimes she had to put conscious effort into not staring at all the bare-headed women and their different colors and styles of hair.

"Ya Allah," she said to Qamar as they approached the bathroom. "I think my legs might fall off."

"We have legs?" said Qamar. "I wondered what that aching was below my hips."

As usual, when they exited the bathroom, Jack stood outside waiting. Shayma insisted that one of the two men always stand guard. It was common in America, she said, for gangs to grab Muslim girls and lock them into one of the big semi-trucks with the idling diesel engines.

Back in the van, Lely sensed the other girls' anxiety. If they had been driving in Syria, before the bombs fell, she could get her friends to do some of the games she and her siblings used to play when they were bored.

How wonderful it would be if she could make faces at the passing cars, the way she did after her first-grade year when her family took a long trip. She and her brother and sisters squished their noses against the windows. She had stretched her brows to look bug-eyed, let her tongue loll as though suffering from a fit. And when someone in another vehicle smiled or honked or gave them a dirty finger, they would roar with laughter

But not here. It was too scary.

Shayma said they must do nothing to bring attention to themselves. They must try to be invisible. They would be safe from gangs in their new home overlooking the lake, but they were not safe from gangs on the freeway.

"I'm in America," she murmured again.

. . .

"Look at the sign! Look. Look." Lely opened her eyes as they shot past a big road sign, lit in a brief flash of headlights. "That second word—it says Seattle," said Shayma. "Down these mountains, past this snow. And Bellevue comes before Seattle. That's where we're really going. We used to live in Seattle, but we had to move."

"Your bird is waiting," said Yana.

Stupid Yana. Teasing about sleeping with a man, teasing with Shayma.

"I hear that birds are elusive," added Sara.

Sara, too. Jokes a girl should never make when men were close enough to hear. They had their own little club in the backseat, Shayma and those two.

An hour later, with rain thumping the roof and a long line of taillights glistening on the windshield, for the first time in America they took an off-ramp inside a city. Bellevue. They turned this way and that, stopped at traffic lights that cycled green and yellow and red and green again before they could pass through. Tall buildings showed the lights of rooms whose contents Lely could only guess. One of them would become what she called home.

Jack turned sharply right mid-street and stopped where a steel garage door slowly rose, exposing a cement warren of lights and vehicles.

"Alhamdulillah, at last!" exclaimed Sara. "Wherever that lake is, once we're out, Jack should drive this stinking van into it."

"It will kill the fish," said Yana.

Jack, Sara, and Yana crammed themselves and their daypacks into the first elevator load. A minute later the elevator doors opened again, and Lely stepped in with her pack, squeezed with Shayma, Qamar, and Majd. They climbed slowly until it opened into a small foyer with a black wooden door, a brown leather chair on one side and a divan of the same material on the other. Shayma, who'd put on fresh lipstick and daubed herself with a scent that reminded Lely of vanilla, entered a code on a keypad and opened the door.

Inside, a short man in a white dress shirt and walnut-colored evening jacket eyed them. His chest was strong, his hair a mixture of brown and gray. In a sheath strapped above his knee, he had a long knife.

"Darsi!" exclaimed Shayma, leaning and kissing his cheek, eliciting half a smile. She looked past him, past the others who'd preceded them, beyond a chest-high table laden with plates of canapes, smoked meats and fish, olives and sliced peppers. An aroma of warm olive oil and garlic infused the room, stirring hunger in Lely—at last, something besides a chicken burger and fries.

"Hawk!" Like a pre-teen girl overcome at the sight of a puppy, Shayma squealed the foreign word. She dropped her pack, hurried around the table to a man with a rounded stomach and thigh-sized arms in a button-down steel gray shirt. He kept his arms at his sides, and Lely saw on one of them the tattoo of a predatory bird with oversized talons.

In a flirty tone, Shayma said something in English, wrapped her arms around his waist, pressed against him, pushed her mouth to his lips. And then ... *ya waily*, it couldn't be, but it was. Right in front of everyone she thrust her hips forward, planted her groin against his.

Everyone in the room, Lely noticed, mirrored her own reaction—everyone who'd been in the van, including the men, and four girls sitting in a lounge off to their left. She stared and they stared as this Hawk brought his beefy hand over Shayma's butt and pressed her closer. Shayma twisted away, whirled, and faced her audience with a satisfied smile.

"Put down your things! Eat something." She gestured toward the table. The girls in the lounge bounced up and moved toward the food. They looked older than Lely, garbed in clothes that outlined evidence of greater physical development—knee-length skirts and short-sleeved t-shirts with English words. Two wore hijabs and two did not. Majd and Jack joined them, picked up plates, and pushed close to the girls until their arms touched.

Lely and her friends stood in a semi-circle near the door and the man with the knife while the older girls and Jack and Majd served themselves. She felt her body almost frozen with shock and she wondered if her friends felt the same. On the other side of the table, Hawk and Shayma, each with an arm around the other's waist, oversaw the room as though patriarch and matriarch. Beyond them, an open passage led to the rest of the residence.

While she waited, Lely scanned the lounge. It was long and narrow, holding three separate seating areas, each with a different style of furniture—black leather, cushiony turquoise, white chenille. On the wall above a gas fireplace, a huge flatscreen television flashed images of gorgeous Arabic women, zooming out and in, zeroing in onto cleavage, the music frenetic and the singer an Arab male. It took a second for Lely to recognize the song—"El-Bint-El-Lebnanyi"—Lebanese Girl.

Majd, who'd shed his jacket so that his good arm, the one with the elephant tattoo, flexed well-pronounced muscles, sang the melody, substituting "Syrian" for "Lebanese."

Syrian girl, Syrian girl
I'm going to have her ...

Turning from the food, Jack produced a leering grin for his buddy before moving a finger down the back of the girl standing next to him, a girl with a turquoise hijab, a sea-green tee-shirt and an orange pleated skirt of a length one would never see in Dara'a. The girl elbowed him, eliciting a laugh from Jack and Majd. Still near the door, Lely backed farther away, bumped into a table, would have knocked over a vase if Darsi had not caught it.

The older girls and the men moved to the lounge area, giving Lely and her friends space to assemble their dinner, while Hawk and Shayma continued in their magnanimous posture.

"When will we see our families?" Yana dared to ask.

"This is your family," said Shayma. "Your sisters and your guardians. You're home now. Eat and enjoy."

"We see you already have your meal," teased Sara.

Lely gasped. At home—the kind of home she had known all her life until she left Za'atari—such a remark would provoke severe punishment. The Hawk looked oblivious. Perhaps he did not understand Arabic. Shayma, however, broadened her smile, licked her tongue around her lips, a gesture that widened Sara's eyes and transformed the tease in her expression to a gape of shock.

What kind of family was this?

CHAPTER THIRTY-EIGHT

Funny—waking up on Christmas with Shayma, and she didn't even believe in Christmas. Thought Jesus was a prophet, just not the son of God. Well, The Hawk wasn't too sure, either.

Still on his back, a single sheet and blanket over the two of them, The Hawk glanced at the back of Shayma's head. Her hair had been oily and clumped when she arrived last night, but she'd showered and shampooed and made the blackness of it gleam, brought out the softness. Now she slept as though she hadn't had a decent rest in a long time—nor a helping of indecency, either. He smiled. She'd mastered the craft, oh yeah. Rose up through the ranks, and she just seemed to like it. Like she liked it last night. Couldn't wait for it. Just dragged him away, right in front of the new girls.

What would his brother and family be doing in Delaware at this moment? Probably sitting around the tree, kids ripping up paper, an orgy of stuff. A day of that and then back to the investment bank, derivatives, hedge funds, credit-default swaps—screwing over people for fun and profit. None of it produced anything. No product. No customer. The fucker felt proud of it, too.

His brother could have his Christmas tree and stick it up his ass. Watch the little star pop out his mouth and plant him in the ground.

Out here on the West Coast, The Hawk ran a bona fide business. Real service for real needs. High value for high rollers. You take a risk. You stick your neck out. You outsmart the competition and you reap the rewards.

Smug. He caught himself feeling it, the very quality for which he condemned his brother. It was a recipe for failure. Take your eye off the road and smash into a tree. Better get his ass out of bed, Christmas or no Christmas.

He slipped out of bed, donned a white robe, walked to his desk. He had work to do.

A new batch of girls and nine men lined up for a virgin at $15,000 a pop. He had only four virgins, so he'd open a bidding war. Now *that* was a merry Christmas. All he had to do was get the girls ready. Docile and smiling. Not as rabidly hot as Shayma, but that wouldn't fit the virgin fantasy, would it?

Jack back. Majd back. End of vacation for the regular girls. Time to make some calls, yeah, we're up and running now, who do you want and when do you want her? Get the damn calendar filled and stop bleeding red ink.

He switched his computer to the webcams.

Just the way Shayma said it would be, bless her tart little heart—each of the new girls locked in her own room. Two still slept, the third sat on her bed, and the fourth stood holding a television remote. The one sitting up scooted onto her back, spread her arms out full length, and rolled from one side of the bed to the other. That was her, wasn't it? Yeah, Lely. *Holiday is just about over, Desert Lely.*

The Hawk rose from his chair, walked to Shayma, tied his robe shut—didn't want to give her any ideas. He shook her by the shoulder and bounced back.

She whirled up naked, arms outstretched, hands open, like she'd scratch out his eyes. Funny how sometimes she still woke that way. She blinked, took in her surroundings, smiled.

"Careful, Hawk. You could be hurt."

"And who'd make you happy then?"

"Nobody. There's nobody but you. I would have to nurse you back to full strength, but I have the equipment to do it."

"Get your robe on. We've got work to do."

She bent her head to peer at her breasts. "I can work like this," she said. "This *is* how I work."

"I thought you did it for fun."

"That is also how I work."

He gave her a quizzical look.

"I am only teasing, dearest," she said.

"We need to talk about the girls. I've got customers."

They sat at a small table next to the desk, overlooking Lake Washington in the dim gray dawn. In the foreground along the shore, Douglas firs leaned eastward, while little whitecaps rolled in the dark water. Except for a few vehicle lights, the floating bridge was abandoned. Raindrops clinging to the window dribbled down in jagged paths.

"That's our last batch of girls," he said. "I'm not sending you back there anymore. It's too hot. You heard what happened to Crabby?"

"No."

"Someone cut his throat."

The Hawk watched fear flicker in Shayma's eyes—just a flash of a second. She was too smart to let it linger, but he was glad to see it. It was healthier for her that way, both the fear and the covering of it.

"I won't miss it," she said. "Your Coast Guard stopped our ship an hour after we left it."

"So I heard. Jack called me."

"I told him to."

"Where are the phones?"

"What phones?"

"Smart woman."

"We bought new ones in Maine."

"Good. Tell me about the girls. You working your magic on them?"

"They are progressing. They will not be as shocked as they would have been. It's all natural, right? I prepared them and yet ... did you notice their surprise?"

"We've seen it before."

"If you put them to work now, they'd be frightened creatures."

"And that's not our market. Close your robe. You're distracting me."

Again she looked down at her breasts and when she raised her head she feigned a pout.

"I thought you liked me."

"Close your robe."

She stood, let the robe fall open a moment while fixing her eyes onto his, and slowly covered herself before sitting.

"Only woman I know who makes getting dressed look sexy."

"Who else have you been watching?"

"Well."

"Besides the girls."

"That's business. And they've been forming ice on their asses with all of you gone, so don't get me started. You want some coffee?"

"Yes, thank you."

He went to the counter to fill the coffee pot.

"Same program, Shayma," he called while the water ran. "Get them ready, one at a time, separately. When you're done, I want them thinking this is the best option they'll ever have. I want each of them believing the others are totally on board. Like they see the necessity of it, and none of them wants the alternative. Let's say five years to pay their debts and then they're free. Any of them going to be a problem?"

"I don't believe so. We—that is, Majd and Jack and I—had to have a private word with one of them. Her name is Lely. She's been fine ever since."

"I know about that one."

"Oh?"

"Crabby told me about her. Saucy. Hell of an artist. Drama queen." He added an extra scoop of coffee to the filter. Strength in all things.

"Try spending two weeks with her."

"She's a leader?"

"Somewhat."

"Then she's the first one. The others will follow. I want her ready by tomorrow night. No point dragging it on. We've got customers waiting."

Shayma moved her hands down her cheeks and turned her head to look out onto the gray morning. That was the gesture she always made when she was worried.

Good. A little anxiety kept a person sharp. She needed to prove her worth, the same as everyone else. Another year, and he'd cut her loose. He'd made a promise, and he always kept his promises.

CHAPTER THIRTY-NINE

On Christmas morning Boyd drove Abboud out of the city, north into rolling hills of mixed pastureland and conifers. Just before ten o'clock, he parked at his grandfather's ranch on top of a bluff, sheltered by Douglas firs. Wispy clouds streaked a pale blue sky. In front of the pickup, pasture sloped downward in varied shades of green until, a mile away, the faint blue of the Samish Bay formed the horizon.

Boyd lowered his window. "You hear that?" he asked.

"Hear what?"

"Nothing, that's what. No traffic. No sirens. Nobody shouting."

Grandpa Boyd marched out of the cedar log house, the crunch of his boots on gravel breaking the spell of silence. He wore a black leather vest over a maroon long sleeve Henley shirt that barely contained his beefy arms and shoulders. He had tied his long gray hair into a ponytail, and a blue paisley bandanna served as a headband.

If one were to meld Willie Nelson with a Harley biker, Grandpa Boyd would have been the outcome.

He strode to Abboud's door and opened it.

"Nawar," he announced as though she were a long-lost friend. "Russ told me he'd be bringing you. First time he's had a woman here since … well, since I don't know."

Boyd popped out of the car. "Grandpa. We're just friends."

Grandpa Boyd extended a hand which Abboud took as she emerged from the car. "Who said I said anything else? Nawar's a woman. What am I supposed to call her? An *it*?"

"Yeah, sure, Grandpa." Boyd resisted a smile. Same old mischief—innuendo followed by innocence.

Grandpa Boyd opened the door to the back of the cab and took out Abboud's coat and overnight suitcase. "Mind if I carry your things?"

"Thank you, Mr. Boyd," she said.

"Johnson'll do. Call me Johnson. That's my first name."

"Russell told me that."

"Can't call me Grandpa if you're just friends. But you never know. That could change, huh?" He winked. "By the way, that's a pretty, um …" He pointed at her head.

"Hijab," she said.

"Hijab. The color reminds me of lavender. Used to have a lot more lavender around here when Claire was alive. Not much of a woman's touch around here anymore."

Halfway to the house, Abboud paused to gaze toward the distant sea. "This is so lovely."

"I've got nothing to do with it," said Grandpa Boyd. "God gets the credit."

Abboud turned to him and smiled. "Yes. God gets the credit."

Boyd, too, admired the view. Clustered among the pastureland, cedars and Douglas firs flourished in the marine air.

Inside the house, Grandpa Boyd stopped at the foot of a staircase. "You sharing a room or—"

"Grandpa, you already know," said Boyd.

"Well, I'm sorry if I forgot."

"We share the same room only when we are under cover," said Abboud.

Grandpa Boyd raised his eyebrows.

Boyd didn't need to glance at her to picture Abboud's mischievous smile. "She doesn't mean blankets. She means when we were in Jordan. We passed ourselves off as a married couple. Nawar is playing with the term *undercover*."

The old man pushed out his lower lip and mocked an expression of puzzlement. "So, playing with the *term* undercover isn't the same as playing undercover. That it?"

"Yes," said Abboud. "Those are very different activities."

While Boyd momentarily wondered if one version could lead to the other variant, Grandpa Boyd turned and bounded up the steps. He and Abboud followed. On the upper floor, a sturdy rail of polished wood formed a perimeter around an open rectangle that looked down on the lower floor living room. Set back from the rail, on three sides open doors led to bedrooms. Grandpa Boyd entered the first one at the top of the stairs and set Abboud's coat and suitcase on a beige wingback chair before returning to the walkway. He pointed past the rail across the gap and nodded at Boyd. "That one over there is yours. When your dad gets here, I'm putting him downstairs."

"Is he on his way?" asked Boyd.

"Called a couple of hours ago to say he was leaving. Looks like we'll do Christmas before dinner tonight." He looked at Abboud. "Russ told me he talked to you and it's okay if we do Christmas."

"It is fine, yes," Abboud said. "In Islam we consider Jesus to be a great prophet. Many imams say we should not participate in a Christmas celebration, but some say it is not so bad. I am in the latter category."

"Your English sure is sophisticated," said Grandpa Boyd. "I hope I can keep up."

"That's why she's an interpreter," said Boyd.

"You learn it in England?" asked Grandpa Boyd.

"No," said Abboud. "I had classes in Syria, and also I listened to the BBC and practiced to sound like I was British. Also, my father received his engineering degree at Oxford."

Grandpa Boyd whistled in admiration. "You been there?"

"No. That was before I was born."

. . .

Half an hour later, in an enclosed horse arena, Boyd and Abboud stood next to Sockeye, a dark brown quarter horse with a white muzzle and white pasterns above his rear hooves. Having already tied a bridle on Sockeye's head with guidance from Boyd, Abboud held an English saddle. She sucked in a breath and lifted it onto the pad on the horse's back.

"Strong arms you got there," said Grandpa Boyd, sitting astride Klink, a walnut-colored quarter horse with a beige mane and tail.

A trio of barn swallows darted from one end of the arena to the other, the echoes of their fleeting chirps prompting Sockeye to prick his ears. Boyd eyed the saddle's position. "It needs to be forward a little. The pommel—you remember which part that is?"

"Yes."

"It needs to be on the highest point of the horse's withers. Lift it a little when you move it forward. You never want to slide a saddle against the direction of the hair growth."

Abboud adjusted the saddle, and Boyd pushed the girth off the top so that it hung on Sockeye's right side.

"And now I buckle the … what do you call it?" said Abboud.

"The girth. It needs to be tight. The last thing you need is for the saddle to slip when you're getting on."

He checked the girth after she buckled it. "Very good. Now I'll just hold the reins while you—"

In a single motion Abboud placed her left foot in the stirrup and pushed herself up and onto the saddle as though she'd done it a hundred times.

"You oughtn't to have done that," said Grandpa Boyd.

"Actually, that looked pretty good," said Boyd. "But Grandpa's right. I was going to explain that you need to make sure the horse is standing square, meaning both his legs are even and all the weight is even. Make sure he's calm and still. If I wasn't helping, you'd need to make sure you had the reins in your hand in case he starts to move. You can use the pommel to help yourself up if you need to, but it's better to spring up just like you did than to pull yourself up."

"You never told me what Sockeye means," she said, leaning forward to stroke the horse's neck.

"It's a fish," said Boyd. "A type of salmon." He handed her the reins.

"Oh, yes," she said. "I have seen that word at the grocery store." She pointed at a gingerbread brown Arabian mare with a black mane and tail, Boyd's other horse, tethered to a rail. "And so, Chinook—is that a fish, also?"

"Another species of salmon."

"If Russ wasn't riding when he was a kid," said Grandpa Boyd, "he was fishing. Both, if he could talk me into it."

"I don't recall having to work very hard to convince you." Boyd kept his attention on Abboud. "Don't do anything yet. Just sit for a minute and let him get used to you. He hasn't been ridden since October."

After shortening the right stirrup, he stepped back and examined the horse and soon-to-be rider. They both looked eager. The arena, too, looked ready, its surface of waxed sand and rubber particles damp. Grandpa Boyd must have watered and rolled it before they had arrived. From the adjoining stalls and overhead storage, a faint smell of grass hay and manure mixed with the familiar odor of horse sweat. It felt like home, more so than his apartment in Tukwila.

Sockeye tilted his head right and swung it up lightly. For a brief moment, anxiousness showed on Abboud's face, but she held her back straight, like a seasoned rider.

"You're sure you've never ridden?" said Boyd.

"Never." She adjusted the reins. "This is like a dream. I thought I would never ride a horse."

"Your posture is excellent. How do you know to do that?"

"When I was twelve and when I was sixteen, I watched the Olympics on television. I studied the riders and imagined I was one of them."

Sockeye swung his head again, but he kept his legs still. "He does that when he wants to get going," said

Boyd. "Most horses get used to not being ridden, but Sockeye's different. He likes the attention. He likes trail rides more than arena work, but either one is fine with him. Anyway, now that we're back from the Middle East, I'll get out here more frequently and give him and Chinook the attention they deserve."

"Russ earned these two horses when he was in the fifth grade," said Grandpa Boyd. "That was after he proved he could handle the chores that came with them. How old are you now, Russ? Thirty?"

"Thirty-one."

"Most likely those horses have got another five years left, maybe more."

"They're a lot more mellow than they used to be," said Boyd. "All right, Abboud, if you want Sockeye to walk, give him a nudge with your knees. Just a little one and leave it at that. The reins work the way you'd think. A light pull left for left, right for right. Lift up if you want him to stop. Let's give it a try."

Abboud set Sockeye moving at a slow walk along a wall that separated a small set of bleachers from the arena floor. Boyd strolled beside her before veering away to stand in the center, as he'd often watched his grandfather do when Boyd Farms used to board more than a dozen horses from affluent families in the Skagit County region. Johnson Boyd coached young riders, mostly girls, in the sport of dressage. Some of them took a liking to his grandson Russell Boyd, but he was shy during his pre-teen and teenage years.

Soon, with minimal direction from Boyd, Abboud and Sockeye were doing figure eights at a trot. She wore a look of entrancement, in that zone where the horse and the rider merge their minds. Scratching Chinook between her ears, Boyd watched Abboud and wondered if there were anything she couldn't do.

He untethered Chinook and mounted. "I'll show you a few more things, Abboud, and then how about all three of us head down to the beach? Is the trail in good shape, Grandpa?"

"Last time I looked."

"And when was that?"

"Yesterday."

. . .

The trail to the beach was muddy, the result of previous rains. They crossed one county road and began crossing a second one fifty yards north of a white farmhouse. Near where the trail crossed, a boy and a girl rode bicycles that looked brand new—Christmas presents, apparently.

"Horses!" shouted the boy, who couldn't have been older than kindergarten age. He changed directions and charged toward them.

By then, Grandpa Boyd had crossed the road. Sockeye, with Abboud on board, was in the middle, and Boyd's horse had a front leg on the pavement. Sockeye stopped cold and turned his attention toward the oncoming bicycle.

Boyd reined Chinook and dismounted. "Easy, Sockeye," he called. The kid was speeding straight at the horse. Was he nuts? Where were his parents?

Sockeye swiveled his head toward the boy and reared half a foot. Abboud held on, but Boyd hurried to the horse.

The boy's face changed from gleeful to terrified. Showing no signs of slowing, he cried out. Sockeye wheeled around and faced the boy. Abboud pulled her feet from the stirrups, sprang off the horse, and landed next to Russell. From the other side of the road, Grandpa dismounted Klink and turned toward them, but there was no time to grab the reins, no time to guide the panicked horse away.

Boyd jumped forward and grabbed the boy's handlebar an instant before he would have crashed into Sockeye. The boy flew forward. His helmet smashed into Boyd's arm, and he tumbled from the bike. Abboud grabbed Sockeye's reins.

"Kenny!" His sister, who'd given pursuit, stopped behind him.

"What's going on, kid?" said Boyd. "You got brakes on that bike?"

But all the boy could do was look at him, dumbstruck with fear. He moved his mouth, but several seconds went by before he sputtered, "I forgot."

Despite the throbbing in his arm where the kid had smashed into it, Boyd couldn't stop himself from chuckling.

"Well, I'll be snookered," said Grandpa Boyd.

Abboud hunched down to face the boy. "Would you like to pet the horses?" she asked.

The worst of the fear left the boy's face, and what looked like a mix of interest and apprehension took its place.

"I would!" called the girl.

From the house, a woman's voice shouted, "Kenny! Angela! Get back here." Boyd looked up and saw a woman wearing what looked like a red Christmas sweater standing on the porch. "I'm so sorry!" she called toward him.

"Not a problem," he shouted back.

They continued on the trail, with only Grandpa Boyd on his horse. After a few minutes, Sockeye calmed, and soon all three were on horseback for the final stretch.

When they reached the beach of sand and pebbles, the wind blew harder, a westerly skimming the San

Juan Islands and the Rosario Strait. Clouds straddled the dark green silhouettes of the islands and the waters of the sound. Peeping as they moved, plovers scurried across the beach, stabbing their curved beaks into the sand. Twenty yards offshore, gulls commandeered a rock, shrieking in their places, eyeing the shallow seawater. There was no surf here, not on the sheltered eastern edge of the Puget Sound, but the tide was low, exposing seaweed and barnacled logs.

Boyd, his grandfather, and Abboud dismounted their horses. The sound of the wind and the calls of the birds harmonized in a soft song. The horses snorted contentedly, and no one spoke. They walked a hundred yards, not another human in sight, reversed course, and reluctantly mounted the horses for the return trip home.

* * *

Just after four, as the day grew dark, Jeb Boyd drove into the parking area in a silver pickup that looked as though it could pull a house off its foundation. Boyd jumped up from the Yahtzee game he was playing with his grandfather and Abboud, and he hurried out the door.

What would the mood of his father be, especially when he beheld Abboud in her lilac hijab? Two times the night before, Boyd had taken out his phone and selected his father's number, but he had stopped short of calling. Maybe now, before the others came outside, he could prepare his dad for the sight of a Muslim woman.

His father had already gotten out of the pickup when Boyd reached the parking area. As always, Jeb Boyd wore the accoutrements of a cowboy—a charcoal gray cowboy hat, twelve-inch boots with intricate stitching on the shaft, blue jeans, a tan canvas field jacket. The garb played well at his steakhouse on the north end of Spokane, but it struck Boyd as strange when he showed up that way at the actual ranch where he had grown up. He hadn't ridden a horse since forever.

"Hey," he called after his father had retrieved a duffel bag from the passenger seat.

"Howdy, son," answered his father.

"How was traffic?"

"Snowing at the pass. Clear sailing ten miles west."

They shook hands and said merry Christmas. His father's long sideburns had grown more gray since they'd last interacted in person, the day after Christmas a year ago in Spokane.

"I brought a friend," said Boyd, "but don't act like she's a girlfriend. She's just a friend."

"She's a girl and she's a friend and she can't be a *girlfriend*?"

"You sound just like Grandpa."

They turned toward the house.

"Her name is Nawar."

"Nawar?"

"She's a colleague from work and yes, she's Muslim. She likes horses, so I invited her."

His father stopped, tilted his head, wore a look of … what was it? Puzzlement? Irritation?

"What day is it today?" said his father, as though he'd forgotten.

"Jesus, Dad, don't do this."

"You forget how you got that scar on the side of your face?"

"It's Christmas, all right? Birthday of the Prince of Peace. I need you to act like it, Dad. I need you to make a promise. Otherwise … otherwise, we'll leave. Is that what you want? Because we can leave right now."

"Hold your horses. I base my judgments on evidence. You brought her here, so she can't be too crazy. I won't say a goddamn thing."

"Just be nice, Dad. Give her a smile. She's not the one who shot me. In fact, she saved my life."

The front door opened, and Grandpa Boyd stuck his head out. "You two coming in or are we eating dinner outside?"

. . .

Everyone exchanged gifts—Boyd gave Abboud a gift certificate for University Bookstore and she gave him a bag of Najjar Turkish Coffee without cardamom but with a package of Neccos taped to the bag. They feasted on a dinner featuring precooked turkey slices and gravy.

Toward Abboud, Boyd's father had projected a professional charm, as though she were the Spokane mayor having a meal at his restaurant. With each glass of wine, he grew more and more friendly, until it seemed Abboud had evolved from the mayor to a daughter or a favorite niece. Now, in the early evening, they sat in the living room, Boyd and Abboud together on the sofa and his grandfather and father on separate chairs, all in an arc facing the fireplace.

Boyd's father leaned sideways and touched the arm of the sofa near Abboud. "Russell tells me you saved his life. How's an interpreter do that?"

She glanced at Boyd, but he didn't know what to say or what gesture to adopt.

"He speaks Ay-rab enough to get himself in trouble." His smile extended—Boyd had seen it too many times. It always came after he'd been drinking, and it always disguised something mean.

"It's FBI work, Dad," he said. "You know we can't talk about it except in general terms."

"So you're still on the case?"

"Yes, we are."

"You know …" His father paused, took a drink of pinot noir, and held the glass in his hand. "How long ago was it"—he directed a stern look at Boyd—"that you told me you'd never set foot in an Ay-rab nation for the rest of your life?"

"Dad," said Boyd.

"Don't you go startin' things up," said Grandpa Boyd.

"Said you can't trust them. You train them and you give them weapons and they turn around and they put a fucking bullet next to your ear. Wasn't that why you didn't reenlist?"

"Jeb, why don't you go outside and take a hike?" said Grandpa Boyd.

Abboud caught Boyd's eyes. She didn't need to speak in order for him to understand her question. Had he really said such a thing?

"What? Are you sending me to my room?" said Boyd's father. "All I'm doing is pointing some things out. Honesty is the best policy, isn't it?"

"Jesus Christ, Jeb. Damn right I'm sending you to your room."

Boyd stood. "Nawar, would you please come with me?"

Abboud rose and Boyd took her hand, and it didn't matter that they weren't a couple.

"I'd send you out to your goddamn truck and all the hell way back to Spokane if you hadn't drunk so much goddamn wine," said Grandpa Boyd. "Jesus, if you won't leave the room, I will."

Boyd pulled Abboud away from the living room toward the front door, while Grandpa Boyd went to the kitchen.

Boyd's father raised his voice. "My, aren't we a sensitive bunch? Go on out with your Ay-rab non-girlfriend. Sure changed your mind about the Ay-rabs, haven't you?"

At the door, Boyd spun back toward his father.

"You know damn well I didn't say those things." Boyd struggled to keep his voice even. Rage seized his body. His jaw was tight. "You're twisting words to fit your warped view of the world, and we're all sick of it."

He stepped into the night with Abboud and closed the door. She pulled her hand free, and he kicked the ground so hard that pieces of gravel rattled off both his and his father's pickup.

He looked at Abboud. "I'm so sorry. You don't have to stay here. I can take you home. We'll come ride another time."

"What is it you were telling me about things you cannot control? You did nothing wrong. Come on. We should walk."

"You don't have a coat."

"Neither do you. We will not go far."

They walked away from the barn to the single-track driveway. Behind them, one of the horses snorted from inside its stall. An owl hooted, gentle and soft. Far in the distance, a train clattered on its tracks. The night was cold and starry.

When they reached the paved road, they slowed their pace. A couple hundred yards in front of them, the Steward house blinked an array of colored Christmas lights.

"I never said what he said I said. That's not how I feel."

"For a while I was beginning to think you were unfair in what you said about your father."

"Yeah. Well, he was hiding it."

"So was it one of the Iraqi soldiers who shot you?"

"Doesn't matter. But, yeah, that's what happened."

"How can you say it does not matter?"

"It matters, but it doesn't matter now. It's history."

"Certainly it matters. Someone you thought was on your side shot you. Did you kill him?"

"Not me, personally, but—"

"Good. He deserved to die. As for your father, an Arab shot his son. I understand your father's anger. I have felt it myself."

They spooked a half dozen dairy cattle, who dashed on pounding hooves away from the barbed wire fence along the road. The Stewarts' house was only a hundred yards away now.

"Bashar Assad is an Alawite," said Abboud while they continued to walk. "Alawite soldiers killed my husband. Alawite gangs terrorized my city of Dara'a. They have a special name, Shabbihas. They pulled young men from homes on my street, boys I had grown up with. They shot them and left them to die. After the Shabbihas left, if anyone came out to help our young men, snipers would shoot them. There was a time when all I wanted was to kill Alawites. It did not matter if I died as long as I could kill at least one Alawite.

"If an Alawite came to Za'atari Refugee Camp, something bad could happen to him. He might be a good Alawite. Maybe he hates Assad and the Shabbihas, but no one would trust him. They would think he is a spy. He would never have a chance to show that he is a good person."

"Your people have suffered atrocities," said Boyd.

"We've suffered casualties. That's different."

"You do not call it an atrocity when Muslim terrorists fly jets into your buildings?"

They stopped short of the Stewart house.

"You're right," said Boyd. "I was just a kid when that happened. But it stuck with me. That's part of why I joined the army. But the scale of it was different. Assad has wiped out whole cities. It's like you've suffered your own Twin Towers over and over again."

"The emotions are the same. I wanted to kill an Alawite. Your father wants his revenge, also."

Christmas lights wrapped around trees, a picket fence, and the roofline at the Stewart house. A giant Santa Claus stood next to a sled pulled by elk-sized reindeer, all the figures draped in blinking reds and greens and blues.

"We're a long way from Za'atari," said Boyd.

"We should turn around, yes?" said Abboud. "I am getting cold."

"You still have that same anger?" Boyd asked as they began the walk back.

"No. But if I am honest, if I were to meet an Alawite, I would be suspicious."

"But you wouldn't automatically hate him? Or her?"

"I hope not. There is an Alawite woman who goes to my mosque. She came to me when she learned I was from Dara'a. She said she was sorry for what her people have done. I must assume there are many like her."

A pair of headlights turned onto the road. They were the headlights of a big truck—his father's truck.

Boyd groaned. "He shouldn't be driving."

It took less than a minute for his father to reach them. The driver's window lowered.

"My bad, son." Although it was difficult to read much in his father's face, Boyd thought he detected remorse. "Nawar, I'm sorry. I know that's not good enough. I'm leaving. I'm going to a hotel, so you don't have to worry about me driving. I don't know what else to say."

The window rose and the truck pulled away.

Abboud clasped Boyd's hand. "Your fingers are freezing," she said.

"So are yours." As his father's taillights faded from view, the growing warmth from her hand eased the churning in his stomach. He tried to push away the memory of what his father had done on this night, tried to focus on the woman next to him. Her touch felt more immediate and consequential. Was it a one-time gesture of solidarity and support, or did it mean something more?

CHAPTER FORTY

Still in her pajamas, Lely lay on her side on the slate tiled floor to peer underneath the door. She saw what she saw yesterday, which was nothing except a few inches of hardwood floor. A moment ago, when she pressed her ear to the wall on the left side of the room, she heard the same thing she heard yesterday: nothing.

She rose from the floor and grasped the handle of the door. It remained locked, just as it was twenty minutes ago. Yesterday it had opened on only four occasions—breakfast, lunch, and dinner, plus a fourth time when Shayma collected the trays and the dishes.

"Why can't I see my friends?" Lely had asked.

"Your friends are fine," Shayma replied. "We will talk more tomorrow."

And this morning meant that tomorrow was now.

She had already studied the heating vents—only a small puppy could squeeze through them, if she could remove the cover. She'd examined the window wall on the right side of the room. It provided a view of a wide free world with a big lake and city buildings, but it did not open to a balcony so that she could climb up or down the way characters in movies did.

She retreated from the door and climbed back onto her gigantic bed. It was big enough to be a raft, and the floor of turquoise slates could easily have been the sea. She imagined her whole family alive on it with her, rowing on the waves, putting distance between them and the killing ground that was Syria. They would land at a lonely beach below a farmhouse where a family would take pity on them. They would start a whole new future.

The room itself was bigger than one of the Za'atari trailers. It had a long wooden dresser with t-shirts and socks and pajamas and jeans and one drawer with nothing in it but panties, none of which was something she would actually wear, not unless she were married and her husband was kind. It had a walk-in closet with eleven luxurious abayas in all the colors of the rainbow. The bathroom had a vanity, a mirror, and a gigantic tub with jacuzzi jets. Above it was the one place in her whole room she hadn't yet checked.

She picked up an upholstered wooden chair, carried it into the bathroom, and placed it inside the tub. After peering up the high wall to judge the distance between her and a thin opening of outside light, she climbed onto the chair and raised her arms, but she could not reach a recess in the wall where the little window was. She jumped straight up. At the apex she glimpsed a flash of gray sky. She jumped again, clutched at the ledge, strained to boost her body up, up, but her fingers slipped, and she landed awkwardly, almost tumbled off the chair.

Her breaths came quicker now, and not just from the effort to rise to the level of the window. She wanted out.

She had not come to America for this.

She sat on the edge of the tub, the chair at her back, and lowered her head into her hands. There had to be a way.

She would not cry.

Perhaps she could burst out her room when Shayma arrived for the promised talk. If Shayma tried to prevent the escape, she'd punch her in the jaw, hard, really hard. No one would stop her. She'd scratch eyes, she'd throw plates, she'd grab the knife from that Darsi old man at the door, and she'd make them open it. She'd leave. And so what if the American police threw her in jail and kept her there for a year and flew her back to Syria for Assad and his soldiers? If she could kill even one of them, it would be worth anything they would do to her.

From her spot on the tub she heard a familiar metallic click, the sound of Shayma inserting the card key she'd seen that first night when they deposited her in this room.

She hopped up and closed the bathroom door. How would she explain the chair in the tub?

"I'm on the toilet," she called.

The knob to the bathroom door turned and she jumped back before it swung open. Shayma stood there in a lemon-colored skirt that did not reach her knees and a tight blue pullover sweater. Attired in a short-sleeved shirt that exposed the elephant tattoo on his unbroken arm, Majd stood behind her, expressionless.

"How was the view?" Shayma asked, eying the chair in the tub. She glanced at Majd and nodded toward Lely.

Lely opened her mouth, but no words came. Majd stepped into the bathroom, collected a handful of her hair, spun her out the doorway and into the bedroom. Grasping her hair as though a leash on a dog, he marched her to the bed and flung her onto to it. Lely scrambled to the midpoint of the headboard and whirled to face them. Majd stepped back while Shayma strolled to the side of the bed, her face calm, confident, assured of her command.

"I've been watching you this morning," she said. "You and Qamar and Yana and Sara. None of them put a chair in their tubs. You'd better hope you did not scratch the surface, because then you would owe us even more. Majd, bring me that chair."

After he retrieved it and placed it where she indicated, Shayma sat, regarding Lely for a while. Lely wedged herself against the headboard as tightly as possible. They'd closed the door to her room. She'd have to get hold of the key card if she were somehow to escape. Probably Majd had it. Shayma had no pockets on the flimsy attire she wore.

"Lely." Shayma's voice was calm. Lely could hear herself panting, heard the gasps escape from her throat.

"Lely, look at me."

She forced her eyes away from Majd.

"You do not like it here? No, no, look at me, don't look down. Majd will do you no harm, not as long as you have my protection. Do you want my protection? Answer me. Look at me."

What would *yes* mean? Agreement that she didn't like it here? Or that she wanted Shayma to protect her from Majd? She nodded, shivering inside.

"I would like to protect you. You are very valuable. But it is clear you do not like it here. No, no. Don't be alarmed. We can offer you a choice."

She put onto the bed a duffle bag she'd been carrying, unzipped it, and tossed some clothing at Lely.

"Put these on."

Lely glanced at Majd standing at the foot of the bed.

"No, no. He stays. Get used to it."

She looked toward the open bathroom.

"No, no. You will change your clothing right here. The female body is a lovely sight. You have nothing to be ashamed about."

Lely brought her knees up to her chest, wrapped her arms around her legs, squeezed into a tight ball. They couldn't make her do it.

"Do you want Majd to do it for you? He knows how to remove pajamas. But I'm afraid his method is ... less comfortable."

No, she did not want Majd to do it. She did not want him to touch her ever again. But she found she could not move, that fright had frozen her on the outside while she trembled on the inside.

"Lely. Lely. Look at me, not at Majd. I will give you five seconds to get started. One ... two ...three ..."

Still pressed against the headboard, Lely turned away from them.

"... Four ..."

She pulled her right arm out of the sleeve, followed with her left arm, reached down and lifted the pajama shirt up over her head. She felt behind her for the clothing Shayma had tossed.

"Good. Keep going."

The brassiere was red and sheer. She put it on, and after that a thin white shirt without buttons at the top. In the same manner, she removed her pajama bottoms, feeling her face flush, her heart beating, her breath tense, and she put on the red panties and the dark purple skirt that barely covered her hips. Finally, she removed her blue and red bangles and set them on her pillow—her mother would die a second time if she saw Lely like this.

"Turn around, Lely."

She obeyed, pressing her knees against the bed, her legs squeezed together and tucked behind her.

Shayma nodded her head—a kind of appraisal, one that a man might give.

"Now, right where you are, stand up."

No, she wouldn't.

"Majd."

He stepped past Shayma. Lely stood.

"Look at me, Lely. Your lips are dry. Lick them."

Majd couldn't make her do that. But he could try.

She licked her lips.

"Good. We're going for a little drive. It's cold outside, so I'll loan you a nice coat. It looks like fur, but it isn't. I hate fur—it's so cruel. We're going to visit a different place where you can live and work if you decide you don't like it here."

Work. Doing what? Where would they bring her in her tiny skirt and the disgusting bra and the shirt that didn't do anything to hide it? But she knew. It wouldn't be a department store or a restaurant or a business office.

"I like it here," she whispered.

"What did you say? Look at me. Speak up."

"I like it here."

"Oh, I do hope so. This *is* the safest place for you by far. But I want you to be absolutely certain, and so we are going to visit this other place. When we are there you will say nothing unless I ask you to. You will make no sudden moves and you will certainly not try to run or any other kind of nonsense, because I cannot predict what Majd will do if you try such a thing. Do you understand?"

"I like it here."

"Answer my question. Do you understand what I just said?"

"Yes."

"Good. I hope you will decide you like it here even more when we're finished with our visit—*if* we decide to take you back. We take very good care of our girls. By the way, you will see them again on the way out. Not your friends—your older sisters. They're watching television in the living area. Tell them hello when we pass by. Can you say hello to them?"

"Yes."

"Good."

Moments later, close to the end of the hallway, she heard Arabic and recognized the sitcom *El Kabeer Awi* and remembered her parents watching it when she was a little girl. They passed a kitchen and reached the lounge, and the four girls, all wearing multi-colored pajamas and no hijabs, moved their eyes from the big television screen to her bare legs and see-through shirt.

Two of them whistled. They all laughed, and Lely burned with shame.

"Remember to say hello," said Shayma, carrying the fake fur coat.

"Salam." Her throat felt so tight it amazed her she could squeeze out the word.

"Special delivery?" called one of the girls. Tall with rose-hued blonde hair, she lounged on the same turquoise sofa where Lely sat two nights ago.

"Shall we take you also?"

"Oh, no, Miss Shayma."

In the parking garage Lely and Shayma took seats in the back of a green sedan, and Majd drove them out into the cold gray day.

CHAPTER
FORTY-ONE

Abboud set the paper plate with the shawarma on the table in front of Boyd, then took her own plate to the chair opposite him. She wore a forest green hijab, lemon yellow sweatshirt, and blue jeans. Those deep-set dark eyes which had seemed haunted when he met her six weeks ago now carried a mysterious aura, intriguing, wise. Funny, how his perception had changed once he'd gotten to know her.

He took a bite. "Wow. This hummus. I don't think I could buy that pre-made stuff in the grocery store ever again."

"What is in the store I call emergency hummus," said Abboud. "Only when one is desperate."

"So, uh, what do you think you'll do the rest of the day?"

She stood up. "Help my aunt and uncle here at the store. Like right now."

A thin woman with an eggplant-colored shawl and a brown scarf over her dark hair placed items from her shopping basket onto the front counter. Abboud went to the register to scan and bag the groceries. Beyond her, by the window, a family of four perched on stools, savoring paper bowls of Bakdash. Boyd decided he'd buy a cone when he finished. It was a damn shame he'd spent a week holed up in Amman without the ability to stop by the new Bakdash parlor, one that utilized the same recipe as the original in Damascus.

Amani Haddad strolled out from an adjoining hallway, carrying a metal pan with kitchen towels draped over the top. Flat bread, no doubt. He set it on a counter against the front wall.

"Mr. Boyd," he said in his customarily animated voice, "you have not told me about horse riding. How did Abboud do?"

"Like she'd been riding for years."

"Not true!" Abboud returned the table, having finished with the customer. "I froze yesterday when a little boy decided to run us over on his bicycle. The boy panicked and I panicked. He forgot how to use his brakes and I forgot how to move my horse."

Mr. Haddad's eyes widened. "He ran into your horse?"

"No. Russell jumped in front and grabbed the ... what do you call those things?"

"Handlebars," said Boyd.

"Ah! FBI agent stops attack. I assume the boy is in jail now?" Mr. Haddad held his arms forward, miming a man in handcuffs.

"Ten years," said Boyd. "He's lucky he didn't get the electric chair."

The shopkeeper looked at Abboud. "Remind me to check the brakes on my bicycle."

He returned to the tray and removed the towel, revealing the flatbread, its fresh-baked aroma mixing with the spices emanating from the meats inside the deli case. "You want a piece?" he asked Boyd.

"No, thank you. I need to leave room for Bakdash."

Close by, Mr. Haddad placed the bread under a warmer. Abboud sat back at the table. By the time she and Boyd finished their shawarmas, the shopkeeper had left the area and returned with a platter of lamb, placing pieces of it in individual paper trays.

Boyd lowered his voice. "I need to give those horses more attention. I figure, every other weekend. Doesn't have to be overnight. Leave early in the morning, come back at night. Less traffic, probably ninety minutes each way. You're welcome to come along. I mean, not every time, unless, I mean, if you want to come every time, that's okay."

"I would like that. Not every time, of course."

"It's okay. Every time, if you want. It's just that I understand you have things to do yourself, and so there might be times you can't." *God. He was sounding like a fool.*

"Of course."

"So I'll let you know when I'm going. It won't be this coming weekend but probably the next one." *When was that? Ten days from now?*

Too long.

He asked, "So, what are you going to do this week? Anything exciting?"

"Besides work? Back to the dojang. Maybe even tonight, if it seems quiet enough here. Certainly on Thursday."

"That reminds me. The way you handled yourself when we were assaulted. I had hand-to-hand combat training in the army and a little at Quantico, nothing like what you did. I was thinking maybe I should take some lessons."

"I agree. You should take some lessons."

"Is there room in your class?"

"I do not actually take a class. I am sparring. Sometimes the sabom-nim watches and tells us things to improve."

"Sabom-what?"

"Sabom-nim. Like an honored teacher. A master."

"Oh. So does your place … your dojang … does it offer lessons to beginners? Is it the same time you're sparring?"

"Yes. In a different part of the building. I know you would be welcome." She showed her mischievous smile. "Every time, if you want. Unless you have something else to do, which I would understand."

"You're mocking me."

"Never."

"Yes, you are. But it's fine. I'm kind of acting like an idiot."

She glanced at Mr. Haddad, who was spending more time rearranging items in the deli case than what was necessary. Outside, the day was growing dark. Soon, the early dinner customers would arrive.

"Come with me," she said. "There is something I wish to give you." She put their paper plates in the trash and led Boyd down an aisle of crackers and chips before stopping next to the cookies toward the back. "My uncle can be … what is it you say? A busy-body?"

"He likes to know everyone else's business?"

"If by *business* you mean their personal lives, yes."

"Is he really your uncle?"

"No. But he and my Auntie Karam are very special to my heart. They have been kind. They have taught me much about America."

She picked up a package of date-filled cookies known as maamoul in the Arab world. "I remember how much you liked these biscuits at Za'atari," she said. "They are not the same as homemade, but you will like them with your coffee."

"Of course I'll pay for them."

"Nonsense. Consider it my share of gas money for our trip to your grandfather's ranch." She leaned closer. "You want us to spend time together. So do I. That is what friends do."

Friends. That sounded okay. More than okay—*excellent.*

A chime rang as the door to the shop opened. Facing the front of the store, Boyd saw a man walk past the aisle, and his breath froze. He turned to hide his face and pulled Abboud by the hand to the back wall, where paper products lined the shelves.

"Someone we know very well just walked into your store," he whispered.

CHAPTER FORTY-TWO

After they crossed the big lake that Lely had seen from the window of her room, she peered at the forest of skyscrapers and the steel beams dangling from cranes that tickled the underbellies of clouds. They passed another lake, this one bearing float planes and numerous marinas with fancy boats like the kind she'd occupied at the Port of Tripoli.

Ya Allah, if only she could be back there now! If only she had been home with her family when the barrel bombs had struck. She pictured her spirit-self elevated off the ground, observing her corpse lying inside a dark and crumbled building. Would there have been pain? How much did her family suffer before they died?

Her mind drifted back to the moment, to this car, its tan leather seats, its English-lettered electronic displays up front on the dashboard. This woman Shayma and that man Majd were going to force her into doing things she didn't want to do, she was sure of it now. Would there be mercy for her in the afterlife? When the blue-faced angels Munkar and Nakir, with their wild hair and big teeth, appeared at her grave, what would they decide?

She shivered, despite the warm coat Shayma had loaned her and despite the increasing heat inside the car.

When they exited the freeway, Shayma opened her purse and removed a tube of lipstick.

"Lean to me. I'm going to pretty you up."

Lely leaned across the seat and offered her lips. She could feel the phlegm at the back of her throat and the taste of fear, and it would be a simple matter to draw it up and spew it out. Splat! What a lovely sight it would be, the mess on Shayma's face, the contorted scowl of her rage. Lely would laugh, even if they beat her.

But she saw instead how like a dog she was, cowering, tail pushed down, eyes pleading for a pat on the head. Ya Allah, how she detested herself, doing exactly as she'd been commanded. Would this surrender matter when Munkar and Nakir pronounced their judgment?

Majd turned onto a four-lane road with stoplights, hamburger places, car lots, motels and large buildings selling tires, garden plants, lumber. She closed her eyes.

Perhaps she could will herself into a kind of hibernation. If she could make her body an empty casement of flesh and bones, she, the real Lely, could flee. She could numb herself, turn as gray and cold as the day outside. In Za'atari she had seen people like this, people who breathed but otherwise showed little signs of life. She imagined herself as one of them.

But her bare legs shook. Her heart raced. Something like a cramp pinched the muscles in the back of her neck. She could not disentangle herself from her body. What was happening was truly happening.

Majd parked on the side of the highway next to what she recognized as a two-story motel. On the walls, beige paint had peeled off to reveal large patches of bare stucco. She counted six bright blue doors across both the top and bottom floors. Only one vehicle, a small pickup with faded black paint, occupied a parking space in front of one of the rooms. Whatever they expected of her at this place, it was going to be bad. Shayma had implied that they might leave her here. She would never see Qamar again, or Sara or Yana. Her life would be hideous.

"Wait for me," said Shayma, who exited the car and went around the back before opening Lely's door. Lely felt petrified, glued to her seat, but Shayma cured the condition by grasping her hand and yanking her out. "If you want me to leave you at this place," Shayma said, "all you have to do is continue to resist."

"I am sorry," said Lely.

"Then you'd best get your sorry self moving, or you'll be even more sorry."

With Majd on Lely's left and Shayma on her right, she strode toward a blue door on the far left of the building. As she walked, Lely tugged down her skirt, providing at best another inch of coverage. Wind wrapped its cold hands around her legs, rose up from beneath her coat to her back and chest. She had not appeared in public without a hijab since she was a little girl. She had not appeared bare-legged to the tops of her thighs ever.

When they reached the building, Shayma pounded at the door six times while

Majd hovered a couple of meters behind them. A television blared inside the room, competing with the sounds of cars and trucks whooshing along the street.

From behind the door a man shouted some short sound, probably an English word, bristling with annoyance. After a moment, the door opened, and a heavy-set man stood there with an unshaven face and the smell of body odor and cigarettes and a megadose of cologne. He wore red pajama bottoms and a gray t-shirt with a cartoony horse and English writing. The outside frigidity and the cranked-up superheat of the apartment collided at the intersection where both parties appraised each other, until Shayma clasped Lely's wrist and walked inside. The man closed the door, leaving Majd outside.

Three women sat on a low-lying blue couch with a rip and a brown cup-shaped stain on the armrest. The nearest, whose face bore Asian features, wore a white t-shirt with no bra, pink pajama bottoms, and fuzzy green slippers. A long length of ash fell off the cigarette pressed between her lips. It joined the gray-blotched carpet that may have once been green or brown. The woman in the middle was white-skinned with brown hair pointing every direction, and the woman on the far end may have been Arab. All three stared at a loud cartoon featuring stunted characters and misshapen faces. The women were either young or they were old—Lely could not decide.

The man led them past the women to a vacant spot in front of an easy chair. Shayma said something in English and the man laughed, his breath an old shoe with a trace of mint. She grabbed Lely by the collar of the coat, pulled her close, and unbuttoned it top to bottom. Stepping aside, she left Lely to face the man.

"Take it off," she said in Arabic.

She had to do it, or else Shayma would leave her there with that man and those women, but ... *ya Allah,* his eyes were drilling into her, his mouth set in a leer.

She felt Shayma's hand, almost like a caress across the side of her head. Like a lover, Shayma put her lips an inch from her ear.

"Either you take it off or he does," she whispered, "Give it to me and I will hold it for you."

Lely stared at her feet, removed her left arm and then her right from the sleeves, but held the coat to her chest. Shayma stepped forward and tugged it away.

"Look up," she said above the noise of the television, and from her peripheral vision Lely noted the woman with Arab features turn her head to observe. Did she understand the language?

Lely raised her head. She felt the man's eyes rip away her sheer shirt and the red bra she knew to be quite visible, and so she peered at a spot on the wall above the easy chair. Her legs wobbled, but she stayed upright. He reached a hand toward her, placed two fingers beneath her chin, and with his eyes demanded that she observe him, after which he let his vision roam down and up her body. He moved his hands to her shoulders, spun her half a turn, and she shivered from the feel of his eyes studying her from behind. He brought her back around, face to face. His eyes never leaving her body, he reached behind him and groped for a lit cigarette propped on an ashtray next to the chair.

She wanted to punch him. She wanted to run. She wanted to cry.

When he finally turned his attention back to Shayma they said things in English until Shayma clutched Lely's forearm and pulled her past the women out the door where Majd still stood, watching the traffic. The smell of cigarettes lingered before the chill blew it away.

"It will take you much longer here to pay for your journey to America and your food and lodging," said

Shayma, still holding the faux fur coat. "Ten years at least. Maybe forever. It is not my concern. But if you stay with us I can promise you no more than five years, maybe less. In this place you will see many more men with much worse desires than what we permit in our home. With us, no man will dare to harm you, but here …"

Shayma glanced back at the blue door and the noise of the television and shook her head. The cold in her words and the cold of the wind caused Lely's body to shake.

"There *is* a family for you in America," continued Shayma. "Us. We already have saved you once. Your precious Mama Amena was about to sell you to a man with a brothel in a city south of Amman."

Lely's shivering jaw dropped agape. She wrapped her arms around herself, around the flimsy sheer shirt. It was a lie, a vicious, creepy lie.

"No, no—this is true, Lely," said Shayma. "I have my contacts. I heard about it as well as the same thing about to happen to your friends. When I told The Hawk, he agreed to pay Mama Amena double what she would have received, plus all the costs to bring you here, keep you comfortable, and make sure only honorable men will enjoy your company, men who will respect your body while you share its pleasures with them."

Lely eyed the street as they approached their car. If she bolted, she'd get only half a step before Majd, pressed close to her side, would grab her.

"Oh!" Shayma raised Lely's coat. "Look at me. I almost forgot." As though Lely were a child or a doll, Shayma clasped her arm and dressed her in the coat. She stepped behind Lely, embraced her around her stomach, and murmured in her ear.

"One more consideration, Lely. Whatever you decide, that will also be Qamar's fate. There are places like this all around the city. We will place her in a different one. Sara and Yana we will keep. And so you are deciding Qamar's fate as well as your own."

She unwrapped herself from Lely and spun her half a turn so that they stood face to face.

"Now is the time to decide. Shall I leave you here? It's a simple knock on the door, and you will be gone, and so will Qamar later this afternoon. Or do you wish to remain under my protection?"

Lely hated Shayma, her tricks and her lies. She shouldn't have to choose.

"Lely, if you do not say your choice, I will leave you here."

If only Allah would strike her dead that very instant—that was the choice Lely preferred.

"Yes."

"Louder, please, so I can hear you. Put your words into a sentence and look at me when you say it."

"I want ... to be with you." Be with her ... punch her face, stab her heart, poison her tea, feed her to the dogs.

"Let's go sit in the car. It's cold."

In the back seat Shayma directed Majd to start the car but to leave it parked.

"We still have to have some understandings," she said. "We have high expectations for our girls. By the way, did our girls seem happy to you?"

Did they? How was she supposed to answer?

"Yes."

"Whether they are or are not, they act like they are. If you're running around in a sour mood, we won't keep you. The men don't like it and neither do we. So you must show good cheer. We won't fight you, Lely. You must do what we say without a fuss. Otherwise, we will sell you to Bill—that's the man you just met. And in case you were wondering, the girl on the end of the sofa used to work for us. No more. And she can never come back. I felt terrible when we had to give her up, but I promise we'll do the same to you, unless you show that you want to be with us."

With a forefinger, Shayma traced the length of Lely's nose, a touch that felt creepier than if it had been a black widow spider. "I have come to care about you. I would hate to see you go. We've been together for a while. And Qamar—I'd hate to lose her, too. So, one more time—to stay with me, these are the terms. Obedience and a positive attitude. Do you accept these terms?"

It wasn't fair, tying the fate of Qamar to her own choice. Would Shayma really do that? And five years— could Lely trust them? And what about after that? Her life would be destroyed—who would marry her? Who would give her a legitimate job?

But her life was already destroyed.

"I accept," she mumbled.

"Oh, I'm so pleased. Look at me and tell me with a smile."

With a smile, Lely looked at Shayma and repeated her acceptance.

"You look so nice with a smile. Let's leave this place, Majd."

As Majd joined the traffic, Shayma took from her purse a headshot photograph of a clean-shaven middle-aged man, his cheeks fleshy, his forehead high, thin strands of dark gray hair combed left to right. The portion of his white shirt and gray sports jacket filled the bottom of the picture.

"Isn't he handsome?" said Shayma. "And he's very wealthy. I used to dream that a man like him would take a great liking to me, enough to take me with him. And now I have that with The Hawk. The same thing could happen to you. This man can certainly afford it. Would you like to know how much he has paid to be your lover tonight? Probably not, so I will tell you. Ten thousand American dollars, Lely. That is how special you are. Smile for the man in this picture."

Lely smiled.

Boyd hunched low, studied a tub of dried figs, then shuffled sideways, motioning for Abboud to do the same. Part of him wanted to fling away subterfuge, storm to the front, and grab the bastard who'd just walked in. But in the overall scheme, this unexpected customer was small prey. It was not yet time to pounce.

He and Abboud shuffled a few more steps, until they were halfway up the aisle, close enough to hear the newcomer.

"So, this is Amani's Market."

Abboud's eyes widened. Boyd's body felt taut, on hyper-alert.

"Amani's Market. Halal meats and Arab groceries, hot food and Bakdash," said Mr. Haddad.

Tamir Pierce switched to Arabic.

"What's he saying?" Boyd whispered.

"He is here for Bakdash. He says the store is on his

way from the airport. He says when he lived in Jordan he heard about Amani's Bakdash."

While Mr. Haddad was speaking, Boyd picked up a canister of Baharat spice blend. They both pretended to examine the mixture of cinnamon, peppercorn, and other seasonings Boyd couldn't recognize.

"My uncle is bragging about the Bakdash," whispered Abboud.

Boyd recognized the sound of the freezer case opening, and Pierce began talking again.

"He says he is from Australia, but he has grown to love Arab cuisine. He does not know how long he will be in Seattle. He is here on business."

"If we play this right, he'll be staying here a lot longer than he thinks."

The lid to the freezer case shut. From his peripheral vision, Boyd caught the shape of Pierce walking past the front of their aisle, perhaps twenty feet away. He put the Baharat canister back in its place and readied himself. There was no doubt in his mind—wherever Pierce was headed, he would be following him. He wasn't going to let Pierce elude him a second time.

Mr. Haddad and Pierce exchanged words at the register.

"He says he would like to stay and shop some more," whispered Abboud, "but he is here with an Uber driver and so he must go."

She scrutinized Boyd with a question in her eyes. Without words, he could see that she wanted what he wanted. He nodded but held up a hand and mouthed *wait*.

The door chime sounded. Boyd darted to the front of the aisle, poked his head beyond it, and looked toward the door. Spooning Bakdash from a dish, Pierce walked to the right and disappeared.

"Mr. Boyd, is something wrong?" asked Mr. Haddad, still behind the register.

"Let's go!" he called. He and Abboud dashed to the door and stopped.

"Your jackets!" called Mr. Haddad.

Pierce was nearing a side street, ten yards from the market. Boyd yanked open the door and immediately spun left, facing the opposite direction from their adversary. Abboud followed his lead. A peek behind them revealed Pierce speaking with a thin gray-haired man who leaned against the rear of a white Scion. The man walked to the driver's side, while Pierce went to the front passenger seat.

"We're going after him!" He grabbed Abboud's wrist, glanced both directions, and ran for the center turn lane, forcing an oncoming driver to hit the brakes. Ignoring the horns of angry drivers, heedless of the darkening dusk, he waited for an opening before sprinting the rest of the way across the street. It took only a few seconds for them to scramble into his pickup.

In his sideview mirror, the Scion pulled from its curb, heading away from them. Boyd backed up, tapped the car behind him, and turned onto the street. Accelerating, he outpaced the traffic in his direction, pulled into the center lane, and swung a mad U-turn the opposite way. Again, horns greeted his action. He sped toward the now-distant Scion, pushing through an intersection just as the light turned red. Easing on the throttle while still passing vehicles, he zigzagged from lane to lane until he reached a distance of three cars behind the Scion. He settled into the flow of traffic.

"Did they teach you this at the FBI training?" Abboud kept her eyes focused on the Scion.

"Nope. Learned it from *The Blues Brothers* movie. You should watch it sometime. Wrecked 103 cars. They were on a mission from God."

The Scion moved into a left-turn lane. Boyd slowed abruptly, allowing a car in the next lane to pass by and eliciting another horn blast from a driver behind him. Wincing in anticipation of a rear-ending that didn't happen, he veered into the turn lane, now separated by only one car from the Scion, which waited at a red light.

Boyd turned on the dashboard media center and pressed *phone*. "Melody Roshan," he said.

Roshan didn't answer. As the light turned green, he left a message: "Call me ASAP. Abboud and I are on the tail of Tamir Pierce right now in Tukwila. You heard me right. Tamir Pierce, our friend from Za'atari."

He called Fisk while following the Scion into the right-turn lane at the next intersection. It was nearly dark—Pierce wouldn't know who was in the pickup, but he might perceive he was being pursued. After they turned, Boyd slowed enough to annoy the driver behind him, who wheeled around and filled the gap between him and the Scion.

Fisk didn't answer his phone, either, and so he called Shonda, his boss's secretary. On the third ring, he received an answer.

"Shonda, this is Agent Boyd. I need you to find Roshan or Fisk immediately. Doesn't matter what they're doing. If they're meeting with Jesus H. Christ, get them out of there and get them on the phone."

"They're not here. They're at the King County Sheriff's. Some kind of task force."

"Call over there and get them out of the meeting and have them call me immediately."

They were on Interurban Boulevard now, heading south. In a couple of miles they'd reach the freeways, either Interstate 405 north or I-5 south. Boyd knew his blood was racing, and yet a strange sense of calm had a hold on him. It was as though he were back in Fallujah, knowing that he and his platoon were driving into an ambush, knowing that bullets and RPG's would be smashing into his rig, that they would have to get out into the lethal storm and push the battle back to the enemy.

"This is crazy," said Abboud.

"No shit."

"There is only one reason why Mr. Pierce would be in Seattle."

"He's not here for a ride on the Great Wheel."

"Do you know what else is crazy?"

"Besides this whole thing?"

"We missed the traffickers in Za'atari. We missed them on the container ship. I cannot sleep through the night because I am sick with anger. But now a bowl of Bakdash ice cream is going to lead us to those girls."

CHAPTER
FORTY-FOUR

Shayma sat cross-legged a foot away from Lely on the fancy bed as big as a lifeboat, the same bed onto which Majd had thrown Lely by her hair. The brute was in the room with them, sitting at a table and scrolling on a cellphone. Shayma smiled at Lely like it was all okay, just friends, and wasn't this fun?

At least Lely had been allowed to change out of the stupid skirt. Now she wore a gray abaya with floral designs on the sleeves, made from a soft cotton, more luxurious than anything she'd ever seen at Za'atari. Best of all, it kept her legs warm.

"Do you know who Wael Sharaf is?" Shayma's voice was gushy, her expression chummy, as though she, too, were a schoolgirl.

Only a blind and deaf person would fail to recognize the name Wael Sharaf. Lely and all her friends squealed whenever they saw a *Bab Al Harah* show on YouTube, the only way they could watch it at Za'atari.

"No," she said.

"What?" It was fun to see Shayma confused. "What about Omar Borkan Al Gala? He's my favorite. Makes me squirm. Did you know Saudi Arabia kicked him out of their country for being *too handsome?* They worried he›d corrupt the women, but they were too late to save me.»

Finally, Shayma said something with which Lely could agree. She was beyond saving.

Like Lely herself. After tonight.

"I'm going to tell you a secret, Lely." Shayma leaned forward. "Whether it's Wael Sharaf or Al Gala or the most handsome hunk of a man you ever saw, that's exactly who you'll be entertaining every time a man comes to your bed. This you must imagine like it's real and you're the luckiest girl in the entire world. You can make every man feel like Omar Borkan. You see, to stay with us, that is your true work. You must do more than satisfy a man's desire. You must make him feel like a movie star. Not every girl understands this, but every girl who gets to stay with us does."

Lely nodded—her life depended on pretending to care. She also understood that when the time came, Shayma would be watching. She wished she could figure out where the cameras were—perhaps the smoke detectors? If at a later time, when she was alone, she stood on a chair and checked—Shayma would see that, too.

Would Allah know of her sin? The Prophet, may Allah bless him, said that Allah would know what was in each person's heart. Would he understand what Lely had inside hers? Had it become evil? Was this the price of her pride?

"Positive attitude, Lely."

She forced another smile.

"There are some things we expect you to be able to do when you're with this man tonight. By the way, his name is Sergey. He is Ukrainian but he knows Arabic. As I said earlier in the car, he knows you're a beginner and so we can assume he won't expect you to have perfect techniques. In fact, that would make him suspect you've entertained others before him."

Shayma reached across to Lely, clasped her right hand as though she were her closest, dearest confidante. "It's okay to be shy. He'll expect that. It's okay to be nervous. Remember what I told you about our customers treating our girls with respect? He will do that. In fact, in order to win this special night with you, he had to agree he will do some things to make you feel … ready … when he is ready. He will kiss you. You will kiss him in return. He will seduce you. You will show him that his seductions are heating you up. I am going to show you how."

Shayma scooted to the side of the bed and retrieved a DVD from her purse.

"Majd, set this up, will you?"

It was the kind of DVD Lely feared. She was forced to watch side by side with Shayma, both of them leaning back against the headboard just like it was a movie theater, except that Shayma continually stopped and started it and talked almost the whole time. Majd abandoned his cellphone and stared at the screen.

"Look at her. Look at her. See the expression on her face? Can you make your face look like that? Look at me." Shayma made the same face and laughed. "Men love that expression."

"Listen. Listen to her." Shayma made the same sounds, only quieter, and this time Majd laughed.

"You like that, Majd? This is the only way you'll ever hear it from me."

Shayma maintained an unceasing string of commentary. Watch what she is doing with her hands, her feet, her hips. See what he's doing. Women do that. Men do that. It was very natural.

By the time Shayma stopped the DVD, Lely's stomach roiled and the back of her neck felt twisted as a wrung-out rag. Sometimes, before she came to America, she had imagined the act of lovemaking. It was warm and affectionate and although she had no face to picture, it was a man who cared for her very much. Those times she had felt warm inside and out, not like she did now, cold and sick.

Shayma sat still, pausing from her incessant blabber. A minute passed. Majd resumed whatever he was doing on the cellphone. A shudder grew beneath Lely's skin.

When Shayma finally broke the silence, she'd dropped the girlishness. She stared at the blank television screen, and her voice was monotone.

"I know this is hard, Lely. I have been where you are. I remember what it was like. Some girls stay and some girls go. There was a woman before me, Latifah, if that was her real name. What I am doing for you, she did for me. She helped me be one of the girls who stayed. I was nineteen years old. This was in the early days of The Hawk's business. Those of us who stayed were supposed to work seven years to pay our debts. Do you know what happened to Latifah?"

"How could I?" said Lely.

"She finished her seven years and was allowed to leave." Shayma placed a hand at the knee of Lely's abaya. "Do this right, Lely, and you will be free in five years. I know that sounds like forever, but it isn't. Then you shall have your life. Not all girls are that fortunate. Certainly not the ones who have to leave. It might not seem like it, Lely, but I do care for you. The same way I care for all the girls. If I were to lose you, I would consider it to be my failure. The Hawk would see it that way, too."

Shayma ended her speech—her lame justification. She obviously expected Lely to say something back, like Lely was supposed to affirm her honor and forgive all the horror she was putting her through. No way. She gritted her teeth—any words that escaped her mouth would teem with hatred.

Shayma sighed, then sprang from the bed and beamed at Lely. "Show me how happy you are."

Lely decided that when the opportunity came, she would run. English or no English, fully clothed or half naked—she would run. Later in the day or in a week or in a month—she would run.

But for Shayma, she smiled.

"What's up, Boyd? It had better be good."

Boyd let out a breath. *Finally*, Roshan had called back.

"Abboud and I are northbound on Interstate 405, past milepost six, following a white Scion sedan. Sitting in the passenger seat of that sedan is our old friend from Za'atari, Tamir Pierce."

Roshan paused. After a moment, she asked, "How certain are you?"

"Very. He showed up at the Arab market in Tukwila where Abboud has an apartment upstairs."

"He was speaking Arabic," said Abboud. "We were close enough to hear him. He told the owner he had just come from the airport. He is with an Uber driver."

Another pause. A red Mustang merged in front of them and slowed, forcing him to touch the brakes. The Scion shifted into the left lane and sped ahead, but Boyd was trapped. The lead car from a long line of tailgating vehicles reached his sideview mirror, while in the right lane, an auto-hauling truck paralleled the passenger window.

"Stay on his tail but don't make it obvious," said Roshan. "We're going to get you some backup."

"We're not going to stop him, are we?" said Boyd.

"Absolutely not. What are you driving?"

The convoy of tailgating vehicles crept forward.

"We're losing him," whispered Abboud.

"What did you say?" asked Roshan.

"Just a minute," said Boyd.

He damn well wasn't going to lose those girls again.

He braked.

The front end of a panel truck suddenly filled the rearview mirror. Anticipating the impact, Boyd squeezed the steering wheel, but luck was with him. The only thing that struck was the blast of a horn.

The automobile hauler pulled ahead, and Boyd shifted into its lane. He had to get around that damn Mustang. What the hell was the driver doing in the middle lane?

"I'm driving a green Dodge Dakota pickup, four-door, extended cab," he said.

"Stay safe and keep this phone call open. I'll be back with you in a minute."

He was almost even with the Mustang.

The car-hauler's brake lights brightened. The Mustang edged ahead.

Abboud slapped the dashboard.

The Scion had already disappeared from sight. He could only guess how far ahead it had gone. In a few miles, there would be a series of exits. They could not afford the loss of contact much longer.

He braked again, allowing the Mustang and the panel truck to clear before squeezing left between the truck and mini-van. The last vehicle of the convoy in the fast lane crept past, and he veered behind it. He drew even with the panel truck, whose driver flipped him the bird, and he caught the Mustang. A little old lady sat behind the steering wheel, while a chihuahua served as navigator, its front legs on her shoulder and its hind legs on top of the backrest.

"Backup's on the way," said Roshan. "Unmarked vehicles. We're trying to get a helicopter."

Boyd cleared the Mustang, swerved into the center lane and hit the gas. If it had been a normal Tuesday evening, traffic would have been going fifteen miles an hour, but it was like a weekend out there. He shot past most of the speeders in the left lane before slowing when he reached a blue sedan. He flicked his brights on and off, on and off.

"I hate it when people do that," said Abboud.

"So do I."

The sedan moved into the slower lane and Boyd sped past the fast-lane convoy.

"There he is!" said Abboud.

Shadowed by night, the Scion merged in front of a Mini-Cooper in Boyd's lane.

"You're mine, you son of a bitch." He felt at once calm and hyper-alert, the way he'd learned to be while under fire.

"He is taking an off-ramp," said Abboud.

"Which one?" said Roshan, still on the phone.

"Factoria Boulevard."

Boyd slid into the right lane and onto the off-ramp immediately behind Pierce, and they stopped at a red light.

"Do you think the driver has any idea who's sitting in the passenger seat?" said Boyd.

"I am sure Pierce said it was an Uber," said Abboud.

"If they know each other, we've got two problems instead of one."

Roshan cut in. "Sheriff's dispatch tells me their unmarked vehicles just entered I-405 off I-90 West."

"Won't do any good," said Boyd. "That's farther up the freeway."

Roshan sighed. "We'll get you someone. Give me a running account of exactly where you are."

"Will do."

When the light turned green, the Scion went south. Boyd slowed. The vehicle behind him bolted around and settled between him and the Scion. It was unlikely that Pierce would recognize them in the dark, but he didn't want to take a chance. A block and a half later, the Scion turned onto a Taco Bell parking lot and into the drive-through line. Boyd followed it into the lot. Keeping his engine running, he parked next to a row of hedges while Abboud relayed their location.

"We've got those cars coming back to you, but there's heavy traffic southbound," said Roshan. "They're fifteen minutes away."

They waited while the Scion crept forward, eventually disappearing in the line of cars on the other side of the restaurant.

"Can we get over there?" asked Abboud.

"It's just that drive-through lane. They can't drive anywhere except forward. We'll see him come out the other side."

Abboud shook her head. "I do not like this."

"Backup an estimated ten minutes from you," said Roshan.

Several minutes went by before the Scion finally came into view. Pierce was not in it.

A loud slap pounded on the passenger door window. Boyd and Abboud whirled toward the sound. Pierce stood outside, a pistol inches from Abboud's face.

"Hands up or I shoot!" he shouted.

"Shit," muttered Boyd. "Pierce is outside—"

"Shut up!" demanded Pierce, apparently reading lips. "Open the fucking door. Now!"

"What's going on?" said Roshan.

"Open it," said Boyd.

Abboud opened her door a crack and Pierce yanked it the rest of the way. "Give me the fucking phone," he said, gesturing toward the center console.

Boyd slowly handed the phone to Abboud. Why the hell hadn't Pierce simply shot them? Why go through all this trouble? What was his game?

Pierce snatched the phone from Abboud and chucked it toward the street. It bounced off a sidewalk and into the pathway of a propane truck.

The phone function on the media center disappeared. "Believer" by the Imagine Dragons took its place, part of the refrain about letting the bullets fly.

Not today, thought Boyd in response to the lyrics. *Please—not today.* When was that backup going to arrive?

His gun pointed at Abboud, Pierce opened the back door and quickly slipped inside.

"Abboud, hands on the dashboard and keep them there. And turn that God-awful song off. Agent Boyd, put us in drive, then keep both hands on the steering wheel. Let's go for a ride."

If he could slow-walk Pierce's command, maybe the backup would arrive. If he ducked-opened-the-door-fell-to-the-ground, he might not get shot—but Abboud would. The pistol in the holster beneath his shirt was useless. Pierce could put three bullets through his brain before his hand reached the shirt.

Someone outside had to have noticed Pierce pointing a gun. Wouldn't that *someone* call the police?

"Boom!" shouted Pierce. "You're dead, just like that. Don't think I won't do it. Get the fuck going."

They left the parking lot, continuing south. Where was the backup? Surely, Roshan had heard enough to dispense with subtleties. She'd want a whole armada, sirens blaring, lights blazing—no escape for you, Tamir Pierce.

But it was quiet, traffic sparse. Pierce directed him to turn right, away from gas stations and fast food, toward the freeway, now a mile or so distant.

Abboud showed no fear—no constricted breathing, no whimpers, nothing. How'd she do that?

If she died, the fault would be his. Chasing after this asshole had been his idea.

Hell, they were both going to die. Maybe Pierce just didn't want to do it in the middle of a taco joint.

"Park underneath the overpass," said Pierce. Interstate 405 loomed fifty feet in front of him. Otherwise, there were sleepy warehouses and empty fields. He parked beneath the overpass and waited for his life to end.

"Keep your hands on the wheel."

What the hell? Still alive? He glanced at Abboud, caught her eye, mouthed the words *I'm sorry.* He didn't want to die, not really, but even more, he didn't want to be responsible for someone else's death. Especially Abboud's. Not after all she'd been through.

In the rearview mirror, Pierce had placed a phone on his knee. He used his gun-free hand to scroll and type.

After a minute, he spoke into the phone.

"Hello. I'm having a bit of car trouble. Could you send a cab?" He gave precise directions to their location. "Five minutes—that would be splendid."

After Pierce ended the call, he glared at the rearview mirror. "How unfortunate that you would be in that little shop at the same time that I walked in. I saw you, of course, through the security mirror. The Hawk will have to decide what to do with you. But it doesn't look good for either of you now."

"The Hawk?" said Boyd.

"My ex-employer. He owes me some backpay."

"He's stiffing you, huh?"

"It's not an insignificant sum. I'd apologize for dragging you into it, but that was a choice you made, not I. Now listen. When the cab arrives, we're old friends. You'll sit behind the driver, Mr. Boyd. You'll take the middle, Abboud. I'll be next to you on the right with a pistol in my pocket pointed at your ribs. I have seen your moves, Abboud. Admirable skill. But do refrain from a demonstration, because it will end badly, not just for the two of you but also the driver. I assume you wouldn't want the death of an innocent on your consciences."

"Why did you help us?" asked Abboud.

Boyd detected a tightness in Abboud's throat. Even she had her limits.

"Do you mean at Za'atari?"

"Yes."

"It was supposed to be easy," said Pierce. "No one expected you to be Bruce Lee, Abboud. My role was to make your bodies disappear, but the only ones who evaporated were Jack and his mates. The truth is, I didn't think it through. I should have just left you there. But seeing how you were going to survive, I thought I'd mess with your minds. And I had you fooled, didn't I?"

"Don't flatter yourself," said Boyd.

"Rather impertinent, aren't you? Considering how your lives are in my hands? The Hawk doesn't appreciate being crossed. He'll have some special ideas for how to dispose of you. It would be an act of mercy for me to shoot you right now. But I rather like the idea of delivering you to him. He values loyalty, and I can't think of a more loyal thing to do than place in his lap the agents who fucked up his Za'atari connection."

"Did you kill Dr. Bergeson?" asked Abboud.

"I think we've spoken enough," said Pierce.

Headlights appeared in the rearview mirror. In a minute, the taxi arrived.

CHAPTER
FORTY-SIX

Lely winced. Her eyes watered, but Shayma didn't object. One of the older girls, Amelia, plucked out another of Lely's eyebrows while she sat in a chair before a mirror in her bedroom. It felt like a bee stings above both eyes. Each tweezed hair seemed like an extraction from her spirit one follicle at a time.

"Finished?" asked Amelia, her own brows minutely cropped, shoe polish black, thin and curving to a point.

Shayma bent down and studied Lely's face.

"Ah," she said. "Our newest sheikha."

After Amelia applied the eyeliner, Shayma handed her a bottle of mascara. "Both sides of the lashes. Wiggle the brush back and forth at the base, then swipe up."

"I know," said Amelia, before applying a coat, a touch of baby powder, and a second coat. One at a time, she pressed a spoon beneath Lely's eyes to apply mascara to her lower lashes.

How could Amelia do this work with a monster like Shayma? Had she once been in the same spot as Lely—terrified, angry, weak, sick? Had Shayma once had those feelings? It seemed impossible that Shayma had ever had any feelings at all, except lust and greed and cruelty. Ya Allah, she thought, no matter how bad things became, she would never be like Shayma.

"You pick the shadow," Shayma told Amelia, leaning to study Lely from an angle. "Nothing gaudy. Something modest, something for a virgin."

"Caramel?"

"A light shade."

Maybe that awful hotel would have been better. There would be no spotlight, no fussing. It would be sordid and dark and horrible, but it would be over and no one would care. But then someone else would …

Ya rabbih, there were no good choices.

"Excellent," said Shayma. "Perhaps one day you'll work as a beautician. Now go get yourself ready."

Amelia stepped away and paused, her face reflected in profile at the edge of the mirror.

"Lely," she said.

Shayma turned at Amelia, who smiled, lowered her eyes and left the room.

Lely. The soft voicing of it—sorrow, empathy. Survival.

After painting Lely's lips coral pink, Shayma daubed her with a perfume scented like vanilla and almonds. Lely changed into a black abaya with carnation pink angled in a vee shape down the chest, a slate gray hijab, and black high heels. Shayma brought her to the lounge.

Qamar, Yana, and Sara were not there. Lely still had not seen them since their arrival. As much as she had yearned for their company, she did not want to see them at this moment—or, rather, for them to see her.

"Go sit with Amelia," said Shayma. "Sergey will be here in thirty minutes."

Wobbling on spiked heels, her legs scarcely able to hold her weight, Lely bypassed the buffet table and its canapes, olives, pistachios, and sliced melon. Beyond the turquoise sofa, where a girl sat with a man, she met Amelia on a loveseat in the section of white chenille furniture. Amelia had accented her hazel eyes with glittering lilac shadows, and she wore a lavender hijab over a black underscarf. Instead of an abaya, she wore tight denim jeans and a thin white pullover sweater. She slid a full glass of white wine across a coffee table after Lely sat in a chair facing her.

"I know it is forbidden. But so is everything else here."

Lely shook her head.

"Drink it," Amelia insisted.

Lely eyed the glass, then glanced toward Shayma, who was dealing cards with that Hawk man at a table on the other side of the buffet. Would Shayma notice if she refused the wine?

Would Jack or Majd beat her? She shook her head again.

Amelia slid the glass back to her side of the table.

"Too good for it? You won't be after tonight."

She gazed at the big screen television on the wall behind Lely, where an American basketball game played on mute. Instead of the game, soft jazz slithered out of hidden speakers.

"Six o'clock," Amelia said, staring at the television. "That's when I get my first man. Two more after that." She drank from the glass she had offered Lely.

On the turquoise sofa, the girl leaned her head against the man's shoulder. She wore a black abaya with three scarlet stripes like claw marks down the front, and no hijab over her alabaster blonde hair. The man had to be at least twenty years older than she. He said something in a low tone, and she giggled—a phony laugh, Lely was sure, just like the phony smiles that Shayma made them show. At the front door Darsi wore brown slacks, a white shirt, and a lighter brown suit jacket, but his knife wasn't visible.

"Have you seen my friends?" Lely asked.

Amelia did not take her eyes off the television. She nodded. "You will be first," she said. "When you're all broken, that's when you'll see each other again."

The girl without the hijab kneaded the back of the man's neck. A moment later, they latched their lips into a long kiss. Lely turned her face away. She heard Darsi open the door, and her heart stopped. Ya Allah, it was not Sergey, not yet. This man was younger, athletic, a black leather jacket draped over his arm.

The girl who'd been in the kitchen, plus another one, both wearing hijabs and Western clothes, stepped in from the hallway. The sight of their smiles—mechanical, as though photo-shopped—caused Lely's stomach to lurch. Shayma set down her cards, guided this new man to a small desk, handed him a paper. It must have been the contract Shayma had told her all customers were required to sign, as though this were some legitimate business which could bring ill-behaved customers to the attention of law enforcement. Supposedly, this paper protected Lely and the other girls from abusive behaviors.

As though they were not already being abused.

Amelia took a drink of wine, drawing Lely's attention back to her.

"Are my friends okay?" Lely asked.

"As okay as the rest of us," said Amelia.

Next to them, the girl and the man rose together and left the lounge via the hallway. In twenty minutes Sergey would arrive, and then … and then, that hallway would seem like a passage to hell.

The newest man, who was short with fluffed hair almost covering his ears, took a place on the newly vacant turquoise sofa, a girl on each side of him. They had plates of hors d'oeuvres and drinks, and they communicated with gestures and hand motions. The man paid more attention to the basketball game than the girls, raising his fist once and hollering.

An idea popped into Lely's mind, accelerating her heart. Her calf muscles twitched. She gulped back a breath.

When Sergey arrived, he'd walk through the same door that athletic man had entered. Outside that door, there had to be a set of stairs somewhere, in addition to the elevator. Outside that door, the foyer was small, so the door to those stairs had to be very close to the elevator.

She would have to get past Darsi.

To do that, she couldn't be sitting with Amelia. The distance was too far. But if she was near the buffet …

She bit her lower lip. This was crazy. Darsi would cut her belly open. Maybe he'd only tackle her, and then they'd bring her to that filthy hotel and the outcome would be the same or worse. But if she timed her sprint well … they wouldn't be expecting it. She could outrun that old man with the knife, and she'd have a big enough head start to get down all those stairs. She'd outrace the elevator if they came after her that way, and when she got to the bottom she'd run into a street. She'd stop traffic. So what if a car hit her?

She looked across at Amelia. "Maybe I will get a glass of wine."

"It will help you. You have to survive."

Lely rose, her knees trembling, her heart trying to beat its way out of her chest. It was hard to take a step, but she did. She wouldn't be a bowl of pudding. She would act with strength, with force. Willing her pounding heart to direct its blood and its power to her legs, her arms, her mind, she strode past the man and the two girls.

Before she reached the buffet, Darsi opened the door again. She hesitated when she saw a man with a scar above his jaw next to his ear and a woman in a hijab, both of them holding their arms away from their sides, their mouths tight, their eyes open wide. Someone behind them grunted something, and they stepped in. Trailing them, a bald-headed man held a gun.

Darsi backed up and retrieved his knife. Lely stood frozen in place.

The Hawk shot up from his chair, while Shayma spun around in hers. He called out in English, and the man with the gun replied. Did these men know each other? Jack walked in, and the group disappeared down the hallway, leaving behind Shayma and Darsi.

The man with the leather jacket rushed past Lely toward the door, but Shayma stepped in front of him. Only then did Darsi move half a step in that direction—what would he and Shayma do to this man?

With a stern expression that Lely knew too well, Shayma spoke to the man, who answered with a tone of anger or fear or perhaps both. Darsi stepped next to her, his arm dangling, the knife twitching. The man's shoulders slumped. His voice changed to something passive. Shayma nodded her head, and Darsi let the man leave.

She glared at Lely. "What are you doing here? Go back to where you were sitting."

Lely glanced at Darsi. "I … is it acceptable to have some wine?"

"Amelia already has a glass for you."

"I said *no thank you,* so she drank it, but I changed my mind."

Shayma stared at Lely—could she guess what was really in her mind? Finally, she nodded. "Those two who just came in—they were trying to steal our van from the garage." Her eyes burrowed into Lely.

Everything Shayma said was a lie, but Lely didn't care about this one, no matter how thin and stupid it was.

She'd blown her chance to escape. In all the chaos, there had been a one-second chance to dash out the door.

Sergey was due in ten minutes.

CHAPTER
FORTY-SEVEN

Boyd knew only that he was in Bellevue, somewhere near the waterfront, in a fancy penthouse that reminded him of the Elliott Bay Hotel and Condominiums. He didn't get over to the east side of Lake Washington very much, so he didn't know Bellevue.

Not that it mattered.

He stood next to Abboud in front of a kitchen sink. His heart banged against his chest and his shirt was damp with sweat. While his reptilian brain clamored for a fight, his logical mind pointed out the likely outcome—dive for the floor while accessing his gun and hope … no. There was no way he could get to his gun before *bang*—a shot in the gut, most likely, followed by one he'd never hear, the one that would penetrate his brain.

The kitchen was large, all the appliances stainless steel. A center island with a black marble countertop occupied the middle. Across from it, Pierce stood near a pantry, his pistol pointed at Abboud, but also, Boyd noted, an easy swivel of the body to account for The Hawk and the smaller of the two men he'd encountered at Za'atari.

"I assume they're armed," said Pierce. "I haven't had an opportunity to check. You should have your men search them."

"The fuck you doing here?" A bird of prey tattoo covered the right forearm of the man who seemed to be in charge—The Hawk, as Pierce had indicated when they were still in the pickup.

"I'm here to collect my wages," said Pierce, his voice calm, his expression unruffled.

"You made that tough to do when you flat fucking disappeared. You didn't exactly leave a forwarding address."

"Survival outweighs the timely delivery of mail. We need to come to an understanding, a severance agreement, if you will."

The big guy with the elephant tattoo entered the kitchen, one arm encased by a hard-shell cast, the other pointing a pistol at Pierce.

"Tell Majd not to worry about me," said Pierce. "You need your goons to search these two."

"Why the fuck did you bring them?" said The Hawk.

"Let's call it a gesture of good will. They disrupted our supply chain. I assume you want them to pay a price for that."

"Which goes to prove you don't know a damn thing about me. I'm a businessman. I've got better things to do than fixate on revenge. But I know all I need to know about you, Pierce. You're a fucking idiot. These two were just doing their jobs. If you'd have taken a crap on the kitchen floor, it would have been an easier mess to clean up than this."

The Hawk turned his attention to Boyd. "Move away from her. All the way to those cupboards. You're a rookie, aren't you? My god, what a way to end a career. Jack, you search the woman. Majd, give me the gun, and you search this prick." He nodded at Boyd.

A minute later, the kitchen's center island contained a Glock 26, an iPhone, keys, wallets, and coins.

The Hawk picked up Abboud's phone and waved it once at Pierce.

"You think you're a fucking genius and you bring this goddamn phone into my house and the fucking cops are probably on their way here right now."

"Keep your gun pointed at Agent Boyd," said Pierce. "If you move it my direction, I'll kill you. As for the phone, the capacity to pinpoint its exact location is a bit of a myth."

The Hawk tossed the phone to Jack. "I don't have time to debate this shit. Jack, bring the phone over to Ashwood Park and leave it in a tree. Majd, go outside, find a hiding spot, and watch for cops. Ring me if they show up. The rest of us are going to take a little stroll to the marina. Jack, when you finish losing the phone, meet us there."

Pierce shook his head. "I'm afraid you don't understand. Floyd, is it? You're not in charge now, Floyd."

"Well, bully for you," said The Hawk. "You know my name and you found my business address. Are you coming with me to the marina or not? Because right now, thanks to your genius fucking brain, that's got to be Job Number One."

Boyd visualized the dark acreage of Lake Washington, miles across to Seattle, even more miles south to north. No one to hear. No one to see. His body and Abboud's, weighted and dropped.

He met Abboud's eyes, and in an instant it felt as though they'd exchanged a hundred thoughts. She did not blame him. Nevertheless, he was sorry. She was afraid to die. So was he. There may have been more for them, not just as colleagues, but as a couple had they remained alive. They both wanted to see how it might have played out.

Could she detect in his eyes his determination to fight? Somehow, between this kitchen and the gloomy depth of night, he would resist. Hell, he'd attack, his whole being absorbed, consumed with the primal will to survive. Without words, he saw the same fire in her eyes.

Jesus, he admired her. If he were to go down fighting, he couldn't think of a better person to be at his side. Except he wished more than any wish he had ever wished in his life that she were not there.

But it was time to push those thoughts away, time to clear his head. There was only one goal now—fight.

"Come on, Pierce," said The Hawk. "Even if you're in charge, you're still a guest and you made a mess. You owe it to your host to help clean it up. Then I can arrange your compensation. Eat your vegetables first, right?"

He turned toward Jack and Majd, both of them waiting at the kitchen entry. "Go on. Do what I told you. Pierce isn't going to shoot me. I'm the goose that has his golden egg."

Jack and Majd left.

Pierce exhaled audibly. "I'll go. But it's only because I choose to go."

The Hawk peered at Boyd and Abboud. "Here's the deal. We're going out the way we came in. You don't do anything funny, we won't shoot you in front of the girls. They've seen enough shit in their lives. They don't need to see any more."

"If you truly cared for them, you would let them go," said Abboud.

The Hawk shook his head. "Yeah, like I'm going to change my mind now. Their lives would have been shit if I hadn't brought them here. This sort of thing happens to girls like them. Better with me than someone else. The ones with me get treated like gold."

"You really believe that, don't you?" said Boyd.

The Hawk showed a brief smile. "I know your game. Keep me talking, hope for the calvary. You should have tried that on Pierce. He'd have bought you a round of beers. But I'm done."

He waved his gun toward the kitchen entry. "Move."

CHAPTER FORTY-EIGHT

Lely raised her glass at Amelia like she'd seen people do in movies, and she downed two big gulps before she knew what she'd tasted. It left a fruity tingle in her mouth and throat, though it had none of the sweetness of sodas or juices.

Amelia slouched against the backrest. "That's right," she said, a soft slur in her words. "You seem like a nice girl. Like I used to be. Ha ha. That was a joke, you know."

"You're still nice." Lely took a sip this time.

"You don't know me. You don't know what I can be. If you see me in a bad mood, you'd better stay out of my way."

Lely glanced at Shayma, who stared at the entry to the hallway while drumming her fingers on the cocktail table.

"They almost threw me off the boat," Lely murmured.

"Shut up," said Amelia.

The two girls who'd been abandoned by the man with the leather jacket rose from the turquoise sofa and joined Amelia. "Well, that was one way to get out of work," said the taller of the two. Her eyebrows looked like Amelia's, black and curving and thin. She contemplated Lely. "So you're the featured item tonight. I wonder how much they got for you."

"Enough to stuff an elephant," said the other girl, who wore a chartreuse hijab.

"More than enough for a flight back home," said the first one, answering her own question.

Lely didn't agree. She was worth nothing. A neon sign blinked, and a voice whispered: *nothing.*

She pushed away the thought. "I'm Lely," she said.

"Jannah," said the taller one.

"Razaan," said the one in chartreuse.

Lely turned to check the television—the current time showed in tiny numbers on the upper left corner of the screen.

Two more minutes.

Maybe he'd be late.

Maybe he would get into a car wreck.

The jazz flowing from the speakers now featured a xylophone. Lely took a bigger gulp of the wine. For a moment her brain whirled. The sensation passed, and resolve took its place.

She examined the three girls in front of her while they gazed at the basketball game.

She was not going to be like them.

Earlier, when the man with the leather jacket arrived, Jannah and Razaan had joined him around the buffet. That was the pattern here—sit in the lounge, eat some fancy hors d'oeuvres, act as though the depravities were tasteful, civilized.

She rose from her chair, noticed how the eyes of the girls twitched at her movement, while the rest of their bodies remained inert. She strolled toward the buffet, holding her wine glass with a steady hand, her eyes fixed on Shayma.

"My … date will be here soon," she said. "I want to be here to greet him. I will give him a smile."

Shayma tilted her head as she considered Lely's proposal.

"This is how I will earn my freedom, is it not?" said Lely.

Shayma smiled, patted the other side of the table where The Hawk man had been sitting before … Lely pushed the memory out of her mind. She sat, forcing herself not to look toward the door, to focus instead on Shayma, whose smile always declared friendship, acceptance, contentment. How did she do it?

"Do you know how to play rummy?" asked Shayma.

"No."

"I will teach you."

While Shayma shuffled the cards, Lely risked a sideways glance. If she moved quickly, if the element of surprise worked in her favor, she could reach the door in four steps. She'd have to burst past Darsi before he could react.

"They will come back this way," said Shayma, still shuffling. "It is the only way in or out of this penthouse. But do not be alarmed. Most likely The Hawk will allow those two thieves to go. We're just trying to scare them. That's all."

She wouldn't try it when The Hawk and his men herded that poor man and woman back out the door—there'd be too many bodies, too many weapons. She'd try it when Sergey entered. She took a sip of wine. She needed to be steel. Steel and lightning.

"We each get ten cards," said Shayma, dealing rapidly. "The point of the game is to collect sets of cards, either consecutive cards of the same suit, or cards with the same value, such as three queens. It always has to be at least three."

Jack and Majd emerged from the hallway, their eyes serious, seemingly oblivious to Lely's presence or anyone else's. Darsi stepped aside, Majd opened the door, and the two men left.

Shayma peered at the door.

The *closed* door, thought Lely. It would have been suicidal to make a dash with those two men side by side with brutality in their eyes. She'd chosen her spot—when Sergey arrived. She would not be a coward. Steel. Lightning. *Boom.*

Shayma put her cards face-up on the table. "Why don't we lay down our cards so that we can see them and we'll play a practice hand. Go ahead. Show me what you've got."

Lely set down her cards.

"Look. You've already got a run and you haven't even drawn yet. It's okay to be nervous. Remember, Sergey will be kind to you. We've already worked that out."

Lely nodded her head, then kicked loose her high-heeled shoes.

"Since I dealt, it is your turn. The first thing you do is take a card, either the one that's faceup next to the stack, which we call the stock—or one that's facedown. And when I see your hand, I see that you should take the faceup card, because that's going to give you three twos. That's a pretty lucky start for you. You're a lucky girl, Lely.

The cards prove it. Go ahead and pick up the discard, and then you can set down both the run and the twos."

Lely did as instructed. She reached for her wine but decided against another sip. She wanted to be clear-headed when the moment arrived.

"Okay," continued Shayma. "You can't do anything else, so pick one of your remaining cards and discard it faceup next to the stock. Probably your king. It's by itself and—"

The man with the scar and the woman with the hijab stepped out of the hall. Behind them, each with a hand in his coat pocket, likely holding guns, came The Hawk and the bald-headed man. They moved past Shayma and Lely. Darsi placed his hand on the doorknob.

She was finished with waiting. There would never be a perfect moment. She tensed her calf muscles, her thighs. She rocked her feet on the low metal bar of the cocktail chair.

The Hawk and the other man stepped past her. Darsi opened the door. She was going to burst between those men and between the captives, too.

Now.

CHAPTER
FORTY-NINE

A shoulder-high female figure wearing a black abaya and a gray hijab banged into Boyd's right arm and tumbled toward the floor.

Boyd never saw her land.

He kicked his right leg back hard, connecting with what felt like The Hawk's gut. A pistol shot exploded as he spun to face his adversary. From the corner of his eye, he saw Abboud had snatched the same moment to turn on Pierce. Before The Hawk could regain his balance, Boyd sent him staggering backward with a kick to the stomach. He dove forward, clasped and yanked The Hawk's wrist away from his side. Another gunshot blasted, and Boyd felt the recoil, felt the heat. They crashed through the open doorway and onto the floor of the lounge.

On top of The Hawk, Boyd bashed his foe's gun-toting hand against the floor. Pierce stumbled into them and tripped backward, bringing down a table and a cascade of playing cards. Boyd pressed the back of The

Hawk's hand against the floor. They were at an impasse as the thick-armed Hawk fought to free his hand. Girls shrieked and jazz bore down from the ceiling, while the crash of smashing dishware resounded from the struggle between Abboud and Pierce.

The Hawk punched the heel of his free hand into Boyd's jaw, a shock of pain like the blow of a monkey wrench. Dizziness seized his brain as the neck injury he'd suffered at Za'atari resurrected. The Hawk threw a second punch, but Boyd retained enough awareness to see it coming. He drove his head down, smashed his forehead onto The Hawk's nose and mouth. He raised his head to repeat the move, but his weakened neck refused to cooperate. He pushed his body against The Hawk's, concentrated his strength on keeping the pistol-wielding hand against the floor. The pain from his jaw and his neck radiated head to toe, sapping his strength. The Hawk slid back, thrashing and twisting. Boyd sensed his control slipping. He managed to deflect another punch, but he felt his adversary start to rise.

* * *

Lely scrambled up as soon as she fell, dashed to the stairway door at the same time a gunshot smashed into the air. A hole splintered the wood of the door inches in front of her face. She gasped, reeled a moment, then clutched the knob.

It was locked.

A second gunshot magnified the sirens in her ears. She had nowhere to go. If only this shot could have pierced her brain—it wouldn't be so bad, not compared to this. She turned and slid to the floor, leaning her back against the wall. A pair of desperate fights were happening inside the lounge. The only two she could see clearly were The Hawk and the man who'd been captured. The woman in the hijab and the bald-headed man moved in and out of view, throwing punches and plates, kicking without connecting.

What did it matter who prevailed? They would all hurt her. It was only a matter of how horrible it would be.

The bald man stumbled backward into view and fell. He bounced up, reached into his pocket, withdrew a gun. Lely lowered her head and covered her face, wished she could cover her ears and every other sense that she had. When no gunshot erupted, she peeked between her fingers. The bald man didn't have a gun anymore. He shook his hand as though in pain while facing the woman, both in fighting stances.

Where was Shayma? Where was Darsi? Had they run down the hall? Were they still in the lounge, out of sight where the other girls had been sitting?

What was Shayma's protection worth now?

An idea popped into her head. She didn't need the stairs. She could take the elevator—there was no one to stop her. She jumped up, pressed the down button. The *down* arrow above the elevator glowed. She would have to wait, probably for too long. If only she could make herself invisible. No one would see her, and when the elevator finally arrived and she was safely inside, only then would she show herself as the doors closed and none of these horrible people could do anything to stop her.

She turned around. The Hawk was scooting his body backward and trying to get off the floor. His hand rose up and there was the pistol, but the other man slammed it back against the floor. The Hawk was going to beat the so-called thief. What had he come to steal? Was it her?

She stepped closer to the doorway, hiding behind the wall while leaning to peek inside.

The bald man pivoted and punched the woman at the same time she kicked him in the ribs. Blood gushed from the woman's nose as they both staggered back. Lely couldn't believe her eyes—here was a woman, wearing a hijab and fighting like a ghazi. She turned and stared at the elevator. The arrow still pointed down.

She returned her attention to the lounge just as … no, it couldn't be. What was Amelia doing? The girl with the hazel eyes and lavender hijab had crept into view. As though mesmerized, she gazed at The Hawk man, still trying to rise, landing another punch on the back of the other man's head. She was so close! A sudden move would topple her. A stray bullet could strike her.

She took one sudden step, raised her spike-heeled shoe, and stomped it down—straight into The Hawk man's eye. He bellowed as loudly as the gunshots had been, and he thrust his free hand onto the wound.

Jannah, the tall girl, sprang into view, and she kicked The Hawk in the side of his head. Amelia added another kick, and then Jannah again, and the man on top was rising up, The Hawk's gun now in his hand.

The bald-headed man turned and ran into the foyer, passing within inches of Lely as he dashed by. He stopped to glance at the elevator—the arrow pointing up was now lit—and he tried the door to the stairs, making the same discovery that Lely had.

Before he could turn around, Lely dove at his legs and tackled him to the floor. He was so strong that he broke free at once, but just as he was pulling away, there was Razaan with a wine bottle in her hand. She smashed it down on top of his head. Glass shattered and red wine drenched his bald pate, mixing with blood oozing from a gash. He groaned and slumped to the floor. The fighting woman dashed into the foyer and stood over him, her nose dribbling blood onto his prone body.

The elevator made its *ping* noise and the doors opened.

It was Sergey.

His mouth dropped open and he reached for a button. The doors began to close, but the woman stepped between them. With one hand she pushed them open and with the other she grabbed Sergey by the collar and yanked him into the foyer.

He looked down at Lely. She didn't know how good his Arabic was, but she spoke to him anyway.

"I am not for sale," she said.

. . .

Boyd and Abboud sat on a chenille white sofa in the middle of the lounge. A small army of law enforcement personnel buzzed here and there, conferred, measured, shined lasers and dusted for prints, took photos, took notes, spoke into phones. Passing in and out of the room were social workers, paramedics, an Arabic interpreter, and a misplaced Cantonese interpreter with nobody to talk to. Paramedics and cops had already marched the whimpering Hawk out, holding a cloth against his eye socket. Shayma and the old guy, who turned out to have a knife, were being questioned somewhere in the penthouse.

Among the crowd was Agent Roshan, who had already questioned Boyd and Abboud, parked them on the sofa, and left each with a water bottle and a granola bar. She would not allow them to see the girls, who were somewhere else in the building with social workers and the Arabic interpreter.

A paramedic had checked Boyd's jaw and neck and delivered shocking news: he was injured. At least, as far as the paramedic could determine, there were no broken bones. Abboud's nose had stopped bleeding. Boyd downed three ibuprofen tablets and pronounced himself good.

The night would drag on for a long time. He'd have to write a detailed report, either at the FBI Building or at the Bellevue PD, wherever the higher-ups decided. Roshan and others would certainly return to him with follow-up questions.

Abboud stared at the big screen television. A basketball game was playing, the Clippers against the Suns. From the ceiling, the damn jazz kept mocking them, cool jazz, easy jazz, elevator music.

"I didn't know you were a basketball fan," he said.

Abboud kept her eyes on the screen. "I would rather watch The Food Channel. I think *Guy's Grocery Games* is on right now."

"*Guy's Grocery Games*? Is that like swishing a five-pound turkey from three-point range?"

"I have no idea what you are saying."

He took a sip of water. "Know what I'd like to do?"

"I know what I would like you to do."

"Dare I ask? What would you like me to do?"

"Take a shower. You stink."

"You don't exactly smell like roses. But you look good with dried blood on your chin."

"I thought I had cleaned it."

"Think again."

She sighed, took a bloody handkerchief from her pocket and opened her water bottle.

"Just kidding," he said.

"You can have the first shower." She took a sip and squirted him from her mouth.

"Thanks." He felt giddy. They were alive. An hour ago, they were about to die.

"So what is it you would like to do?" Abboud asked.

"Thank that girl Lely and her friends before the social workers take them away."

"Future FBI agents?"

"There's an idea. They've got the moxie."

"Roshan said I could not see them yet."

"Yeah, but she didn't say for how long, and unfortunately, she's not here for us to seek clarification."

"Russell. I cannot."

"I'll say it was my idea. I insisted."

"Just like the first time I saw you, Agent Boyd. Intruding on a place we are not authorized to go." She rose from the sofa. "What is it you say? Onward?"

"Yeah. *Onward* will do."

Lely blinked. Had she stepped through a secret portal and ended up in Dara'a? Nawar had told her it was an Arab store with hot food, but she hadn't expected *this*. From the deli case, aromas of tabbouleh, falafel, shawarma. On the counter along the window, condiments and dips and … her eyes zeroed in on a beige concoction with a texture like lumpy pudding—was that baba ghanoush? It was too much to hope for.

Farah, Lely's temporary foster mother for the past week, had served her pita bread with hummus, but it was from the grocery store and it wasn't the same, not even close. Maybe she could convince Farah to come to this Amani's Market. But Farah didn't speak Arabic. How would Lely explain about this store or tell her its location?

She waited with Agent *Rus-ul* near the entry while Nawar went ahead to greet the owner. At the window counter, one of the two men hunched over plates of food glanced at Lely. Each with dark and curly hair, both men appeared old enough to be in college or in their early working years. She shuddered, and the men returned their attention to their meal. A month ago, she might have decided they were cute. Now, their attention repulsed her. Ya Allah, how she had changed. Would she ever get back to her old self?

"So this is Lely!" A rotund man, bald at the top of his head and sporting a blue blazer, opened a half-door and stepped out from behind the front counter. Although he was with Nawar, he was still another man with his eyes on her. He put his hands to his heart. "Marhaban," he said.

"Shokran jazeelan," she replied, also putting a hand to her heart. "I feel like I am back in Syria."

"I'm so glad," said the man. "Call me Amani. Nawar is like a daughter to me. She told me you saved her life."

Lely averted her eyes. "She is the one who saved me." Why did everyone keep exaggerating what she had done? All she had wanted was to escape.

"You're heroes, all three of you," said Amani. "Allow me to treat you to lunch."

"You're too generous," said Nawar.

"Am I?" Amani tilted his head. "Then allow me to charge you double."

"Ouch," said Nawar. "I take back the compliment."

"That was a compliment? I'm a businessman. I took it as an insult." He returned his attention to Lely. "Nawar tells me you are from Dara'a, the same as she."

Lely looked down again. "Yes." Did this man know how close she had come to unspeakable shame? Did Nawar tell him? *This is the girl who came within minutes of prostituting her body.* Is that what *everyone* said about her? Perhaps even before she entered the store, Amani, who knew about her because of Nawar, had announced to the men eating at the counter that there was a girl coming who'd worn a skirt the size of a washcloth to a hotel with prostitutes. Perhaps that was why the men had scrutinized her.

Stop it. How she wished she could squelch those stupid thoughts! She blinked again. She was in a store. Her legs felt a little wobbly, but she was safe.

"She's kind of a quiet girl," Nawar told Amani.

"That's fine." Amani opened the half-door and gestured for them to go to the table behind it. "If talk is silver, then silence is gold. Wait here. Let me get you some food."

Nawar said something in English. *Rus-ul* nodded and came with them to the table.

Amani went to the deli case, picked up a piece of flat bread and held it for them to see. "What will you have? Shawarma? Falafel? Shish tawook?"

They ate their meal. Halfway through, Nawar asked Lely when she would be going to school. Farah had told Lely that she would begin in three days at a school where there were other Middle Eastern girls who spoke Arabic and wore the hijab, but Lely didn't want to go, not yet. How would she hide what had happened to her from the other girls? She would never tell, of course, but they would see it in her face. The boys would see it, too, and so would the teachers, and so would the whole world.

Ya Allah—those thoughts again!

"Monday," she answered. She wished she could say more, just like she wanted to eat more, when all she chose was flatbread and the baba ghanoush. The kick of the spices in it would normally have heightened her senses, but now all it did was make her feel like leaving it on her plate. She ate small bites, chewing slowly. It would be rude not to finish.

She smiled at them, though she knew it lacked feeling. She was not the girl she was presenting. She was more than this.

Rus-ul, on the other hand—he didn't lack feeling. Did Nawar notice how he looked at her? He had pulled out a chair for Nawar before they sat down. Of course, he did the same for her, but he didn't show the same expression he did for Nawar. His eyes nearly glowed! It was kind of funny, the way he doted on her. He couldn't participate in the conversation, not that Lely herself had much to contribute, but he did try to say some things, like when she sneezed, he said *Rahimaka Allah.*

And Nawar—she pretended not to notice *Rus-ul's* attention, but she didn't fool Lely. A woman knew when another woman was pretending. An extra invisible energy whirled in the air around the table where they sat, and it didn't all originate from *Rus-ul.*

Watching those two feign indifference toward each other made Lely feel more at ease. Next to her, at this very table, was the America she had always heard about—the kind of place where people from different cultures and religions and nations could meet and maybe grow to love one another, maybe even get married, which didn't mean that was going to happen with Nawar and *Rus-ul*, but it might.

She wrapped her fingers around the red and blue bangles on her wrist, and a spark of warmth radiated near her heart.

"You don't have to finish," said Nawar. "It's okay if you're not hungry. But you must save room for Bakdash. Did you know what actually led to your rescue? It was Bakdash, right here from my uncle's shop. I will tell you the story while we're eating it."

AFTERWARD

Many amazing organizations do tremendous work in assisting war-ravaged peoples throughout the world. If you're moved to offer support for this work, there are two organizations that I particularly admire. Mercy Corps has long been present at Za'atari Refugee Camp as well as in many other refugee camps and impoverished areas around the world. They deliver aid to meet urgent needs while collaborating with local peoples to develop long-term solutions for lasting change. Almost anywhere you find people in crisis, you will find the International Rescue Committee helping them survive, recover and regain control of their future. The IRC also helps countless numbers of refugees find safe homes away from the violence and fear that have besieged their homelands.

ACKNOWLEDGEMENTS

I am grateful for the assistance I've received from two special individuals, Dr. Baher Butti, a former professor of psychiatry at the University of Baghdad and now a leader among the Iraqi community in Portland, Oregon; and Ghaith Alhallak, a Syrian journalist based in Italy. The violence of war has driven both of these individuals from their homelands. Their advice regarding cultural norms and language has been immensely valuable. I am grateful also for the stellar feedback I've received from my critique group: Renae Canon, Janelle Child, Glenn Harris, Jennie Mansfield, Jackie McManus, and Vernon Wade. Thanks also to Alicia Dean for her meticulous editing, to Elise Hitchings for her eagle-eyed proofreading, and to Laura Boyles, for her wonderful cover art and interior design. Finally, I'm deeply grateful for the encouragement and input I've received from my wife April.

AUTHOR'S NOTE

Thank you for reading *Sinister Refuge.* It is the first book of a series that will feature Russell Boyd and Nawar Abboud. The second book is slated to be published in 2022. You can be among the first to know of its publication by signing up for my occasional email newsletters and also receive special offers exclusive to email subscribers. I promise I won't share your email address, nor will I bombard you with emails.

Meanwhile, I've written two other novels, both published in 2019, that have received very positive reviews.

In *Vengeance Burns Hot*, a firefighting helicopter pilot tries to help his adult son escape from a deadly anti-government militia.

In *Cooper's Loot*, a young reporter believes she's got the story of a lifetime when she joins an odd collection of characters on the hunt for the hidden loot of the notorious hijacker DB Cooper.

Learn more about these books on my website, www.rickegeorge.com.

www.ingramcontent.com/pod-product-compliance
Lightning Source LLC
Chambersburg PA
CBHW051209190726
48288CB00006B/1872